Thickums

Thickums

Blake Karrington

www.urbanbooks.net

Urban Books, LLC
300 Farmingdale Road, NY-Route 109
Farmingdale, NY 11735

ISBN 13: 978-1-62286-669-4
ISBN 10: 1-62286-669-X

First Trade Paperback Printing January 2018
Printed in the United States of America

10 9 8 7 6 5 4 3 2 1

This is a work of fiction. Any references or similarities to actual events, real people, living or dead, or to real locales are intended to give the novel a sense of reality. Any similarity in other names, characters, places, and incidents is entirely coincidental.

Distributed by Kensington Publishing Corp.
Submit orders to:
Customer Service
400 Hahn Road
Westminster, MD 21157-4627
Phone: 1-800-733-3000
Fax: 1-800-659-2436

Thickums

by

Blake Karrington

Chapter 1

Being a big girl from the hood wasn't easy at all, but Nora didn't let that stop her from reaching her goal of becoming a registered nurse and landing her dream job at a hospital near her home. She had been working at Presbyterian Hospital for a little over five years and had recently been promoted to head nurse. Now making close to sixty grand a year, she was one of the youngest head nurses in the city. Nora had everything she wanted, except for a man to share it with.

"So, what do you plan on doing for your thirtieth birthday?" Nina, a nurse's assistant, asked as she walked up behind Nora.

"Child, please. I gotta work on my birthday. By the time I get off, my feet won't allow me to go anywhere else but home," Nora replied, hardly taking her eyes off the chart.

"Well, me and a couple of the nurses were going to Lucky's to get our drink on. You should come by before you go home," Nina suggested.

Nora didn't want to hurt Nina's feelings or seem rude by declining her offer, but the last time they had gone out, it was a disaster. Nina drank so much that Nora and the bouncers had to carry her to the car. Then Nora had to carry her up two flights of stairs once she got her home. Remembering that night and how tired she was after it, Nora quickly declined in her mind, but left it open ended with Nina.

"Girl, I will try, but I'm not making any promises," she responded. "Now, if you don't mind, I'm going on break." Nora chuckled. "Mr. Ruffin needs to be prepped for surgery, and Ms. Peters has to have her blood drawn. You think you can handle that while I eat my lunch?"

Nina playfully saluted Nora. "Yes, ma'am."

Nora shook her head and laughed as she walked off.

"I'm about to go meet up with the girls. Do you want anything while I'm out?" Andrea asked her boyfriend, Garnett, as she walked into the living room where he was playing X-Box One.

"Did I tell you that you could go meet up with those bitches?" Garnett yelled back, not once taking his eyes off the TV. "Did you clean our room, the bathroom, and the kitchen?" he asked with an attitude. "And did you take the trash out?"

"Yes, baby, I did everything you asked me to," she answered.

Garnett was an asshole, and he treated Andrea like crap, mainly because she allowed him to. The fact that she didn't have a job and wasn't bringing in a steady income, coupled with her weight and her many struggles in life, made Andrea dependent on Garnett. That was her only reason for putting up with his nonsense. That, and the fact that he occasionally made her feel loved. Today definitely wasn't a day for him to show love.

"Well, you forgot something," Garnett, said, reaching down and unzipping his pants. "Take care of me before you leave," he instructed her while still playing the game.

"Are you serious? The girls are waiting on me," Andrea pleaded.

"Do it look like I'm fucking joking with you? Bring ya big ass over here and suck dis dick," Garnett snapped.

Andrea sighed, put her bag down by the door, and made her way over to the couch. Garnett didn't even look at her, he simply spread his legs wide enough for Andrea to get down on her knees between them. She reached in and pulled out his soft dick, jerking it a few times before putting it into her mouth.

It didn't take long for it to get hard, and when it did, Garnett looked down at her and smacked her hands away. "No hands. You know the rules. And you better not stop sucking it until I cum in ya mouth," he spoke, then went right back to playing his game.

Andrea didn't feel like sucking his dick, but she had to. It was the only way to avoid a vicious verbal assault from him, and the possibility of being smacked around. Having been with Garnett for a little more than a year, Andrea knew what would keep him cool and relaxed. He loved head and demanded it more than he did pussy. That was the reason she was so good at it; she had perfected what it took to get him off quickly, and after about eight minutes, Garnett was splashing off into her mouth.

"That's what I'm talking about," Garnett grunted out, dropping the controller and grabbing the back of Andrea's head. "Drink every drop of it," he continued while pushing her head down.

Andrea did as she was told, even though she hated swallowing his cum. She sucked his now semi-hard dick until nothing was left.

Garnett grabbed a fist full of her hair and pulled her up to his face. When Andrea went to kiss him, he put his whole hand over her face then mugged her. "Carry yo' ass on, and don't be out there stuffing yo' face wit' those hungry ass bitches. You don't need to gain anotha muthafuckin' pound," Garnett insulted.

Andrea didn't even respond to his ignorance. She simply got up, fixed her hair in the mirror by the door, then left. She didn't even have the energy to fight with him, plus she had to be at the hospital in one hour to pick up Nora.

Nora walked into the nurse's lounge with one thing on her mind, and that was to rest her feet and grab a quick bite to eat. Today she had a four cheese, five-layer chicken lasagna that she'd baked yesterday for dinner. It was mean and seasoned to perfection. Nora had brought a big bowl of it too. She sat at the table wiggling her toes, watching while the microwave heated the amazing dish. A rumbling sound coming from the mop closet was the only thing that took her attention away from the food. She looked over and saw the door moving slightly, but then it stopped.

"What da hell?" Nora mumbled, getting up from the table and heading for the door.

Nora had watched one too many scary movies and wasn't about to fall victim to a psycho murderer jumping out of the closet. She stopped the first male figure she saw, which was Travis, a nurse from the maternity ward. He was gay as a fruit basket, but he was going to have to do right now.

"Open it," Nora whispered, pointing to the moving door.

Travis was a little scared too, and for a second, they went back and forth, whispering about who was going to open the door. Finally, Travis gave in. He reached for the doorknob then slung it wide open. He and Nora both jumped back, not knowing what to expect. When they laid their eyes on what or who was in the closet, both their jaws dropped to the floor. Nora couldn't believe it. Alice, her coworker, was bent over, holding onto the back wall for support, while Carl, the janitor, was long stroking her from behind. They were so into it they hardly noticed the door was open.

"Oh, shit," Carl said, looking over his shoulder and seeing Nora and Travis standing there.

For a moment, Alice acted like she didn't want Carl to stop, but he pulled out, only seconds away from making Alice reach her peak. She struggled to get her footing. Her knees were weak, and from the looks of things, Nora and Travis could see why. Carl was packing. He had a long, fat anaconda of a dick, and it was slightly curved at the tip. The sight of it made Travis blush. Nora wasn't impressed though. As the head nurse, she was going to be the first person to be held responsible if her supervisors got wind of what was happening under her supervision.

"Oh my God, Nora, I'm so sorry," Alice said as she put her scrubs back on. "Please don't tell Jake."

Unfortunately, Jake was Alice's husband, who just so happened to be a doctor at the hospital. Not only could she lose her job, Alice was also about to ruin her marriage.

Nora walked over to Travis and spoke. "Not a word of this," she said, before dismissing him and Carl. "And you, take a seat," she told Alice, pointing to the lunch table.

Nora closed the door behind Travis and Carl, then locked it. As she sat at the table, Alice's white skin turned pale, as if she had seen a ghost. Nora sat at the table across from her. "What in the hell has gotten into you?" Nora asked then paused. "Wait, let me rephrase the question," Nora said, already knowing what was inside of her. "What is going on with you? I mean, you got a great job, a loving husband. Why would you—"

"Everything's not what you think it is," Alice cried, wiping the tears from her face.

"And what's that supposed to mean?" Nora asked. "You say that, to say what?"

Alice wasn't just a coworker, she was somewhat a friend to Nora, much like all the nurses she worked with.

The relationship Nora had with Alice was a little deeper because ever since the first day Nora began working at Presbyterian, Alice had her under her wing. Although Alice was white and Nora was black, they had gone through a lot of the same issues in life. They could relate to each other in so many ways.

"Look at me, Nora. Do you really think Jake still got the hots for me?" she asked, looking down at her body. "He's a thirty-eight-year-old doctor, and I'm his forty-year-old-wife, fat and out of shape. He hasn't touched me in months, and sometimes I catch him staring at me like I was the biggest mistake of his life," Alice explained. "You have no idea what I'm going through."

"I have no idea? Are you crazy, Alice? I'm six one, two hundred eighty pounds, with breasts the size of watermelons. I'm large in every sense of the word, and can't find a man with enough courage to climb this mountain," Nora spoke. "You plump, but hell, at least you got a man, and don't look like you got problems with getting another." Nora smiled, then walked over to the microwave and got her food out.

"So now what?" Alice asked, concerned about what was going to happen next.

"Well, I get off in a little while," Nora said, digging her fork into the lasagna. "I'll have a word with Travis and Carl. It's an isolated incident, so don't worry about it getting upstairs to administration, nor to your husband. In the meantime, I suggest you sit down and talk to your husband about how you feel. Jake's a good guy, and I think he'll understand," Nora told her. "Now get back to work and let me finish eating my food."

"Thank you, Nora," Alice said getting up from the table. "You are a true friend," she said and leaned over to hug Nora.

Before Alice left the break room, Nora had one more thing to say to her. "Oh, yeah, Alice," Nora said, stopping her at the door. "Stay out of the closets, and don't think for one minute that this conversation is over with. I better get a phone call from you later on tonight."

Alice nodded and smiled before leaving the room. Nora didn't waste another second and went right to work on her lunch. She didn't have long before Andrea would pick her up from work, and she was determined to finish her meal before then.

Before Andrea made her way downtown to pick up Nora, she had to run a few errands, most of which were for Garnett. The first stop was the dry cleaners to pick up his clothes, and then it was off to Wal-Mart to refill his prescription for Viagra. Garnett was so needy.

"Damn, girl, you late, and my feet are killing me," Nora said the moment Andrea finally pulled up to the front of the hospital.

"I know, I know. Just get yo' ass in the car." Andrea laughed while moving her bags from the passenger's seat. "And how was work today?" she asked.

Nora couldn't wait to gossip about the events that had taken place with Alice and Carl. This was the first time something this juicy had happened on Nora's wing, and although she was more professional at work, when Nora clocked out for the day, she was as ghetto as they came.

"I caught two people fuckin' in the mop closet today," she began. "We opened the door, and the man was in mid stroke, tearing Alice's big white ass up," Nora laughed.

"Alice? The white girl that went out to lunch with us a while back?" Andrea asked, shocked because she remembered that Alice was married to a doctor.

"Yes, girl, and Carl is black. That man's dick is the size of my arm. Hewwww my god that man is blessed," Nora sighed, unable to get the visual of it out of her mind.

Being deprived of dick for so long, Andrea got a chill just listening to how Nora was describing it. As she sat in the car thinking about it, she wished she was Alice for the day.

"Let's not talk about dick right now," Andrea said, putting the car in drive and pulling into traffic.

"Why, what's goin' on with you and Garnett? You got that in-house dick, so you should be good as gold."

"Yeah, I should be good, and I swear I wish I was, but . . ."

"But what? You better tell me, girl," Nora insisted. She was dying to know what in the world could be wrong.

Despite the fact that Garnett had a nasty attitude and everyone disliked his disposition, he was a handsome guy. Tall, light skinned, a little on the chunky side, but he wore it well. Always dressed nice, and kept himself groomed every day out of the week. If he knew how to be a gentleman, he might've been a good catch.

"Girl, I shouldn't say it," Andrea said, shaking her head with a huge smile on her face. "I swear, if I tell you, you better not say a word to anybody, especially Darleen.

Nora crossed her heart and kissed her finger up to God.

"Girl, Garnett's dick is little as hell. But not only that, he can't keep the muthafucka up long enough to make me cum."

"Oh, shit, you lying." Nora laughed. "He got a wee wee," she said, holding out her pinky finger.

They both laughed so hard Andrea had to pull over. The laughs only continued when Andrea pulled out his prescription for Viagra and showed it to Nora. All kinds of little dick jokes came out, and if Darleen had been there, it probably would be even funnier. She was the jokester out of the three.

"Ah, shit. Let's go pick Darleen up before it gets too late," Nora said as their laughing winded down.

So far, the day had been a little exciting and full of laughs. It was only going to get better once they picked Darleen up. She was always full of surprises and had a million and one stories to tell, all of which happened at the job. In her line of work, something crazy was an every day occurrence.

Chapter 2

Andrea sat at the kitchen table with a large bowl of Cinnamon Toast Crunch, looking over the food menu she had prepared for one of her clients' baby shower. Her small catering business was starting to pick up, which kept her busy. In the next two months, she had a wedding, two baby showers, and surprisingly, a divorce party scheduled. A huge Christmas party was also a possibility, depending on how well she did with the divorce party. If done right, Andrea could clear fifteen thousand in her bank account before the year was out, and that wasn't including what she could make if she got the Christmas party. That was a nice piece of change, considering the rough year she'd had. It made the new year look a little more promising.

"Garnett . . . Garnett," Andrea yelled upstairs, trying to get him to bring her laptop down to her. "Lazy ass," she mumbled when he didn't respond.

She grabbed her bowl of cereal and headed up the steps. Thinking that he might've fallen asleep, Andrea quietly walked down the hallway toward their bedroom. Whispers coming from the bathroom caused her to backtrack a few steps and put her ear to the door.

"Nah, I'm at work right now," Garnett said to the young lady he had on the phone. "We can go wherever you want. Just make sure you wear something sexy," he seductively told her.

Andrea stood there, eating her cereal and listening to the whole conversation. He was laying his mac game down thick too, and it became a source of entertainment for Andrea. She always had a feeling Garnett was talking to other women, but this was the first time she'd caught him in the act. She started to kick the bathroom door in, planning to throw the bowl of cereal at him and try her best to kick his ass, but instead she just sat there and listened to him talk. The latter idea was probably the worse option because Garnett started telling the female how beautiful she looks and all the things he liked about her. He didn't quite tell her that he loved her, but Andrea could tell that this wasn't a chick he'd just met. It almost sounded like he had feelings for her.

Andrea was getting sick and had lost her appetite. The hurt was starting to sink in, and all she wanted to do now was lay down, and hope that she woke up and realized that it was all a nightmare.

Nora lay in bed looking over at the clock on the dresser. She was about to get up and prepare herself for work when she realized that it was her day off. Instead, she snuggled back under the covers and nearly fell back off to sleep, but the ringing of her cell phone interrupted her slumber.

"Now, who in da hell is calling me right now?" Nora mumbled. The phone stopped ringing for a moment then started up again.

"It better be important," Nora said before picking up the phone and swiping the answer key. "Hello," she answered politely, not recognizing the number that popped up on her screen.

"I hope I'm not bothering you on your day off," Ronald spoke.

"No, Ronald, you're not bothering me. And where are you calling from?" Nora asked as she wiped the sleep from her eyes.

"From a phone in the hospital. I'm on break."

Ronald worked at Presbyterian Hospital also. He was a pharmaceutical technician.

"I hope you're not calling me because they need me to come in to work today, because they can forget it," Nora joked.

"Nah, that's not why I'm calling you. I was just wondering if me and you could go out and get something to eat when I get off?" he asked, shocking the hell out of Nora.

"Uh, uh . . . are you serious, Ronald?"

"Yeah, why wouldn't I be serious? It's not like I'm asking you to marry me or anything. I just wanna have dinner with you," he explained in a sincere manner.

Nora couldn't remember the last time someone had asked her out. Nora wasn't ugly by a long shot, with a caramel complexion, long curly hair that reached just below her shoulders, and a set of golden eyes that were hard to resist staring into. She was a very pretty woman by all accounts, just a little big for the average man's taste. That's sort of the reason why she was so shocked that Ronald was asking her out. He was too fine for himself, and from what Nora had heard through the hospital's grapevine, he was quite the ladies' man and had broken a few hearts. Nora wasn't trying to be the laughing stock of the week.

"I think I might have to pass," Nora answered, regretting it the moment after it left her mouth.

"That's cool. But if you change ya mind in the next couple of hours, give me a call. Do you still have my cell?"

Nora wasn't sure if she'd kept his number from before, so Ronald gave it to her again just in case. It seemed that as soon as the call ended, loneliness began to settle back in. Decisions like the one she'd just made are what actually kept her from allowing the right guy to step up.

Andrea lay in her bed watching as Garnett got dressed up to go out with the female he had been talking to on the phone. She wanted to say something to him about what she'd heard, but she knew that it would only start an argument that she was destined to lose. Knowing him as well as she did, Andrea knew that Garnett wasn't going to stick around to argue anyway. He had his mind set on going out tonight, and there was nothing she could do to stop him.

The one thing Andrea did do while Garnett was in the shower was hide all of his Viagra pills; the new prescription and what was left of the old ones. She almost couldn't hold in her laugh as he looked around the room for them, and Andrea dared him to ask her for them. That was going to be the straw that broke the camel's back. Garnett wasn't stupid enough to ask for them, though. There wasn't going to be any fucking for him tonight, and if he tried without his little blue pill, he wasn't going to do anything but embarrass himself.

Andrea's cell almost vibrated off the nightstand before she grabbed it. It was Darleen calling. "Wassup, D," she answered, watching as Garnett headed out of the bedroom.

"Nothing, at work and can't wait to get off." Darleen smiled and looked back at The Cannon, who was trying his best to keep himself from cumming. "You gotta work harder, baby," she told him.

Darleen was right in the middle of making a movie. The theme today was seeing what veteran porn star could make Darleen submit before they busted a nut on themselves. She was a half hour into the shoot and had already knocked down some of best porn stars in the industry. Jake da Snake lasted every bit of six minutes before he splashed off. Mr. Steel made it to ten minutes before Darleen's soft, gushy pussy made him cum. As bad as The Cannon tried to hang in there, he too caved to Darleen's wet box. For a big girl, she sure did have some good good. Her pussy was deep too, so six, seven, eight and nine inch dicks didn't stand a chance no matter how much girth they were packing.

"What in da hell is you doin', girl?" Andrea asked, getting out of the bed and walking over to the window.

"Working. But look, can you pick me up at six? I don't feel like catchin' no cab, plus I wanted to kick it wit' you tonight. We can hit Mr. Ted's Lounge and get our drink on," Darleen said, sitting up on the edge of the bed while The Cannon walked off set with his dick in his hand.

The whole time Darleen was talking on the phone, the studio cameras were rolling. The producer thought that it made the movie even better. Nobody was able to wrestle with Darleen's big ass. Her thighs were about fifty inches around, and her ass was wide as a house. Breasts were 44FF, lips were full and juicy, and to top it off, Darleen had the nerve to be cute as hell. She was half white, half Native American, with long straight hair that reached down to her butt. Big girl, but sexy as they came.

"Well, I could use a drink. This nigga got me mad as hell right now," Andrea said, watching Garnett's car pull off down the street. "So I'll see you at six, girl."

There was silence on the other end of the phone. "Darleen!" Andrea yelled, wondering if she was still on the line.

Darleen was on the line, but she was in awe when Gordo, the Spanish rookie with a twelve-inch monster dick, walked onto the set. His dick hung low, damn near reaching his knee, and he wasn't even hard yet. Darleen had heard rumors about the foot long bandit, but never did she think he would ever be on the same set as her.

"Girl, I'ma have to call you back," Darleen said, and hung up the phone in Andrea's ear, then turned to give Gordo all of her attention. "I'ma have fun wit' this dick," she said, walking up to Gordo. Darlene grabbed his hand and led him over to the bed. "Watch and learn, fellas."

Gordo wasn't trying to hear none of what Darleen was talking about. His only purpose for being there was to do what he did best, which was beat the pussy up. He took control immediately after she sat down on the bed. Standing there with one foot up on the bed like he was Captain Morgan, before Darleen could say another word, he grabbed a handful of her hair and pulled her face up to his dick.

Darleen took it into her mouth like the dick sucking pro that she was, but the wetter her warm mouth became, the harder his dick got. The harder his dick got, the larger it grew. Darleen's heart started pounding at the sight of his bat. It was so long and thick, she could only get a little more than half of it down her throat without gagging. Gordo didn't care, he shoved another inch or more into her mouth until it reached her esophagus. Darleen could hardly breathe, and her eyes started to water. When he finally pulled his dick out of her mouth, she turned her head to the side to let him know it wasn't going back in.

"How you want it?" Gordo asked with a devilish smirk on his face. "Don't get scared now," he teased.

It didn't matter what position he fucked her in, Gordo was going to make sure she took in every inch. Darleen didn't mind because she wanted everything he had.

"Let me ride this big ass dick," she said, pulling him down onto the bed. "You gon' remember dis pussy," she promised.

She climbed on top of Gordo, grabbed his member and sat down on it. Ten inches in, her canal was just about full, but Darleen didn't stop there. She reached back and spread her ass cheeks apart then sat down on the rest of it.

The producers and the cameramen cheered Gordo on, seeing the pleasured look on Darleen's face.

Gordo was even a little shocked to see how she was trying to handle his mini me. "Oh my fucking God," Darleen yelled out, bouncing her big yellow ass up and down on his dick. Her two large breasts rested on both sides of his face as she continued riding him.

He sat up slightly, reached around and palmed the top of her ass, just below her lower back. Every time she bounced, he slammed her down onto him harder. Darleen was no more good. This was the first time anyone had ever gone deep enough inside of her to tap against her back wall. She was just about at the point of having an orgasm when Gordo took her right areola, put it in his mouth, and bit down on it. That was it. Darleen's walls tightened up around his dick, her eyes rolled to the back of her head, and she dug her nails into his stomach. The orgasm hit her so hard it temporarily paralyzed her voice box, not allowing her to scream out his name. Her juices poured out onto Gordo's dick and balls like she was pissing. The camera man zoomed in on it, catching the images of her cum splashing all over the place.

Gordo didn't even cum. He didn't want to for that matter. All he wanted to do was come through and take care of business like he said he would, and was paid to do.

Darleen was stuck. She didn't have enough energy to dismount, and it took Gordo along with the producer to roll her over onto the bed.

Gordo got up, looked down on Darleen then spoke. "You gon' remember dis dick," he said, then turned around and walked off the set.

***

Nora stood at the front door, waiting for Ronald to pull up. Sitting in the house, staring at all four walls, gave her the courage to call Ronald back and take him up on his offer to go out for dinner. At first she was a little nervous, but then she came to her senses. It was only dinner.

Ronald pulled up in a cream BMW 750. The few nosey neighbors who were outside stopped to see who he was there for. He got out of the car looking nice, although what he was wearing was basic. A pair of dark blue Seven for All Mankind jeans, some all white low top shells, and a blue with white striped button up Polo shirt. She couldn't help but to notice the nice watch that complemented his whole outfit. He cleaned up very nice outside of his work clothes.

Ronald looked so good, Nora thought that he may have been a little out of her league. She never attracted men who looked this good, and she was almost ready to cancel because she still wasn't sure what Ronald had in mind for her.

"Nora. Nora!" Ronald called out, snapping his fingers in front of her face through the screen door. "Are you coming or not?" He chuckled, snapping her out of her trance.

"Oh, shit, yeah boy, I'm ready," she said and stepped out of the door. "You definitely look different outside ya work clothes."

"You don't look too bad yaself." He smiled as he walked her around to the passenger's side and opened the door for her.

"Now where do you plan on taking me?" Nora asked when Ronald got into the car.

Ronald had decided to take her to a Jamaican restaurant not too far from where he lived. She was familiar with the place but had never eaten there before. It always looked crowded, and tonight was no different.

"Are you okay? You look a li'l worried," Ronald said.

"I would just like to know what's going on in that mind of yours," she said jokingly.

"What do you mean by that?"

"I mean, you all of a sudden asking me out. What's up with that? I didn't think I was your type."

"My type? And what's not my type?"

"You know, a full size woman," Nora clarified.

"Whoa, whoa, I see somebody has some self-conscious-ness with their weight," Ronald said, waving for the waitress to come over and take their orders. "What if I told you that you were wasting energy? Life is too short to be worrying about the wrong things."

Nora looked at him like he was crazy. She couldn't believe he had the nerve to say that she had issues over her weight. It was true, but who was he to speak on it? Nora could see that dinner was going to be over fairly quickly.

"You know, you shouldn't worry about what other people think of you. At the end of the day, their opinion doesn't matter. To be honest wit' you, most men don't want a skinny chick. They're outdated and very much overrated. Better in a rap video or on the cover of men's magazines, if you ask me."

"Yeah right," Nora shot back, dismissing his claim.

"Nah, seriously. Let's look at the facts. For one, most skinny chicks can't cook for shit." Ronald chuckled.

Nora couldn't help but to laugh a little herself. Before Ronald could continue, the waitress had walked over to take their orders. Ronald ordered oxtails and brown rice, while Nora had the curry goat, brown rice, and sweet potato bread.

"Back to what I was saying," Ronald continued. "It ain't nothin' wrong with a plus size woman like yourself.

You're a very attractive woman, thick in all the right places. Mmm," Ronald complimented, looking Nora directly in her eyes when he spoke. "And let's be real, it'll take a real man to be able to handle someone like you in bed."

Nora almost choked on her own spit. "Boy, you better slow down. Don't think you gettin' some of this kitty tonight." She laughed, but she was blushing on the inside from his words.

"Byyyye, Gordo," Darleen waved, blushing as she and several cast members left the Onyx Building downtown.

He waved back, giving her a wink before disappearing into his car. It took Andrea yelling at her for Darleen to realize she was about to walk into traffic.

"Girl, get yo' ass in this car," Andrea said, beeping her horn. "You said six. Bitch, I been waiting out here for almost an hour," she complained.

"Shut up, girl, I'm sorry. I got you, though. Drinks and dinner on me."

Darleen definitely could afford it, especially since she'd just been paid thirty-five hundred for the movie she'd just made. She wanted five grand since there were multiple sex scenes all wrapped up in one, but she'd negotiated the thirty-five hundred, which wasn't bad for one day's work. The porn industry was her hustle, and she quickly had become a household name in the industry, having well over thirty movies out and many more to come.

"Girl, you crazy as hell. I can't see how you can do it," Andrea said as she pulled into traffic.

"Shit, I make two grand per scene, averaging two or three scenes a week. I make an extra fifteen hundred on my photo shoots once a week, not to mention the fact that I get to have sex with some of the finest men in the United States," Darleen said, rolling her eyes at the thought of all the good dick she'd taken in today. "Shit, maybe I need to get you in one of my scenes," Darleen joked, reaching over and playfully pinching Andrea's titty.

Darleen wasn't your ordinary big girl. She had spunk, confidence, and knew beyond a shadow of a doubt that she was the shit. You couldn't tell her anything different. She kept her hair done, nails done, and dressed to impress every day. Sometimes she even got clothes from high-end designers custom made to fit her body. Not too many plus size women in the city could do that.

"So, look, my cast wants to have an industry party in two weeks, and I was wondering if you wanted to do the catering for it. I told my boss I had somebody to do it."

Andrea's first instinct was to decline, but then she remembered that she couldn't afford to turn down any work, plus she needed her small business to get all the attention possible. "Yeah, why not? Just give me a couple of days to come up with a good theme that you can take back to your boss."

Darleen was happy Andrea had agreed. All she wanted to do was show her some love and help her make some money. That's the kind of person Darleen was. If she could, she would help anybody, especially her sistas. She went hard when it came to them, and just about everything she did and all the moves she made were to make sure she was in position to help either of them if they were ever in need.

Chapter 3

When Nora finally woke up, a splitting headache just about put her back to sleep. She could barely remember how she got home last night, and for some odd reason, her pussy felt swollen like she'd been having sex all night. But those were the least of her problems. Nora looked over at the clock and saw that she was more than three hours late for work. Her cell showed over thirty missed calls and around twenty text messages. She was astonished and flopped back on the bed in confusion. Her mind was telling her to get up, but her body was calling all the shots, and it wasn't trying to move another muscle.

"I see you finally woke up," a male voice spoke, startling the shit out of Nora.

She looked up, and Ronald was walking into the room with two cups of coffee in his hand. Nora quickly grabbed the comforter and pulled it over her body. She was only wearing her panties and bra. "How did you get in my house?" she asked, watching Ronald walk over and take a seat on the bed.

"I never really left, except to go get you one of these, which I knew you were going to need," he said, passing her the cup.

"What in da hell did I have last night, and did we . . . ?" Nora didn't even want to fix her mouth to ask if they had sex. She was scared of the answer.

"Well, what you had was called Rude Boy Juice. It's a popular drink in Jamaica, which only few can handle.

By God, you surely wasn't one of them." Ronald laughed. "You were acting a fool at the restaurant. I thought what I did was bad. Whew!"

Ronald was talking about the time he had drank a Rude Boy drink for the first time, just a week ago at the same restaurant. He ended up stripping on top of the table then dancing until he fell off of it. Chicks were throwing money at him and everything. That's the reason why some of the people were snickering and giggling when he and Nora walked in. They had to have been the regulars at the restaurant.

"As far as us having sex last night, we didn't. As much as you wanted to, I couldn't see myself taking advantage of a drunk woman," Ronald told her.

Nora sighed in relief, maybe a little too early, because Ronald wasn't done telling the whole story. Before he could even begin to get it out, Nora felt one of her dildos under the blanket.

"However, you did make me watch you please yourself. I was shocked, but impressed with how well you knew your —"

"Okay, okay, okay," Nora said, waving him off. "Oh my God. I can't believe I did that," she said, very much embarrassed.

Nora was known to do some crazy stuff while she was drunk. That was mainly the reason why she didn't drink that often, and if she did, it was light. Here she was, on her first date with a good looking man, and she had done something like this.

"I would love to stay and chat with you, but I gotta get to work, unlike yourself," Ronald said as he got up from the bed. "I took the liberty of calling Ruth this morning and telling her that you weren't feeling good. She told me to tell you to get some rest, and she'll see you tomorrow."

"Thank you, I appreciate that," Nora said, taking a nice gulp of the coffee. "And Ronald, I'm sorry about last night. That's really not who I am," she tried to explain.

Ronald smiled, walked over and kissed Nora's head then turned around and walked out of the room. Unlike most men, he was such a gentleman. Nora liked that about him and hoped that her little antics didn't turn him off. Only time would tell, and Nora was definitely going to monitor his behavior in the future to see if his actions were sincere or just game.

Garnett swore he was being slick, leaving the house in his uniform like he was going to work. Andrea was hot on his tail, dipping in and out of traffic like she was a private investigator. The little stunt that he'd pulled the night before had her on a mission. She wanted to see for herself what type of female he was chasing after and willing to risk losing something good at home for.

"I see ya sneaky ass," Andrea mumbled to herself, watching as he pulled over and changed his clothes in the car. "She better be worth it."

"Fuck that. That bitch better know how to fight," Darleen chimed in. "I told you this nigga wasn't shit, girl."

Bringing Darleen might not have been the best idea, but Andrea needed some type of backup in case Garnett and his chick started acting stupid. Garnett knew Darleen very well and was well aware of her wretchedness. Darleen knew how to hold her hands in a fight, whether it was a male or a female.

Garnett drove a short distance, then pulled into a parking lot near Fourth and Market Street in downtown Philly. Andrea didn't want to follow him inside, nor did she want to lose him, so she immediately pulled over and double parked, not caring if she got a ticket. "Come on, girl," Darleen said, reaching for the door.

Andrea stopped her, wanting to get a visual on Garnett before they moved. A good five minutes went by before he emerged from the garage with a bright eyed, bushy tailed female under his arm. The female was the total opposite of what Andrea thought she would be. Andrea couldn't believe Garnett had pulled somebody so cute. She had to be no older than twenty-one, a red bone, thin with long, jet-black hair. Nice breasts, thin waist, and a fat ass, which complemented her curvy frame. Andrea was sick, and it was sad to say that she was also jealous.

"Aww, hell no," Darleen snapped, getting out of the car.

Andrea was right behind her, and before Garnett realized what was going on, Darleen cracked him from the blind side.

"Bitch!" he yelled out. "You lost ya fuckin' mind?"

"Who da fuck is this, Garnett?" Andrea shouted. "Did you know he had a girlfriend?" Andrea asked the girl.

The young woman had the nerve to say "yeah," with a no-care attitude. Ultimate disrespect, and Andrea reacted the only way she knew how. *Crraaack!* She punched the girl clean in her mouth without a second thought.

The girl fought back, striking Andrea several times in her face within a matter of seconds. She was getting the best of Andrea until Darleen stepped in, grabbed the girl by the hair, and started slinging her all over the place. They jumped the girl for a hot second before Garnett intervened. He smacked Andrea so hard she fell to the ground. Darleen hit the girl with several more upper cuts before she finally let her go.

Garnett looked like he was about to do the same thing to Darleen, but she stood there, gritting her teeth. "Nigga, you know my brother will kill you if you put ya fucking hands on me," Darleen yelled, making him think twice.

He knew her statement was true, so Garnett grabbed his female friend and walked off. He didn't want any trouble with Wax or the crazy crew he ran with. Everybody in North Philly knew not to get on Wax's bad side, and the quickest way anybody could do that was by messing with his baby sister.

"Come on, girl, get up," Darleen told Andrea, pulling her by the arm. "He gon' regret smacking you like that."

Andrea's face started to bruise instantly, and she could taste the blood in her mouth. Garnett's actions had left a scar, but not the apparent physical scar to her lip. Garnett left an emotional scar on Andrea's heart. One that was deep, and hurt more than anything she'd ever felt before.

Nora got the call from Darleen about the fight downtown and was informed that Andrea was going to need a couple of stitches. Nora had her first aid kit ready by the time they pulled up to her house. Darleen was still hype and wanted to go do something to Garnett, and after seeing the cut in Andrea's mouth, Nora felt the same way.

"Why didn't y'all come get me?" Nora asked, sitting Andrea down in the kitchen where there was plenty of light.

"Bitch, you ain't look at ya phone yet? I been trying to call you all morning," Darleen said, pacing back and forth. "I should have fucked dat bitch up some more," she said, bouncing, bobbing, and weaving while throwing a couple of jabs.

"Darleen, sit ya ass down somewhere. I can't concentrate wit' you shadow boxing behind me like you Floyd Mayweather," Nora told her. "Now, as for you," she said, directing her attention to Andrea. "Don't worry about dat nigga. God gon' deal with him. Just make sure you don't go running back to the muthafucka. Let's face it, we been down this road before." Nora leaned Andrea's head back to clean the wound. "And every time, you turn—"

"I know, I know," Andrea said, cutting Nora off. "I swear this time it's over. I'm getting my shit out of that house tonight, and that's it."

Andrea had reached her limit with the physical and verbal abuse, and today's incident had tipped the scale. Going back to Garnett wasn't an option, at least that's how Andrea felt right now. Just like Nora said, they had been down this road before, and somehow, some way, Andrea and Garnett would always ended up getting back together.

"Well, if you do go back to him this time, I'ma beat yo' ass and his," Darleen hissed, jumping back to do some more shadow boxing.

Nora couldn't help but to chuckle at Darleen's silly self. At times, she was so animated, but then again, Nora and Andrea knew that Darleen was serious. She was the fighter, and Nora was like the mother bear. For each of them, they were the best support system, and that's exactly what Andrea was going to need in order to put Garnett in her rearview.

Chapter 4

"Ms. Emma, are you ready for your bath?" Nora asked, walking into her patient's room.

"Yeah, but I want one of those sexy male nurses to wash me up," Ms. Emma joked in her groggy voice. "I need . . . I need . . . I need him to lotion up my body too, and if he's up for it, he might as well—"

"Ooookay," Nora said, cutting her off. "You better stop being nasty, Ms. Emma. Besides, you wouldn't know what to do if one of these young tenderloins got a hold of you."

"Chile, when I'm done with him, he gon' think I invented sex," Ms. Emma said, quoting her favorite Trey Songz tune.

Nora busted out laughing, and so did Ms. Emma until she started coughing. Ms. Emma was one of the few patients Nora enjoyed being around. Aside from being funny as hell, Ms. Emma was knowledgeable and wise. That came from old age, and experiencing just about everything life had to offer her.

"Ms. Emma, can I ask you something?" Nora said, standing at her bedside. "Do you think I need to lose some weight? I mean, I'm only asking you because most men are intimidated by my size. It seems like I only attract the weirdos and all the good handsome men want something a little more . . . ."

"A little more what, baby?" Ms. Emma asked, seeing Nora freeze up.

"Thinner, smaller, model like," Nora responded.

Ms. Emma chuckled and placed her hand over Nora's. "You are beautiful just the way you are. Don't get caught up in what America thinks a woman should look like. It's plenty of men out here that love and appreciate a big girl and let me tell you this: you don't have to lower your standards, either. You just have to be patient . . . and know . . . you just have to be patient and know your worth," Ms. Emma said as she tried her best to keep from falling asleep.

She couldn't help it, and by the time Nora looked over at her, Ms. Emma was asleep. Nora simply smiled, tucked Ms. Emma in, and left out of the room so she could get some sleep.

"Yo, you think it's cool if I invite Nora to the Thanksgiving party?" Monti asked Ronald out of the blue.

"Man, fuck no. You already got Kim, Niki, Paula and a bunch of their crew coming. You know how Niki be trying to act like we still together, and me and Nora just getting started. I don't want to have her up in no drama this soon.

"Damn, nigga, you can't keep your hoes in check? Besides, you know I like to see a little drama every now and then." Monti laughed

"Well, see it on your own shit, not mine. If you going to invite Nora, tell Niki and her crew not to come."

"Nah, homie, you know I'm trying to fuck Paula fine ass, so we better not say nothing to Nora.

Andrea had spent the night at Darleen's house and didn't have time to go pick up all her things like she planned. After getting the stitches, then taking the pain medication Nora gave her, Andrea was too tired to do anything. Darleen was on point, though, and made sure

Andrea got up bright and early this morning. She wasn't trying to give her friend the opportunity to go back on her word. Andrea had said that it was over this time, and Darleen was making sure of it.

"Now, when we get in here, make sure you don't do no talking. Get important shit like ya birth certificate, social security card, and other important documents," Darleen explained as she turned onto the block. "Don't worry about clothes and shit like that. He can have all that, cause as soon as we leave here, we're going shopping for a whole new wardrobe," Darleen said.

She pumped Andrea up real good, but the moment they walked through the front door, Andrea deflated like a flat tire. Garnett was sitting on the steps with his head down in shame. His face was wet like he'd been crying all morning, and from the look he had in his eyes, Andrea could tell that he was hurting. She'd never seen this look in his eyes before, let alone seen him crying.

"Baby, I'm sorry," Garnett said, getting up from the step. "Please forgive me," he pleaded, walking up to her.

"Bitch, don't go for that. Get ya shit and lets go," Darleen spoke up, pushing Andrea up the steps past Garnett. "Keep ya fuckin' distance too, pussy," she warned, pulling a taser from her bag. "I'll zap da shit out of you in dis bitch."

"Why don't you mind ya fuckin' business?" he barked at Darleen before taking off, up the steps behind Andrea.

He ran into the bedroom with Andrea, slammed the door behind him, then locked it to keep Darleen out while he talked. "Baby, come here," he said, walking up and wrapping his arms around Andrea's waist. "Look at me, baby," he begged, turning her chin toward his face. "You know I love you, Muffin. I swear I will never treat you wrong again. I know I fucked up. Just don't leave me."

Andrea stood there, looking into his eyes. Tears began to fill up hers as well. Andrea hadn't realized how weak she was for him until now. Him kissing her forehead, her cheeks, and her bruised lip softly didn't make things any easier.

"Don't do it Andrea!" Darleen yelled, kicking the door as hard as she could. "Fuck him, girl," she continued. "I swear to God."

Andrea reached up and placed both of her hands to the side of his face. She pulled his face to hers and kissed his lips. "I forgive you," she said, looking into his eyes with sincerity.

Garnett knew that he had her now, at least that's what he thought.

"I love you, Garnett, but it's over," Andrea said, pushing away from him slowly. "I deserve so much better," she added before heading toward the door.

Garnett couldn't believe what he'd just heard, but before he could stop her from leaving, she got the bedroom door unlocked. Darleen was standing there, popping the electricity on her taser, wishing Garnett would do something stupid. Garnett wasn't trying to get electrocuted, so he kept his distance, but at the same time, he showed his true colors.

"Bitch, you gon' leave me? Ain't nobody else gon' want you. I'm the only nigga that's gonna want ya ass," he yelled, following Andrea and Darleen down the steps. "You fat, you ugly, and ya pussy stink." He continued with his vicious verbal assault until they were at the door. "Fuck you bitch. Fuck you too, Darleen, you fat bitch."

He was doing fine until he started calling Darleen out of her name. As she and Andrea were walking out the door, she slowed up a little so that Garnett could catch up to them. He got to about two feet behind them, still cursing up a storm and calling them all kinds of bitches.

Darleen, without warning, spun around, taser still in hand, and zapped Garnett in his gut. She tried her best to fry his insides with how many times she tased him. Garnett fell to the floor, shaking, with his teeth clinched and his eyes wide open.

Darleen went to shock him again, but Andrea grabbed her arm. "You gon' kill him, Darleen, chill," Andrea said, pulling her away from him. "We out, girl, come on," she yelled at Darleen.

Having made her point clear, Darleen jumped back into the car and sped off down the street at high speed.

Nora stopped past the pharmacy to check up on Ronald, that and to get some supplies for her first aid kit. Monti's simple self was at the front with a huge smile on his face when Nora walked up. She looked right past him for Ronald.

"What can I do for you today, thickness?" Monti smiled.

"Is Ronald here?" she asked, ignoring the nickname he called her.

"He's in the back dispensing pills right now. But whatever you want, I can get it for you," Monti told her.

"Nah, it's cool. I can come back later," she responded.

Monti could see that Nora was feeling Ronald, and thought that he'd start a little shit. "Hey, Nora, I'm having a Thanksgiving party next week, and I was wondering if you could come through. Ronnie Ron gon' be there," he joked.

Since Ronald was going to be there, Nora went against her better judgment and decided to accept his invite. She really must have really liked Ronald, because she didn't do parties at all.

"A'ight, thickness—and make sure you bring some of ya girls wit' you too. We gon' turn up," Monti assured.

"Bye, boy," Nora said, waving Monti off before walking away.

Nora almost made it to her wing before her phone began vibrating in her scrubs. It was Darleen calling, so she had to answer it to find out what happened with Andrea this morning. Andrea was cracking up laughing in the background, which was a good sign.

"Girl, I electrocuted da shit out of that nigga." Darleen laughed into the phone. "He might be on his way to the hospital from all these volts I sent through his body," Darleen said.

"Y'all, that's not funny," Nora said, chuckling herself at the thought of Garnett on the ground, shaking from the shock.

"We goin' out tonight, girl. We celebrating. Dis bitch really broke up wit' dat crazy ass nigga. We goin' to Jolly's Live, and all drinks are on me," Darleen shouted into the phone then hung up in Nora's ear.

Nora just shook her head and headed to her wing, where there was more than enough work for her to do. Going out tonight with the girls really didn't sound so bad after all.

"Drop down and get ya eagle on, girl, drop down and get ya eagle on, girl," blasted through the speakers at Jolly's Live.

Darleen wasted no time running to the dance floor, pulling Nora along with her. Dancing was another one of Darleen's talents, and she could do it well. She knew how to move, winding her hips, poppin' her ass. With no problem, she dropped all her thickness to the ground, then brought it back up. She had stamina too, breezing through a couple of songs without breaking a sweat. "Awww, dis my shit," Darleen yelled.

"Watch out for the big girls, watch out for the big girls, watch out for the big girls," turned the party up.

Every thick chick in the building hit the dance floor, shaking and gyrating all over the place. Nora was getting busy too on the floor, bouncing her big titties to the music. Everyone was having a ball, even Andrea, who sat in the back because she didn't want to pop her stitches. She did manage to get her drink on, knocking back two strawberry daiquiris.

"Let me see you shake dem titties, pop dat pussy, doo doo brown. I wanna rock. I wanna rock. I wanna rock!"

Jolly's Live was going crazy tonight. The DJ was rocking, and it wasn't too many people in their seats. Darleen had her hands on her knees, throwing her ass everywhere, while Nora raised her hands to the sky. Darleen whipped her hair side to side, and Nora did the same with her weave. They were letting it all hang out, literally. Finally, a corny song came on, giving Nora and Darleen a break. They two-stepped their way over to the bar, where Andrea was.

"Girl, my feet are killing me," Nora confessed, unzipping the sides of her shoes. "I ain't goin' back out there tonight. Can I get something to drink?" she yelled at the bartender. "And what you over here thinking about?" Nora asked Andrea, picking up her daiquiri and drinking some of it.

"I know it better not be that nigga," Darleen cut in.

The daiquiri and the single shot of Patrón had Andrea thinking about a lot of stuff. One thing in particular was the way all the thick girls in the club took over the dance floor when certain songs came on. They shut it down, and in moments like that, Andrea was proud to be a plus sized woman. She wanted all the big girls worldwide to feel what she felt.

"I think we should start our own modeling company," Andrea said. "A modeling company for plus-size women like us."

"Girl, how many drinks did you have over here?" Darleen joked.

"Shut up, girl, I'm serious. After seeing what I saw tonight, I believe we have the potential to start a movement.

"Yeah, she had one too many." Nora laughed. "What made you come up with that idea?" Nora asked as she threw back a shot of Patrón.

"I don't know. It was a vision I had watching you two out there dancing. Y'all are rockin' the hell out of those outfits, and to be honest wit' you, y'all are the prettiest chicks in here," Andrea complimented. "Every big girl in here followed y'all two out to the dance floor, and now look," Andrea said, pointing to the dance floor, which was now empty.

Since Darleen and Nora had been at the bar, not one thick girl was out on the floor dancing. Nora thought that it was a coincidence, but Darleen didn't. She was starting to see what Andrea was seeing, and in a flash, she could see herself on the runway.

"Well, look, have a few more drinks, think about the idea some more, then get back to me with ya thoughts," Darleen said as she waved for the bartender. "I don't know, maybe that's something we can explore.

All three women raised their glasses and toasted to that. Andrea definitely had her thinking cap on, and if given enough time, she was going to come up with something that was sure to change the way America looks at plus sized women.

Alone and feeling stupid, Garnett sat in the house recovering from being tasered by Darleen. His pride and ego were bruised more than anything, and it wasn't until then that he realized he'd messed up a good thing. Andrea had done everything for him. Cooked, cleaned, and gave him any kind of sex he asked for, on demand. She even put up with his verbal and physical abuse. It wasn't a chick in the city willing to go through or do as much for Garnett as Andrea had. He knew and understood that now, and wished he could go back in time and change his evil ways. He wished he could have been a better man and treated Andrea with love and respect. He wished he could have done a lot of things, but now it was too late. She was gone and wasn't coming back, and it killed Garnett to think about the precious jewel he'd lost for the next man to find. All he was left with was a sad reminder of how he'd messed up.

Thanksgiving party

Monti threw some of the best holiday parties around this time of year, and from the looks of things, he was not going to disappoint his guests tonight. Pulling up to his house was like pulling up to a club on a Saturday night. The forty-degree weather didn't stop females from rocking their shortest skirts and heels, and it wasn't just them. Everyone was on dress-to-impress status.

"I'm not tryin' to be here all night," Darleen said, thinking about a date she had with Thunder, one of her costars.

"I'm only stayin' for an hour or so," Nora informed as they got out of the car. "I still gotta go to work in the morning."

"Shit, I'm trying to take one of these fine-ass niggas home wit' me," Andrea joked, looking at a couple of well-dressed men walking past them and heading for the house.

As soon as Nora and the girls walked through the door, heads turned. Monti was clearly drunk at this point. He jumped up from the couch and playfully danced over to the door. Nora knew he was about to say something stupid.

"Y'all bitches can eat all y'all want," he joked, cracking up at his own self. "Nah, fo'real, come in and enjoy yourselves."

Nora looked at Darleen and then at Andrea. "Forty-five minutes," she mouthed as they followed Monti.

Going deeper into the house, Nora noticed a familiar face sitting off to the side with a cute female on his lap sipping on a drink. It was Ronald, and it seemed as if he was enjoying his company, feeling and touching all over her body while whispering in her ear. This didn't even look like the same Ronald that Nora knew. Instead of busting his groove, Nora took to the mini bar with Darleen.

"Where da hell did Andrea go that fast?" Nora asked, looking around the room.

"Where you think?" Darleen shot back, nodding toward the kitchen.

Nora hadn't been at the party for twenty minutes, and she was already ready to leave. The only reason she came to Monti's party was to see Ronald, but he'd been so mesmerized by the young model-figure female, he still didn't know that Nora was in the building.

"You want me to go say something to that nigga?" Darleen hissed, seeing Nora stare at Ronald across the room.

Nora didn't even have time to respond before Darleen was making her way over to Ronald. Nora didn't know whether to stay at the bar or follow behind Darleen, who was sure to make a scene. Nora chose to stay and throw

back a double shot of whatever the bartender had poured
in the cup for Darleen. It was strong, too, just the way
Nora needed it to be.

Darleen walked through the crowd of people until she
made it to the living room. This group must have been
the "it" crowd. It looked like the VIP section, with Monti
and a couple of his boys sitting on a couch on one side of
the room, while Ronald and another one of his homeboys
sat on a couch on the other side of the room. Women
and bottles of champagne were scattered about, and it
seemed like everybody was having fun.

"Are you Ronald?" Darleen asked, walking up to him on
the couch.

He looked up at Darleen in confusion, not knowing if
he should answer the question. One of the females that
was sitting next to him on the couch busted out laughing
at Darleen, mainly because of how Darleen was standing
there.

"Don't get ya ass beat, little girl," Darleen quickly
checked. She turned back around to face Ronald. "Look,
my girl Nora over there wanted to have a word with you,"
Darleen told him.

Ronald sat up and looked over toward the bar where
Nora was throwing back another drink.

"Oh, yeah, my nigga, I forgot to tell you that ya girl was
here," Monti said and threw a couch pillow at Ronald.

"Oh, shit, nigga you got two bitches here?" one of the
fellas laughed, causing just about everybody else in
the room to laugh too. But the female who was sitting
on Ronald's lap wasn't laughing. She looked at him,
awaiting his response.

"I don't have but one lady with me, and she sitting right
here," Ronald answered, tapping Niki on the leg.

Darleen was hot when she heard that come out of his
mouth. She wanted swing on him but decided against it.

She simply smiled then walked off, but not before getting the last words. "You sitting here acting like you don't be all up on my girl. You know what that makes you: a fuckin' coward," Darleen said, then walked off.

Monti and the crew laughed at him a little harder. "Yo, I swear I know that chick from somewhere," Monti's friend leaned over and told him.

Darleen walked back over to the bar, and Nora could tell by the look in her eyes that something had happened. "What happened, girl?" Nora asked, passing Darleen a drink.

Darleen threw back the drink, then slammed the glass on the bar. "Let's just get out of here, girl."

"Why, what's going on?" Nora asked in a concerned manner.

After a brief explanation of what took place, Nora was ready to leave as well. She couldn't believe Ronald had responded like that, after all the shit he had told her. Part of her had expected this from him, and it looked like his player reputation was well deserved.

"I told you I knew that broad," Monti's friend laughed, pointing at the laptop screen. "Oh, shit, that's her."

Everybody gathered around the laptop to watch Darleen deep throat a ten-inch dick in one of her films. Monti cracked joke after joke and had mostly everybody in the room laughing so hard they cried. "Wait, wait, don't leave," Monti playfully pleaded, seeing Nora, Darleen, and Andrea heading for the door.

Darleen glanced over and saw herself on the laptop screen. The harder everyone laughed and pointed, the worse she felt.

"Well, at least I get paid to suck dick and fuck. You bitches doing it for free!" Darleen shouted before shutting the door.

***

The car was silent during the ride home. Everyone was soaking in their own embarrassment, and at one point, Darleen had shed a tear or two. "Y'all wanna come in and chill out for a little while?" Nora asked when Andrea pulled up to her house.

"Nah, I'm good. I just wanna go home," Darleen responded as she browsed through her phone.

Nora was about to say something, but her phone began to ring in her bag. She was almost 100 percent sure that it was Ronald trying to call and apologize, but to her surprise, it wasn't. It was Betty, her coworker at the hospital. She informed Nora that Ms. Emma was doing bad, and might not make it through the night.

"Can you please take me to my job?" Nora asked Andrea.

The love and respect Nora had for Ms. Emma was deep. Through the years of caring for her every time she was admitted into the hospital, Nora felt like she was family. If Ms. Emma was dying tonight, Nora wanted to be there.

"Y'all don't have to stay. I can catch a cab home," Nora said when they pulled up to the hospital.

"Nah girl, we here wit' you," Darleen replied, wanting to support Nora if she needed it.

Nora raced through the hospital up to her wing, where she was met by Betty. "Ms. Emma's been asking for you," Betty informed.

When Nora entered the room, she along with Darleen and Andrea walked up and stood next to Ms. Emma's bed. It took a few minutes, but eventually, Ms. Emma opened her eyes. She looked around the room at each of their faces then smiled.

"You must be Darleen . . . And you Andrea," Ms. Emma pointed. "You girls are . . . beautiful," her weak voice spoke. "And why you look so bitter?" Ms. Emma asked Nora. "I hope you're not believing Doctor Floyd . . . he . . .

he always tell me I'm not gonna . . . make it . . . through the night. He must don't know Jesus. Jeeeessuusss," she sang, then went back out.

This time, when Ms. Emma closed her eyes, she didn't wake back up. She died a few minutes later, and although her immediate family didn't surround her, Ms. Emma didn't die alone.

When the girls finally stepped out of Ms. Emma's room, they were approached by a well-dressed white man. "Hi, is your name Nora Baker?" he asked.

"I'm Nora Baker. How can I help you?"

"I know this isn't a good time, and I'm sorry for your loss, but I was Ms. Emma Washington's attorney. There's some paperwork that needs to be signed," the lawyer stated.

"Paperwork? What do you mean paperwork?"

The attorney walked Nora and the girls into the break room then sat at the table. He pulled a thin folder from his briefcase and began to explain that Ms. Emma had provided for Nora in her will, all while passing Nora an envelope. She was hesitant but opened it. Inside was a relatively short letter, but a letter nonetheless. It read,

Dear Nora,
Thank you for looking after me during my final days. You are an angel. I'm leaving behind some money for you in hopes that one day you'll consider pursuing what you dreamed of. Ms. Emma loves you, baby.

Nora wiped the tear that fell down her cheek, then placed the letter back into the envelope. She couldn't help but to wonder what Ms. Emma was talking about pertaining to what Nora dreamed of.

The lawyer pulled out the paperwork for Nora to sign. When Nora saw how much Ms. Emma left her, her jaw dropped. She covered her mouth, looking down at the release forms for one-hundred thousand dollars. Nora couldn't believe it, but she quickly signed the form before the lawyer changed his mind. Before he left, he informed Nora that the check would be ready in five business days, and for her to stop by his office to pick it up next Thursday or Friday.

"Damn, Nora, what are you gonna do with all that money?" Darleen asked.

"Hopefully you'll buy a nice car," Andrea joked.

Nora honestly didn't know what she was going to do with the money. It was all still fresh, and Nora was trying to figure out what Ms. Emma was referring to. She pulled the letter out and read it again and again, trying to decipher the few words. Then it hit Nora like a ton of bricks. She remembered the conversation her and Ms. Emma had about Andrea's idea of starting a modeling agency for plus-sized women. Nora remembered telling Ms. Emma she had a dream she'd strutted down the catwalk in the middle of Broadway in New York City. It was a dream Nora didn't think would ever come true, that is until tonight. Ms. Emma had not only left behind the financial means to get started, but she also left behind a set of encouraging words that made a huge impact on her soul.

Nora turned to Andrea and Darleen, and with every ounce of conviction she had in her, spoke words that would change everyone's life.

"We're starting that modeling agency, and I don't care what it takes. Are y'all wit' me?"

Neither of the two needed to say a word. They would ride through the gates of hell with Nora. On that Thanksgiving night, the seed was planted. The world was about to witness the unbelievable happen, right before their very eyes.

Chapter 5

Darleen damn near jumped out the bed when she woke up and saw Gordo asleep next to her. She couldn't remember for the life of her the last time she had a man spend the night, and she definitely didn't think that it would be someone like Gordo. The whole idea of dating people from her job was out of the question, and how Gordo managed to change her mind was a mystery in itself.

"*Hola, mami. Buenos días, mi amor,*" Gordo greeted when he woke up. He was half-black and half Puerto Rican, and spoke both English and Spanish fluently. He sounded sexy as hell when he was doing it. Now Darleen was starting to remember how he had smoothed talked his way into coming back to her place last night.

"*Buenos días*, my ass," Darleen joked and playfully punched him on his arm. "This a one-time event, so don't get used to it."

Gordo smiled and scooted over closer to Darleen. "I don't think you mean that," he said softly, rubbing her bare waistline. "I think this might be the beginning of something special."

"Oh, yeah? And what makes you think that?" Darleen shot back, trying not to get turned on by his soft touch.

In the porn industry, Gordo had sex with all kinds of women, in all different shapes and sizes, but his personal preference was thick women. He loved everything about them and had no shame in it.

"You might not be able to see it right now, but eventually, I'ma make you my girl," he said, turning Darleen onto her back and rolling on top of her.

Darleen laughed at him, finding his words to be cute. Though she found them hard to believe, it was some part of her that wished those words had some truth to them. Every time a good man tried to take it further than sex with Darleen, her insecurities kicked in, and she ended up pushing him away before she got hurt. So just like the rest of the men that came and went in her life, Darleen immediately put Gordo on the chopping block, with two strikes against him. One was for being so damn handsome, and the other, for having a twelve-inch dick he knew how to work oh, so well.

Andrea pulled up to the hospital to drop Nora off at work, but not before getting an earful of Nora instructing her on things that needed to be done in order to get the modeling agency up and running. So much time and effort needed to be put in, and for the most part, Andrea had more than enough time on her hands.

"And make sure you stay within the budget that I gave you," Nora reminded her as she gathered her things in the car.

Andrea looked over at her friend and was amazed by how serious Nora was about modeling.

"Girl, you really serious about this, huh?" Andrea asked.

Nora stopped then turned her face to Andrea.

"I'm dead serious," she answered, then went back to getting her things. "We been thick all our lives, Andrea, and I think it's fine time we show people that being thick is a beautiful thing. Hell, we already done changed their thoughts on a big ass—you know them white girls used to do everything they could to lose theirs, but now they getting ass implants," Nora said as she got out of the car.

Nora's mind was made up, and once she had it fixed on something, she was the type of person that was going to see it through. "I'll call you on my lunch break," Nora told Andrea as she closed the passenger's side door.

After watching her disappear into the hospital, Andrea pulled off and got her busy day started.

Darleen lay in bed, staring at the ceiling as her body settled back down from the massive orgasm she'd just had from Gordo eating her pussy. He finally picked his head up from between her legs, wiping the residuals of her cum from his chin. This was the first time she'd had her pussy ate in this fashion, and not for nothing, she was impressed.

"Can I ask you something?" Darleen said as she rolled over onto her side to face Gordo. "What's your real name?" She smiled, feeling like she just had to know after that episode.

"Julio Jimenez," he said, pulling her closer to him. "And what about you? What's your real name?" he shot back.

"Darleen Grubbs," she giggled. "And you better not tell nobody," she added and grabbed a handful of his dick. Darleen always thought that her name sounded funny when she said it.

Gordo thought that it was a little funny too, so they ended up sharing a laugh. Before Darleen knew it, they were laughing and joking about a whole lot of stuff. It was to the point that she had forgot about the task she was supposed to do for Nora. Her phone ringing on the nightstand was the reminder that she needed.

"Oh, shit," she blurted out, rolling over and grabbing her phone. She didn't even have to look at the screen to know who it was.

"I'm doing it right now," Darleen said into the phone as soon as she picked it up.

"Where the hell are you?" Nora asked as she walked through the hospital hallways. "And ya ass better not be in the bed."

"I'm not in the bed," Darleen lied, getting up from the bed and heading to the bathroom.

Her job was to find a professional photographer and a place to hold their first show. She too was on a budget and had to make do with what she was given.

"A'ight. I'm on it, big sis," Darleen told her as she turned the shower on.

"See, bitch, I knew you was still in the house," Nora complained. "Get it together. It's now or never," she said, then hung up the phone.

Over the past few days, Darleen could hear in Nora's voice how dedicated she was to the project. It made her want to stop messing around and get the ball rolling. She definitely didn't want to be the reason why none of this panned out the way it was supposed to. She wouldn't hear the end of it from Nora and Andrea. Putting her quality time in with Gordo was going to have to wait, at least for right now.

"Nora, Nora," Ronald yelled out from behind the pharmacy station.

It had been a few days since the incident at that party, and every day she came to work, she didn't speak to Ronald or even look his way for that matter. As far as she was concerned, Ronald had died the same night he played her in front of everybody. She was only giving him one chance to pull a stunt like that.

"Nora, hold up," he yelled again as he jogged behind her down the hallway.

When he went to grab her hand from behind, Nora snatched away, spun around, and looked at him like he was crazy.

"Don't fuckin' touch me," Nora snapped, balling her fist up as if she was about to swing at him.

He took a step back and put his hands in the air. "Whoa, I just wanna have a word wit' you," Ronald said as he slowly lowered his hands so he wouldn't draw any attention. "Look, Nora, I'm sorry about what happened at the party. I did some nut shit, and I regret it," Ronald tried to explain.

"And now what? You expect me to just forgive you and things just go back to normal? You want me to pretend like none of that ever happened, like you wasn't booed up with some chick after telling me you wasn't seeing anyone?" Nora shot back with plenty of attitude.

Ronald lowered his head. The last thing he wanted to do was hurt Nora, but him and Niki had history, and he knew how she got down. If he had acknowledged Nora and dissed Niki in front of their mutual friends, Niki and her girls would've gone to town making fun of Nora. He thought that he was doing the right thing and protecting Nora, but now he was regretting that decision. Before he could lift his head to respond and offer a reason for his actions, Nora had turned around and walked off on him.

Nora wasn't interested in hearing his apologies, nor would she accept any of his excuses. She was at the stage in her life where she was completely focused on her modeling plans. Thickums was her main priority now, not some light skinned wannabe player.

As soon as Darleen stuck the key in the door, she could smell the strong scent of weed coming out of the studio. The thick heavy smoke smacked her in the face, giving her contact before she could get a chance to turn around and lock the door behind her. Tuesdays wasn't a filming day, but that didn't stop Wood, the head producer, from having an all out orgy on one of the sets. He, along with three women, were enjoying the slow day. Darleen was about to turn around and leave, but Wood spotted her from afar.

"Delicious, bring ya sexy ass over here!" Wood yelled out from across the room. He was sitting in his director's chair getting head from a white girl. "Come on over here, don't be scared," he joked.

Darleen walked over to him, cutting her eyes over at the girl bobbing her head up and down on his dick. She kind of felt sorry for the girl, because everyone except her knew that Wood never busts a nut from getting head. The girl looked determined to make it happen, though.

"I need a favor from you, Wood," Darleen said.

He briefly took his eyes off the young lady and looked up at her. "This should be interesting."

"I was wondering if I could use one of the sets so me and my girls can do a photo shoot. It would only be for an hour or two, and we can do it on a day when there's no filming," Darleen explained.

Wood threw his head back in thought, not at all paying attention to the girl that was sucking his dick. He took a long deep puff of the Kush-filled dutch, then blew it out like a dragon.

"You wanna use the studio?" he asked, frowning slightly. "This is a place of business. If I let you do it, then—"

"I'll pay you if I have to," Darleen interrupted, cutting him off. Only two things could get Wood's attention, and that was money and sex. "A'ight, give me twenty-five hundred and you can use the patio for ya shoot," Wood offered.

That would have been okay, but the background was horrible, plus it was too small.

"Come on, Wood," Darleen complained. "How about I make a deal wit' you?" she said, getting his attention.

"Now you talking," he answered, rubbing his palms together. "Talk to me."

"Well, if I can make you cum from sucking ya dick, you let me use any room in the studio, my choice, for as long as I need to next Tuesday," Darleen said.

"Okay, what if you don't? What's in it for me?"

"If I don't, I'll do one scene for you at no cost, and you can use any theme ya nasty li'l mind can come up with," Darleen proposed.

Wood sat there for a second, looked down at the female who was still working his member, then looked back up at Darleen. This was the kind of challenge he liked. Not only was the task of making Wood cum from oral sex difficult in itself, but to make matters even harder, he had to take a piss, which made it nearly impossible for him to cum at this point. It was easy money, in his mind.

"I'll give you fifteen minutes and not a second later," Wood offered.

"Good, cause all I need is ten," Darleen shot back as she put her bag down and let down her hair.

She nudged the girl, who was more than happy to come up off her knees.

"Watch and learn," Darleen said, then went down on Wood's dick.

"Nora, can I have a word with you in my office?" Ms. Hill, a member of the hospital board and Nora's supervisor said, poking her head in one of the patient's room where Nora was reading a chart.

Whenever Ms. Hill had to come out to the floor, somebody was either in trouble or was about to be promoted. Nora didn't want either of the two. She knocked before entering Ms. Hill's office.

"Nora, I'm going to get straight to the point. It has come to my attention that you walked in on Alice and the janitor—"

"Whoa, whoa, where did you get that information from?" Nora asked, getting out of her seat. She did a quick process of elimination, and the only person she could see doing some shit like this was Travis. He always wanted to be the head nurse on their wing.

"Look, if there's any truth to it, you have to let me know now before it gets to the board. I can sanction you, fire Alice, and report the janitor. But if this gets to the higher ups, I won't be able to save your job," Ms. Hill said.

Nora was stuck between a rock and a hard spot. No matter what she did, the consequences were going to be stiff. Alice was her friend, but Nora couldn't afford to lose her job right now. Too much was going on with the modeling agency, along with the everyday bills that needed to be paid. It was a hard decision, but Nora caved. Ms. Hill made her explain in detail what she'd seen, and she had to include times and dates and anyone else who may have been there. She left out of the office feeling like a snitch, but in her defense, Alice was the one who had put her in this situation in the first place.

"Do you think I can take the rest of the day off?" Nora asked, wanting to get some air from the hours' worth of grilling.

"Yeah, I guess you can leave, but make sure you're back in my office first thing in the morning so I can hand down your sanctions," Ms. Hill concluded before finally dismissing Nora.

The only thing Nora could think about was getting a drink. Never during her nursing career had she ever had any misconduct on her record. This was like a smack in the face. Nora felt like she had come too far. No matter what the sanctions were going to be tomorrow, it would never equal the shame she felt inside.

***

Darleen stood in the bathroom, looking at herself in the mirror. After putting her hair back in a ponytail, she reached into her bag to retrieve her phone. She could still hear Wood and the girls outside the bathroom laughing and talking about how crazy it was. Darleen wasn't in a laughing mood; she was more about her business right now.

"Hey, girl, where you been at all day?" Andrea asked as she drove down the street on her way to pick Nora up.

"I been working my ass off trying to get us a place for the photo shoot," Darleen said, lowering her head.

"And did you find a place?"

Darleen looked to the ceiling and let out a loud sigh. She envisioned Wood's dick and the moment she had gotten him to splash off in her mouth. It turned out, deep throating his dick was the problem. Sucking and licking around the head of his rod was his sensitive spot. It took Darleen every bit of five minutes to find that out, then another five minutes to make him cum. It was so crazy that the other females gathered around to watch the event. Just the thought of that brought a smile to Darleen's face.

"Yeah, I found a place. Come pick me up, and I'll tell you all about it," Darleen said, looking in the mirror at herself.

When Darleen got off the phone, she noticed that it had gotten quiet. She walked out and saw the girls just lounging around, and Wood was nowhere in sight. "Where is he?" Darleen asked one of the girls, who pointed to his office.

She walked to the back and opened Wood's office door. She looked in and saw him punching numbers into his safe. He picked his head up and pointed a gun at her.

"Girl, don't be sneaking up on me like that," Wood said, lowering his pistol.

Catching a peek at what was in the safe, Darleen was surprised to see what looked like coke or heroin inside. No wonder he was so paranoid. She closed the door behind her to keep his business out of the streets.

"Damn, nigga, you hustle too?" Darleen asked, walking over and picking up one of the four bricks of cocaine that was sitting on the desk. Due to her older brother, PooMan, being in the streets, Darleen knew a thing or two about the drug game, and she knew exactly what she was looking at.

"I hope you don't think I got rich off of you bitches fuckin' on camera," Wood responded, taking the brick from Darleen and putting it back on the desk. "And make sure you let me know what set you gon' be using next week, cause I got some shit going on next week and I don't want us clashing.

Darleen barely heard a word he said. She couldn't take her eyes off the several other bricks of cocaine in the safe. This made her look at Wood in a whole new light. Darleen had always liked a bad boy.

"A'ight, see ya ass out, and make sure you bring ya ass to work tomorrow. You and Iron Man is doin' a scene called 'Dipped in Chocolate,'" Wood told her.

He always had some freaky shit up his sleeve, and Darleen could only imagine what he planned to do with the two jugs of chocolate sitting in the corner.

Chapter 6

Nora walked into the bank and handed the teller the check she'd gotten from Ms. Emma's law firm. This was the most money she'd ever had at one time, and she was more than eager to do something good with it.

"Could you please give me twenty thousand in cash?" Nora requested.

Though the check was a cashier's check, the teller had to clear it with the manager. The process took a little longer, but after about forty-five minutes of waiting, Nora was walking out of the bank with two hundred crispy one-hundred dollar bills. Darleen and Andrea were standing outside eating McDonalds when Nora came out.

"A'ight y'all, I gotta get back to work. I got a meeting with my supervisor," Nora said when she walked up to Andrea's car. "Here, this should take care of the photographer, the catering, and the club rental," she said, passing Andrea the money from the bank.

"Damn, I'm glad I have both of you here," Andrea said, licking the Mac sauce from her fingers.

Remembering that she needed to finish up some paperwork pertaining to their business, Andrea popped open the trunk and grabbed her big bag with all the forms and information she needed to go over with them. "So each of us owns thirty-three percent of Thickums, and the remaining percent will go into a trust fund for the company," Andrea explained, pulling out the packages for them to read and sign.

This was the reason Andrea was in charge of the business aspect of the project. She had her own catering company, so she knew the ins and outs of contracts, licensing, and just about everything else there was to know about running a business. She had even retained a lawyer to make sure that everything she did was within the law.

"Here's to the beginning of something big, literally," Nora said, raising her pen to the sky like she was toasting with a champagne glass. Everyone raised their pens, and right there on Andrea's car, they all signed, making Thickums, Inc. official. It was go time now.

Nora had all eyes on her when she walked into the east wing, and from the look Ms. Hill had on her face, Nora knew that it was a problem. The meeting for her sanctions wasn't being held in Ms. Hill's office, which raised the first flag. Instead, Nora was led to the conference room where several board members sat around a large oval table. The only person she recognized out of everybody besides Ms. Hill, was Mr. Gant, the Administrative Director.

"Have a seat," he told Nora as he looked through the incident report.

Two seconds later, Travis walked in and took a seat at the table, right across from Nora.

You disloyal muthafucka, Nora thought to herself, realizing that he was the one behind all of this. He'd always wanted Nora's job, and this was the perfect chance for him to get her out of the way.

"Today we will be handing down the sanction on the matter of the incident that took place on November fifth involving Nurse Davis, Nurse Clark, and a member of our janitorial staff," Mr. Gant said, wanting to get the proceedings started.

Nora immediately looked over at Ms. Hill, who had her head down the whole time. "Wait, I thought my supervisor, Ms. Hill, was going to hand down the sanction," Nora spoke as she looked around the room.

She knew that the sanctions from the high ups would be harsher than if they came from Ms. Hill. However, the word about the incident had spread through the hospital like wild fire, so the administrative body had to step in and handle the problem, quickly and quietly.

"Ms. Davis, considering all that has happened, the administration has made the following recommendations in regards to your attempt to cover up this incident and not report it back to your supervisors, as you should have. Sex scandals in this hospital will not be tolerated, in any way, shape, or form," Mr. Gant went on.

Nora wasn't the type to sit and say nothing. "With all due respect, sir, sex scandals go on in this hospital every day with employees. Alice is a great nurse, and I made a judgment call not to say anything, just as the work affair ended," Nora tried to explain.

"Well, that wasn't a call for you to make. We have protocol, and you, along with everyone else, has to follow it," Gant spoke. "Now, this administration has ruled, and the sanctions are as follows," he said, reading from the paper in front of him. "Mrs. Clark, who declined to come in today, was informed via telephone that she has been terminated from employment, and this incident will be on her record. Janitorial staff member, Carl Jenkins, has also been released and is no longer employed here." Gant paused and took off his glasses. "I'm sorry to inform you, but it was unanimously voted that your employment here at Presbyterian is also terminated.

"This is some bullshit," Nora snapped. "Termination though? Are you serious? This doesn't even qualify for termination."

"I know you're upset, and you're a great nurse. That's why this incident won't follow you to the next hospital you work in. This administration will be the only people who know about this, and you can even use me as a reference," Gant explained.

Nora wanted to flip the table over and beat the shit out of everyone in the room, especially Travis, who was sitting there looking stupid. Ms. Hill wanted to say something, but Nora was done listening to everybody. Without saying another word, she simply got up from her seat and left. To lose her job like this was devastating, and it had Nora's head all messed up. Just leaving was the better option than to stay and trip out.

Andrea pulled up to her house and was immediately irked by Garnett sitting on her steps with a sad puppy dog face. She had so much on her plate right now, and dealing with his nonsense was the last thing she felt like doing. A month had passed since that last awful day, and Andrea had grown a lot. Without his constant put downs and disrespect, she had found her voice, and there was no way she would allow him to take her back down that insecure path.

"Wassup, Garnett . . . Why are you here?" Andrea asked when she walked up on the steps. "And how did you get my address?"

"I didn't come here to cause any drama. I honestly wanted to have a word with you," Garnett spoke softly. "I got your address from the forwarding order sent by the Post Office."

Garnett had a different look to him. He didn't look like the rough, tough, and abusive man she once knew. He even dressed different, more like a grown man, instead of looking like he was about to hit the block. He had a fresh haircut and smelled good. Even when he spoke, he sounded a lot different. The whole nice guy demeanor threw Andrea off, and for some odd reason, she wanted to hear what he had to say.

"I don't have long," she said as she leaned against the railing.

"Cool, because this won't take but a minute," Garnett replied, standing to his feet. "Look, I'm not here to try to get with you or anything like that. I really just needed to apologize to you. I know I did it before, but this time is different. This time I really mean it. Man, I treated you like shit, and it took me having to lose you to realize how stupid I was." Garnett shook his head. "I guess a sober mind got me thinking different now. I'm not the same person I used to be."

"Oh, so you don't drink anymore?" Andrea questioned.

"I don't drink, I don't smoke, and I go to counseling once a week for my anger. Nothing happens overnight, but I'm fighting every day to make my life better. Hell, I even got a new job." He laughed.

Now Andrea was really impressed. She could see a change in him that she wished she could have seen when they were together.

"You know, I'm glad that you're getting your life together," Andrea said, reaching in her bag to get her keys. "But I really have a lot of work to get to."

"No, no, no, I understand," Garnett said, cutting her off. "I gotta get out of here too. And look, Andrea, even though we're not together, I want you to know that I will always be here for you. The least I can do after everything is try to be a good friend to you," he said walking down the steps.

Andrea watched as he walked off. It was even more shocking that Garnett had traded in his obnoxious, lime green old school Chevy Impala for a black 2002

Buick LeSabre. It wasn't a fancy looking car, but it looked good on him.

Nora didn't call anyone to come pick her up from her job. Instead, she got on the bus, mad as hell. She was still in disbelief, wondering how something like this could happen to her, especially considering how much of a hard worker she was. Nora put in hours and worked more overtime than any other nurse in the building. Not only was she kind and caring to all of her patients, she was the same to her coworkers. Nora had every right to be pissed about them letting her go.

"Aww shit, there she go! The love of my life," an all too familiar voice yelled when Nora walked up the street. It was Bugsy, a well-known corner boy who Nora saw just about every day. He hustled out of a Chinese store right around the corner from her house and stood out there by himself from sun up until sun down. Many times, he worked the graveyard shift and was out there well after the store had closed.

"Don't be coming up in here looking mean today," he said, stepping to the side so Nora could enter the store. He could tell that she was mad about something. "Come on, talk to Bugsy," he said when she walked up to the glass window.

"I don't feel like no bullshit today. I got fired from my job," Nora said, grabbing some money from her bag.

"A'ight, so fuck that job. They stupid as hell for letting somebody like you go. Besides, that means I can take care of you now," he joked and leaned in to kiss Nora on the cheek. If anybody could make her laugh, it was Bugsy. He was funny as hell, something that Nora had always liked about him. That, and the fact that he playfully hit on her every day.

"When you gon' get ya butt off this corner, boy?" Nora asked while she paid for her food.

Bugsy didn't have a job, no kids, and he wasn't in a committed relationship, so it was nothing for him to hug the block all day and night.

"I tell you what. If I could come home to somebody like you every night, I'll get off the comer and get me a real nine-to-five gig."

"Boy, you better stop playing. You know I don't do young bucks," Nora responded, playfully pushing Bugsy away from her.

"See, that's why you keep missing out. A nigga like me would have ya ass glowing every day," he flirted.

He had Nora blushing for a minute. Bugsy wasn't a bad looking guy. Dark chocolate, around six feet two inches, and he had a baby face with only a few strands of hair. But, he was only twenty-two, and not the kind of man Nora needed in her life. A friendship was the only thing she could see for the future.

"Bye, Bugsy," Nora said, after grabbing her things.

Bugsy stood at the door, watching her walk away. *Nora isn't going to be able to resist my advances for much longer,* he thought.

"Come on, Dave, that's a lot of money for one day," Darleen complained, looking around the club.

After a tour of the place, she tried to negotiate a reasonable rate, but the owner wanted twice as much money as the other clubs in the city, and it was only for one day. A late afternoon event at that. The only thing was that Club Onyx had the perfect setup for what she wanted to do with the show. Space meant everything, and David's club had plenty of it.

"A'ight, look, thirty-five hundred is the best I can do. That will give you unlimited access to the whole building for eight hours. Dance floor, the stage, open bar, and the keys to the kitchen," David explained. "Look, I'm canceling out another event that day, which I could be making a lot more money than what I'm charging you. I'm only doing it because we're cousins.

Onyx was one of the most popular clubs in the city, and for this show, the girls wanted to turn up as much as possible. This was the price Darleen had to pay. In the long run, she knew that it would be well worth it.

Nora felt a little better once she got home and was in relax mode. That only lasted an hour, then the stresses of not having a job started to kick back in. The whole process of getting another job was another issue; one Nora didn't feel like getting into right now. The only thing on her mind was taking a hot bath. It was one of her stress relievers and the main thing that could bring some type of happiness to her life. Right in the middle of her thought process, Nora could hear the phone ringing in the other room. She didn't feel like talking, but she had to answer it just in case it was Darleen or Andrea calling. When she got to the phone and looked down at the screen, the number was unfamiliar.

"Yeah, who's calling?" she answered, walking back toward the bathroom.

"Please don't hang up on me, Nora," Ronald yelled. He had called from another number because he knew she wouldn't answer if she saw his number.

"What do you want, Ronald?" Nora asked in a frustrated tone.

The only reason she didn't hang up the phone was because she wanted him to get whatever it was off his chest, so she could tell him not to contact her anymore.

"I heard about what happened earlier. That was fucked up. I just want you to know that if you need me for anything, don't hesitate to get wit' me."

"As a matter of fact, there is something you can do for me. I know you feel guilty about the whole situation at the party, but I would really appreciate it if you didn't call me anymore."

"Damn, is that how you feel?" Ronald asked, seeing that Nora didn't have any interest in him.

Nora would never forgive him for what he did at the party, so there was no need for her to befriend him. He blew it, and keeping it moving was the best thing.

"Yeah, Ronald. Have a nice life," Nora said then hung up the phone on him.

"Where are you taking me?" Darleen asked Gordo as she looked out the passenger's side window. "I don't like surprises. The two had been together for most of the day. Gordo had picked Darleen up after she finished her business at the club. From there, they went to get something to eat, and now Darleen didn't have a clue as to where they were going.

"I want you to meet some of my friends. I think they'll like you," Gordo said, looking over at her.

Darleen wasn't sure about that, and almost immediately, her insecurities kicked in. She didn't want people staring at her like she was from another planet. Her biggest fear was not being accepted by his people because of her job. It was crazy the treatment that male actors received by the public versus the females. The men were looked at as gods who had the pleasure of fucking beautiful women and being paid for it. Whereas the women were viewed as hoes who would do anything for a quick buck.

"Gordo, I don't think that's a good idea," Darleen said, becoming more nervous by the second.

He looked over at her and could see the concern on her face. It made him pull his car over so he could get some clear understanding about what was going on.

"What's wrong? I just want to take you to meet some of my friends. It ain't like we're about to get married." He chuckled. "Trust me, you have nothing to worry about.

Going against her better judgment, Darleen nodded her head in approval. Her ego, pride, and self-confidence were on the line, but for some reason, Darleen wanted to see where this was going to go. Gordo didn't live in Philly. He was actually a New Jersey native and lived right across the bridge in Cherry Hill. The sun was still out, but it was starting to set by the time they got to his sister's house. The neighborhood looked nice, and so did the houses. It was the way Darleen had pictured Gordo living.

"Hey li'l bro," a heavyset woman said as she walked down the driveway with a bottle of Cîroc in one hand and a cigarette in the other.

"Darleen, this is my sister, Lyne. Lyne, this is my friend—"

"Boy, shut up," Lyne said, cutting him off and pushing him out of the way. "Hey girl, never mind him. Come on," Lyne laughed, threw her arm around Darleen, then led her into the house.

Lyne was a beautiful, full-figured woman. She only had Darleen by a few pounds, and they looked good on her. 100% Puerto Rican, long black curly hair, big hazel eyes, and a cute squeaky voice. Darleen made a mental note to keep Lyne in mind for Thickums once they were up and running. As soon as Lyne kicked in her front door, a large group of people yelled out "Heeeyyyy" with their glasses or blunts raised to the sky. It was 6:45 in the evening on a Wednesday, and it was turnt up in Lyne's house. Another round of "Heeeyyys" sounded off when Gordo entered.

Darleen smiled ear to ear as Lyne walked her around the house introducing her to everyone. Reggaeton music played in the background, all kinds of drinks were everywhere, and on the coffee table in front of the couch, they had about a half pound of weed and a couple ounces of powder cocaine. This was a party for real, and within thirty to forty-five minutes of being there, they had made Darleen feel like she was a part of the crew. Before she knew it, Darleen had a bottle of Belvidere in one hand and a blunt in the other, standing on the couch partying like a rock star with Gordo's folks.

Chapter 7

"She's still not answering the phone?" Nora asked Andrea, who kept calling Darleen.

Today, all three girls were supposed to head downtown to a modeling school for a crash course on strutting the runway. This three-day class wasn't flexible, nor was it cheap, so Darleen couldn't afford to miss prepaid and non-refundable class.

"Dis bitch is trippin'. We gone have to go without her," Nora said, opening the passenger's side door.

"That's crazy, 'cause I just talked to her last night, and she said that she was going to be up," Andrea added as she got into the car. "You gotta be on point, baby girl," she mumbled.

The photo shoot was tomorrow, and three days after that was the show. The catering situation was taken care of, along with the location. Promoting the event proved to be successful as well, covering all points. Facebook, Instagram, Twitter, flyers, posters, and a number of shout outs from one of the major radio stations in the city. The word about Thickums had got around quick, and Nora didn't want to disappoint anyone who showed up to support the cause.

Darleen woke up in Gordo's bed after another night of partying with him and his people. Feeling drained, she reached over and grabbed the small sandwich bag of powder, stuck her pinky finger inside, and took it to her nose. The cocaine ran through her system, giving her a burst of energy. She went back in the bag and hit her other nostril with the flavor. Darleen hadn't been on cocaine this hard since the beginning of her porn career. Having only been clean for seven months, she was right back at it.

"You got some for me?" Gordo asked when he walked into the room. "I hope I'm not a bad influence on you." He smiled and took the bag from her.

"Boy, please, I'm from the hood," Darleen shot back, wiping the cocaine from her nose. She jumped up and walked to the bathroom so she could freshen up before it was time for her to go to work.

Gordo was getting her undivided attention, and he had her not wanting to do too much of anything but be around him all day. Darleen didn't have to worry about anything. Going to work was optional, and the only reason she did was to fulfill her contract with Wood. After today, she would no longer be obligated to the porn industry, and that's exactly what she wanted so she could spend even more time with Gordo.

"Now why do you have the sad face on like you just lost ya best friend?" Andrea looked over and asked Nora after parking the car.

Nora hadn't told the girls yet that she was without a job. She didn't want people to feel sorry for her, nor did she feel like explaining the whole situation. It would only make her upset all over again, but then again, she couldn't just lie to her bestie.

"Spit it out," Andrea said, knowing that something was wrong.

Nora was quiet for a second, and then she let it out. "They fired me over some bullshit," Nora snapped. "All because of—"

"Wait, wait, they fired you?" Andrea asked in disbelief.

"Yeah, all because another chick was in the maintenance room screwing the janitor. Remember I told you about that a while back?"

"Oh, yeah, I do remember. I thought it was squashed, though. Didn't ol' girl get it together with her husband and stop seeing dude?"

"Yeah, she did, and that is what pisses me off. I handled it and kept it from becoming a scandal, but it came back to bite me."

Andrea sat there in awe listening to Nora break down the reason she had been fired. It sounded crazy, but hospitals have all kinds of rules and regulations. Everyone bends the rules, but if you get caught, that is usually your ass.

Nora went in, and the more she talked, the more she got into her other problems in life. "And on top of that, I'm almost out of money, and there's still work that needs to be done with the company," Nora explained.

Nora only had fifty thousand to work with. Thirty-five hundred went to renting out the club for the show, five thousand for promo and invites, the photo shoot was fifteen hundred, hair and make-up were fifteen hundred, the modeling classes were three thousand, catering and decorating was another five thousand, and hiring staff to help with wardrobe was another twenty-five hundred. The five thousand apiece for clothes shopping had really put the dent in Nora's pocket. Thirty-seven out of fifty had left her with thirteen thousand, and who knows what else was going to pop up in the next few days.

"We're going to need some more money, or this may be the first and the last show that Thickums puts on," Nora said with a stressed look on her face.

Andrea looked over, placed her hand on top of Nora's, and promised her that everything was going to be all right. It looked ugly on the outside right now, but Nora believed that what Andrea said was true.

Wood picked his head up after hearing a knock on his office door. It was Darleen, just the person he needed to see. "Damn, I'm glad you're here. I needed to go over the next six roles you'll be playing, along with the dates—"

"Whoa, slow down, Wood," Darleen said, cutting him off as she stood in front of his desk. "You might wanna rewind that. My contract is only for two more scenes," she countered.

Wood had a confused look on his face as he got up from his chair and walked over to the file cabinet. He pulled out Darleen's file, and said, "I could have sworn I had you for six more." Wood was quiet for a moment as he looked over the contract. "Yup, six more," he told her, passing her the folder with the contract inside it.

Darleen couldn't believe her eyes when she saw that the contract was for thirty skits and five interviews. Already having done eighteen scenes, the number she owed was twelve. She thought that she had only signed for twenty roles, but if she was going to blame it on anything, it would be all the cocaine she had put up her nose. Cocaine, pills, and liquor were the main drugs she used in the beginning of her career. She, like so many other girls, had been introduced to all the above by Wood. It was his way of keeping control of everyone, and he knew what he was doing when he would get them high before signing their lives away. In any event, Darleen wasn't doing another twelve scenes. She didn't have the time, plus she wanted to keep her word to Gordo about them starting their own XXX company.

"I'm not doing twelve more scenes. I'm doing two more, which makes twenty, and then I'm done."

Wood didn't have a problem with it, but he had a few tricks up his sleeve. "Well, if you opt to not honor our contract, you're gonna lose a lot of money," he said, sitting back in his chair and interlocking his fingers.

Darleen's rate was two thousand for every movie, and she had already been paid a twenty thousand dollar advance for the first ten. At twenty skits, she would get another check for twenty thousand, and the same when she got to thirty skits. But, since she now wanted out of the contract, and Wood was about to lose money, he wasn't going to give her another dime.

"So, you just gonna take my money like that? That's sixteen thousand you owe me," Darleen snapped. She pleaded and begged for her money, but Wood wasn't trying to hear any of it.

Darleen didn't know it, but Wood had already heard about her and Gordo's plan to run off and do their own thing. If she wanted out, she was going to have to leave as is, and that was without pay. Darleen was hot about it.

"Keep ya fucking money. This piece of shit of a studio ain't gonna last anyway," she based, smacking a bunch of papers off his desk. A stiff middle finger was the last thing he got from Darleen before she stormed out of his office.

Wood could hear her yelling at people and knocking things over on her way out of the building. When he got up to see the path of destruction she had left behind, he shook his head and was more than happy to see her walk out the front door. He had played more than his share of former porn stars with the same game. He would always give them the advance first, knowing that they would fuck up the money and be in need of the remaining cash from the additional scenes he would sneak into the contract. Normally they would give in when he threatened to cancel the deal and not pay any more money, but it looked like Darleen was going to play hardball. Either way, it didn't matter to Wood, since he knew there would soon be some new chick knocking on his door for an opportunity to make some fast cash.

Gordo laughed when Darleen got back into his car. Being in the industry for a little more than a year now, he knew the game and knew that Wood wasn't coming off of any money since Darleen wasn't honoring the contract.

"Stop laughing at me," Darleen said, smacking Gordo's shoulder.

"Awwww, the baby didn't get her money," he teased.

"Shut up. That nigga gone give me my money. He got me all the way fucked up," she commented, looking up at the building as they pulled off.

Darleen sat in silence for a moment when out of nowhere, it hit her. "Oh, shit," she said, pulling out her phone. It had just dawned on her that she was supposed to meet up with Nora and Andrea for the modeling classes today. She tried to call both of their phones, but neither of them answered.

"What's going on? Is everything cool?" Gordo asked at the concerned look she now had on her face.

Nora was going to give her an earful, and Darleen wasn't even suited with a good enough excuses to get a pass on this one. Partying like a rock star with Gordo and his folks was starting to take a toll on her, and picking up the old habit of snorting powder again wasn't helping it at all. She needed to get herself together quick, fast, and in a hurry, before she lost control.

***

Nora and Andrea stumbled out of the front door of the school laughing and joking about modeling and several other aspects of fashion. It wasn't as easy as they'd thought, and this three day crash course was nothing compared to the bigger picture. It was so much more they needed to know.

"Oh, look who decided to show up," Andrea said, seeing Darleen get out of Gordo's car and wave good-bye to him.

"I know, I know, and I'm sorry," Darleen said before Nora and Andrea could say anything. But that didn't stop Nora.

"We damn sure ain't got money to waste, and we can't get a refund for it either.

"Come on, D, we supposed to be in this thing together, and if we expect this to work, we all need to be on point," Andrea added.

Darleen stood there taking it all in, realizing that her role in this project was just as important as everyone else's. It may have seemed harsh, but Nora wanted to give everybody a clear understanding that this wasn't a game, nor were they doing it for their health. It was a purpose behind the success of Thickums. This was something huge in the making. It was something for all the BBWs, but the fact remained that it all started with them.

The Board of Directors sat in the conference room waiting for the meeting to begin. When Mr. Gant walked into the room, all the small conversations came to a halt. He sat at the head of the table, adjusting his glasses before opening his folder.

"Okay people, we have a lot to get to this morning, so if you hadn't already used the bathroom or gotten your coffee, now's the time to do so. We'll be here until lunch," Mr. Gant advised, looking around the room.

Nobody moved, so the meeting began.

"Before we get into anything else, I thinks it's imperative that we reevaluate some of our policies pertaining to personal conduct, at work relationships and so forth. Particularly the situation that happened with Alice and Nora," Gant began.

When he initially fired Nora, it was because of the way the incident was brought to him and his desire to take immediate action. But after further review and careful consideration, he deemed that firing her wasn't the best solution at all. In fact, it had caused more problems, because as of yesterday, Doctor Holland, the best Neurosurgeon in the county, had resigned. He was also the husband of Alice. Two of his surgical team members followed him without question.

"So, what do you expect for us to do, simply allow for medical staff to have sexual relations on the job without any repercussions?" Ms. Hill asked, confused as to where Gant was going.

"No, but I think that we have people in certain positions to handle problems like this. I think as the head nurse, Nora handled the situation well, and that was proven because there were no recurring issues. It showed that she was in full control of the situation, and the sanctions that she handed down worked. So with that being said, I made an executive decision to re hire all parties that were involved in that incident. I'll entrust Ms. Hill with the task of getting our medical staff back on board. Now, does anyone have a problem with that? Good, then let's move on to the next topic," Mr. Gant said before anyone could protest his decision.

There wasn't a person in the room who was willing to challenge Gant and his ruling. For the most part, it made sense, and it seemed like the hospital lost more from handling it the way that they did, rather than coming up with a better conflict resolution approach. If anyone had caught the bad end of the stick, it was definitely Nora.

"You might wanna consider getting yourself a car in the near future," Andrea said when they pulled up to the studio for the photo shoot. "Especially if you plan on lugging around all this shit," she said, referring to all the clothes.

"Yes, Nora, I never understood that. You got a license, but you never wanna drive," Darleen chimed in.

"Don't nobody got time to be driving. Plus, you know I get road rage quick. I can see me now, running somebody off the road," Nora laughed, getting out of the car.

Almost immediately, Darleen noticed Kim, the photographer she'd hired, standing at the front door of the studio. She had a confused look on her face as though something was wrong.

"Are you sure we're at the right place?" Kim asked when the girls walked up.

"Yeah, this is the place. Why, what's going on?" Darleen asked as she walked up to the door.

Jesse, one of Wood's boys, was standing behind the glass, saying something. The thick glass muffled his voice a little, but Darleen knew that he was saying something smart because he always did.

"Open the damn door, Jesse," Darleen yelled.

Jesse just yelled back, something that they couldn't quite hear, and made no move to open the door.

It pissed her off something serious. She backed up from the door and started looking for something to throw at the glass.

"What's going on?" Andrea asked.

Darleen didn't even answer her as she continued her search.

A large rock sticking out of the curbside caught her eye. She pulled it out of the dirt and walked it over to the door. "Open the fuckin' door," she yelled again, this time cocking the rock back as though she was about to throw it. It worked, because Jesse unlocked the door. He knew that she was crazy enough to do it.

"Move," she said, pushing him to the side.

The photographer was too scared to go in with her, but Andrea and Nora rushed right past Jesse.

"Who da fuck told you to let these bitches in here?" Wood yelled from his director's chair.

"She was about to throw a rock through the window."

"You better watch who you calling a bitch, Wood. And today is the day you told me that I could use the studio," Darleen snapped, walking up to him.

"Yeah, that's when you was employed here. So take you and ya fat friends and get the fuck out of my studio. Oh, and I'ma need ya key, too," Wood added.

"Who da fuck is you calling fat? Don't get fucked up in here," Nora shot back. "Fuck him and this studio," Nora told Darleen, pulling at her arm so they could leave.

Darleen wanted to flare on him, thinking about having to suck his dick in order to have the photo shoot there. Now he was sitting there being disrespectful with his mouth. If it wasn't for Nora, Darleen probably would have swung on him.

"You gon' get yours," Darleen promised Wood before allowing Nora to pull her out of the studio.

Right before she got to the front door, Darleen turned around, went into her bag, and peeled one of the keys off her key chain. She threw it as hard as she could, trying to hit Wood with it. She missed him by an inch. Wood walked behind the girls, laughing and calling them out of their name. Nora had to literally hold Darleen back as she kept trying to get away in order to get at Wood.

"Fuck you, Wood. You pussy!" Darleen screamed on her way out the door.

Once outside, Darleen saw the large rock, picked it up and attempted to throw it at the large window.

"No," Nora shouted, grabbing her arm before she got it off.

"Don't get fucked up out here," Wood yelled after seeing what Darleen was about to do.

"He ain't worth it, girl. Come on and get in the car," Andrea said, walking around and getting into the driver side.

Reluctant and angry as hell, Darleen got into the car. The photographer got into her car, too, and wasted no time pulling off. Before Darleen decided to jump back out of the car to get at Wood, Andrea peeled off from the scene.

"Damn, brah, you been moping around here for the past couple of days," Monti said, coming into the back where Ronald was sorting out medication. "I know this ain't about ol' girl."

Monti was referring to Nora, and as bad as Ronald didn't want to admit it, she was the only thing on his mind lately. "I played myself, homie, and the crazy part about it is, she really liked a nigga," Ronald replied.

Monti had to take a good look at his boy. He hadn't seen him this sick ever, especially over a female. Monti was starting to feel bad about that Thanksgiving escapade.

"You really like shorty?" Monti asked in a serious manner.

"Yeah, she was a good girl. And keeping it one hundred wit' you, I was really feeling like she could be the one," Ronald admitted and walked to the front of the pharmacy.

Monti followed behind, listening to Ronald talk about how he really had a thing for Nora.

"Have you tried to call her since the party?"

"Yeah, but she told me not to call her phone again. Then I found out the other day that she got fired."

"Damn, homie, my bad. But the good thing is, there's plenty of good looking thick girls out there," Monti joked, getting Ronald to crack a smile.

What he said did have some merit to it. There were more single plus size women in Philly than anything else. Only a few men appreciated a good size 18 and up. They were hidden gems, and only smart men like Ronald knew their worth. That's why he was so sick about dropping the ball with Nora.

It was silent in the car until Darleen spoke. "I'm so sorry, y'all. I keep messin' shit up," she said.

Nora wasn't going to let her blame herself for Wood's actions, nor was she going to let anybody feel sorry for themselves.

"Hell nah, if you in ya feelings about that disrespect, then come out of it," Nora spoke to her girls. "This shit ain't nothing but motivation for us to go even harder."

"Yeah, but the photographer is gone, and we don't have anywhere to shoot," Darleen cut in.

At the same time, both Andrea and Nora looked over at each other. It was like the same light bulb lit up in their head. On the first day of modeling class, the instructor had taught them how to improvise when taking photos. Spontaneous pictures sometimes came out better than taking them in a studio setting. Nora jumped right on the phone. She was hoping to catch Kim before it was too late.

"What's going on?" Darleen asked.

As Nora talked to Kim, Andrea looked in the rear view with a smile on her face.

"You should have been in class the first day," she said then turned her attention back to the road.

Wood sat in his office, stuffing money into the money machine, counting up the day's take. He wanted to have it ready for the bank run in the morning. The XXX business was doing all right, but his cocaine dealings made him one of the richest thugs in the city of brotherly love. The porn industry was a perfect cover for him, too. For tax purposes, he claimed that he made a lot of his money selling his DVDs in the streets. It was an excuse for him to deposit large amounts of cash into banks all around the city. Of course, he didn't sell half as many DVDs as he claimed, but the IRS really wasn't trying to investigate the matter so long as they received their money. He was doing it big in the hood, and it appeared to be legal.

"Yo, those fat bitches was crazy as hell," Jesse said, coming into the office and taking a seat in the chair.

"Yeah, well Delicious better not bring her big ass up in here. She always got some drama brewing," Wood said as he wrapped up his money.

"Yeah, I feel you, dog. But yo, wassup wit' the new connect?" Jesse inquired.

"Aww, man, he's blessing me, brah. I'm getting Nineties prices, and I'm selling this shit like crazy."

Wood had recently started buying his coke from Teddy, the man who pretty much supplied Philly, New York, Virginia, DC and New Jersey. He was the real deal, and you had to be copping twenty kilos or better to have his number. Wood had just now started making the cut and was moving up in the drug game.

"So when you gon' put a nigga on?" Jesse asked.

"Learn how to keep those bitches from storming my studio first, then you can make some money," Wood told him right before he dismissed Jesse like a two-dollar whore.

Jesse didn't like it, but he did what he was told. It was times like this he wished that he could go out and do his own thing, but Wood wasn't feeding him or the rest of his employees good enough to venture out on their own. He did that for a reason, so the people who depended on him would have to stay close and would do just about anything for him.

The city of Philly became the girls' studio, seizing moments in Love Park, the middle of Broad Street, the Art Museum, the Liberty bell, and several other historic places. Kim followed them around everywhere, getting some amazing shots.

"Let's go, Andrea, work it," Kim said, snapping away with the camera. "Give me a side shot, a back shot, hands in the air, look happy, look mad," Kim directed as she took the final shots. "You guys did a great job. I can't wait to develop them," she said as she put her equipment away.

Wood had tried to throw a monkey wrench in the game, but he ended up making the situation better. Had they taken the pictures in his studio, they would have come out dull and basic. So in the end, something good did come out of that situation. Darleen hated his guts, and she had something real big planned for him in the near future. But for now, all she wanted to do was enjoy the moment.

Chapter 8

A wild and crazy dream of a man stuffing his tongue inside of Nora's pussy had her moaning in her sleep. His mouth was extra wet, and he bit down on her clit like it was a Georgia peach. Even though it was a dream, Nora had to see who was making her feel so good. Hoping it was John Legend or Musiq Soul Child, Nora lifted his head up.

"Shitttttttt," Nora complained, waking up from her sleep. "It had to be you," she mumbled to herself, cracking her eyes open for the first time all morning.

This was the first time in a long time that Nora had slept in, and she probably would have slept a little longer if Bugsy hadn't invaded her dreams. Before she could get out of her bed to get her day started, the phone on her nightstand began to ring. She wasn't going to answer it until she saw the hospital's number pop up on the screen. Wondering what they could possibly be calling about, she quickly cleared her throat, sat up in the bed, and answered.

"Nora, I got your job back," Ms. Hill lied. "I got the board to look at the incident again, and they all agreed to reinstate you.

"What about Alice?" Nora asked, still concerned about her friend.

"I just got off the phone with her, and she'll be back tomorrow," Ms. Hill explained.

Nora wanted to scream for joy, but she didn't want to give Ms. Hill the satisfaction of hearing it.

"So I guess I'll see you on Monday?" Ms. Hill asked.

Nora sat in silence for a moment. She was a little suspicious of Ms. Hill, and how all of a sudden and out of the clear blue sky the board would reinstate her. "So what's the catch? What am I missing?" Nora quizzed, feeling like something was fishy.

"There's no catch, Nora. The hospital need nurses like you and Alice, and I think that you handled the situation well," Hill said, using some of the thoughts Mr. Gant had voiced in the meeting.

Nora still had her concerns, and as much as she wanted to get back to work, she needed to make sure she wasn't being played in the process. There were many things that needed to be done by the administration, and the first thing at the top of Nora's list was to be exonerated from any wrongdoing. That was her main thing, and before she did anything, she wanted that fact to be clear.

Darleen parked around the corner from the studio in her brother's car. Her heart was racing a million miles per minute, thinking about what she was about to do. Friday mornings at the studio were slow, mainly because everyone was home getting rest for the night's events.

"Fuck that mutherfucker," Darleen mumbled to herself, looking at her reflection in the mirror. She took one last hit of the cocaine, wiped her nose, then stepped out of the car.

Kids darted past her on their way to school as she headed for the building. She was scared to death, hoping that she didn't get caught. At the same time, she was determined to get what was hers, and maybe a little something extra if the opportunity presented itself. When she arrived at the front door, she looked up and down the street, then she cupped her hands to the window of the door and looked inside. There wasn't any movement at all, exactly what she expected. She stuck the key in the door, thinking how it had turned out to be a good thing that in the midst of her anger, she had thrown the wrong key at Wood.

Once she was inside, she locked the door back. It was total silence throughout the studio, and Darleen didn't hesitate to make her way back to Wood's office. She damn near shitted on herself when she heard a voice coming from one of the sets. She crept up to the open door, looked inside, and saw Jesse sitting on the couch smoking a blunt with a chick named Joy riding him reverse cowgirl. He was so into it, he was oblivious to anything else going on around him.

Darleen hit Wood's office and went straight for the safe. She only had the last three digits to a four digit code, so it took her a few times before she finally got it open.

"Jackpot," she mumbled to herself, reaching in and grabbing a stack of money. To her surprise, it was only one dollar bills, probably equaling up to about a thousand dollars. "Shit," she said, looking deeper into the safe.

Six bricks of cocaine, a handgun and about a half pound of weed were all that was left inside. Wood owed Darleen close to twenty thousand, and she wasn't about to leave with nothing. She looked around the office for a bag and ended up grabbing a trashcan liner. *This should be enough,* she thought to herself, placing one of the bricks into the bag. Then Darleen got to thinking. He was very disrespectful to them on the day they were supposed to do the photo shoot. So, she said fuck it, took four more bricks, and threw them in the bag. It was only right that she take the gun too, just so he wouldn't be able to use it on her in the event that he put two and two together. She tucked the bag under her arm and headed out of the office.

Darleen ran right into Joy, who had come from the set, probably to get something to drink. They stood there staring at each other. Joy looked down at the bag under her arm and then back up into Darleen's eyes. The only thing that stood between her and the outside was Joy. She was tempted to pull the gun out and shoot her.

"Come on, girl. Get ya fine ass back in here," Jesse yelled from the room.

Fortunately for Darleen, she didn't have to pull the gun out. Joy stood to the side and cleared the path for her to leave.

"Thank you," Darleen whispered then headed for the door.

Nora sipped on her hot cup of tea while sitting at the kitchen table with her laptop open. Kim had sent the photos from the shoot early that morning. Nora immediately uploaded the good ones onto the Thickums Web site and onto her Facebook. She also sent copies to Darleen and Andrea's e-mail. The show was tomorrow, and so far, it was getting a lot of attention. The Internet was going nuts, and Nora had well over two hundred new friend requests. All the pictures she put up got a bunch of likes, and people wanted to follow. A couple of haters threw shots, but the majority of the comments were positive. That really meant a lot to Nora, and it motivated her even more. The smile she had on her face was from ear to ear.

"Oh my God, who in the hell is this?" she uttered when the doorbell rang.

With her tea still in her hand, she walked to the front and answered the door. When she opened it, the only thing she could see was the back of a man standing on her porch. She almost dropped her tea when Monti turned around.

"How da fuck do you know where I live?" Nora snapped when she opened the screen door. "And why are you here?"

"I got ya address from hospital records, and I'm here because I need to talk to you. It's important."

"We don't have shit to talk about. Come back to my house again, and I'm calling the cops on ya ass."

She turned to head back in the house, mad as hell.

"He's in love wit' you," Monti said, getting Nora's attention before she closed the door. "I'm serious, yo."

"What did you just say?" she asked, stepping halfway back out on the porch.

Monti couldn't be around his boy another day without trying to fix his wrong. "Man, Ron is in love wit' you. The boy is sick right now. All he do is talk about you all day, every day."

"Ya boy, Ron, should have thought about that when he tried to—"

"That wasn't his fault, at least not completely," Monti said, cutting her off.

He explained that he set the whole thing up, and Ronald didn't know she was coming in the first place. He said he tried to make it out to be one big joke.

Nora never expected Monti to say that, and though it didn't excuse Ronald's actions, she somewhat understood how it felt to be put on the spot like that.

"Nora, if you wanna blame somebody, then blame me. Just give my boy another chance," Monti pleaded.

A part of her wanted to crack Monti over his head with the coffee mug, but she decided not to. Instead, she just turned around and went back into the house, but not before letting Monti know that she'd think about calling Ronald. She definitely was still in her feelings about the whole situation, and even if she did decide to call Ronald, that didn't mean she was going to be so quick to forgive him for his role.

***

Darleen took the razor and cut through the thick plastic of one of the bricks, then stuck her pinky finger inside. Not sure what she was about to put in her nose, she tasted it with her tongue first. Instantly, her whole mouth became numb. The cocaine turned into a liquid form then drained down the back of her throat. That's when the high hit her. It was a high she'd never felt before. The cocaine was grade-A.

Damn, I can't feel my fucking face, she thought, while rubbing her cheek.

Out of nowhere, a burst of energy had her up and on her feet, walking around the apartment with the urge to clean something. When Darleen heard a knock on her front door, she froze like a statue right in the middle of running some dishwater. Paranoia set in quick, and she knew for sure that it was Wood coming to kill her. The knocks got louder, causing her to walk over to the coffee table and grab the .45 automatic. She was high as hell as she grabbed the brick of coke and placed it back in the bag.

"D, it's me," a familiar voice yelled from the hallway.

Darleen was so high, she'd forgot that she called her brother over to pick up his car. She quickly ran the bag back into her bedroom, then went to answer the door. "Damn, nigga, you banging on my shit like you the police," she snapped.

"Shit, if I was the police, yo' ass would be in jail," PooMan said, walking in and seeing some of the cocaine on the table. "You back putting this shit up ya nose?" he asked, pointing to the powder residue.

PooMan hated when Darleen was messing around with the White Girl. That's how she was bold enough to get into the porn industry, which was another thing about her life he disapproved of.

"Boy, I'm grown. I can do whatever I want. Shit, besides, I got this shit from you and daddy," she shot back.

PooMan rolled his eyes at her, mad that she still was using that as her excuse. He hadn't snorted coke in almost two years.

"PooMan, I need you to check something out for me before you leave."

She ran back to her bedroom, grabbed the brick she had cut into, and busted it in half. Coke fell all over her dresser, but she managed to put about eighteen ounces in a Ziploc bag and brought it out to him. "How much is this worth?" she asked, handing him the product.

PooMan had run through so much coke in his day, he could eyeball it and tell that it was close to half a brick. "Where did you get—"

"Boy, don't worry about all that. Just tell me," she said, cutting him off.

PooMan raised the bag in the air then looked at it carefully. He could smell the coke through the bag, which was a good thing. "If it's what I think it is, you might can get about fifteen thousand as it is. If you cook it up, I might can get you more."

"Well, cook it up for me, bro. I'm trying to get as much money as I can for it," she said, taking a seat on the edge of the couch.

PooMan wasn't as active in the game as he used to be, but he still had a couple of blocks he could move the product on if he wanted to. He was more concerned about his little sister, knowing that she'd done something out of pocket to get that amount of coke. It was a must that he knew what happened, in the event he had to protect her. He could look in Darleen's eyes and tell that she was high, so the chances of getting any information out of her was slim to none. He had better chance if he waited until she sobered up. Until then, he was going to have to play her close and see what magic he could do in the kitchen.

"Give me a Pyrex pot, some baking soda, and fill the sink up with ice water," PooMan instructed.

Andrea walked into the restaurant, not knowing what to expect out of Garnett. She didn't know what compelled her to have lunch with him, but there she was, walking up to the table.

"Glad you could make it," Garnett said, getting up to greet her. "You look nice," he said as he pulled out her chair for her.

Andrea was a little impressed with his manners, something he'd never displayed before. She also had to admit that he looked nice too, and smelled good as hell.

"So, how have you been? I mean, what have you been up to besides modeling?" He smiled.

Andrea didn't even think he knew about Thickums, but then again, it was all over the Internet.

"Well, we do have a show tomorrow, and on some real shit, I'm nervous as hell," she admitted for the first time.

"Why would you be nervous? It can't be that hard."

"I don't think I'm fit to be a model. Oh my God, I can't believe I just told you that," she said, cupping her hands over her mouth.

It was weird expressing herself to Garnett like this. She was so used to him always putting her down instead of uplifting her.

"Let me tell you something, Andrea. You are a very beautiful woman from head to toe, and there's no reason why you should feel the way that you do. The people are going to love you when you go out there and do ya thing."

It was mind-blowing for Andrea to hear Garnett speak so highly of her. Compliments like this were always missing in their relationship, and she wished that he would have been half as nice to her when they were together. It would have gone a long way. Andrea was starting to like the new Garnett. She wasn't sure how long he was going to be able to keep up this new act, but for now, she was going to enjoy it.

PoohMan had turned eighteen ounces of powder cocaine into twenty-four ounces of crack, give or take a few grams. There was no one there to test it, but PooMan knew his work and guaranteed that it was the bomb. He calculated in his head the possible kick back by two different methods. Darleen could sell it by weight and bring back twenty-one thousand, or she could chop it down, bag it up into dime rocks and bring back twenty-four thousand. Either way, she was going to have to subtract a couple of grand for PooMan moving it for her.

Wanting the most for her product, Darleen decided that she wanted to sell dime rocks. PooMan promised that it would only take about a week for her to make the money, but he also informed her that she was going to have to put in a little bit of work, which she didn't mind. When it came to money, Darleen was always down for whatever.

Nora picked her head up from the laptop and looked at her phone. She was tempted to call Ronald, but she wasn't sure how the conversation would go. At one point, she did like him, but so much had changed from then until now. Monti confessing to deliberately sabotaging what they had was a head banger, and it left the worst taste in her mouth. But, Nora wasn't the type to allow herself to be hurt more than once by the same person. After their first mess up, they would become no more than a memory. Whether she liked it or not, that was the stage she was at with Ronald, and she no longer had desired to be with him. The most important thing going on was the show tomorrow, which was going to be here in a blink of an eye. That's where her focus was right now, and that's where it needed to stay.

Chapter 9

"So, you expect me to believe that somebody broke into the studio, cracked open my safe, and took all of my shit, all while you were in the other room sleep?" Wood asked Jesse with his face twisted up in disbelief.

It sounded so lame, Jesse didn't even want to answer the question. Nothing he could say would convince Wood that he didn't have something to do with the robbery. He was good and pissed off. Darleen had only left the stack of one dollar bills, a brick of coke, and the weed.

Wood was glad that he hadn't left more money in there, because it, too, would be gone. "Are you sure you wanna go down this road?" Wood asked, walking over to the couch where Jesse sat, shaking like a leaf.

When Jesse realized that he, Tech, and Wood were the only ones in the studio, he began to plead. "Come on, Wood, you know I would never take anything from you," he said, looking up at Wood.

Wood looked back at Tech and chuckled. "Can you believe this guy?" he asked, poking Jesse in the head.

On that, Jesse tried to jump up from the couch and make a last ditch effort for the door. He didn't make it three feet before Wood yoked him up from behind and put him in a vicious choke hold. Jesse couldn't get loose for nothing, and the more he struggled, the more pressure was applied. Panic set in, and Jesse began swinging his arms and legs wildly. Wood took a couple of smacks to the face, but he didn't let go. He choked Jesse until his body went limp, and then continued to choke him for an extra minute or two, just to make sure that he was dead. Not only was Jesse dead, he had pissed and shitted on himself during the ordeal.

Smelling the foul odor, Wood finally decided to let Jesse go. His lifeless body dropped to the ground like a bag of weights. Wood stood over top of him with a sinister look on his face, then he looked over at Tech. "Clean dis shit up before people start coming in."

The last thing he needed was a homicide case. "I gotta make a few calls," he told Tech then walked off and headed for his office.

Just as he was instructed, Tech began to make Jesse's body disappear into thin air.

Nora had to take a break from running around all morning, trying to make sure everything was good for show time, which was only about three hours away. Club Onyx was decked out. The bar was fully stocked, bright lights lit up the place, and Andrea had done an excellent job with the catering. Reserved tables had bottles of champagne on them with gift bags for each seat, and the food Andrea prepared with the assistance of a renowned chef, was nothing less than amazing.

"Girl, my feet hurt like hell," Andrea complained when she walked into the dressing room where Nora sat in a chair in front of the lighted mirror.

"Shit, I feel like I already did the show." Nora laughed as she reached down and massaged her feet. "Have you seen Darleen?"

"Hell no, and I tried to call her, but she's not answering. I swear that girl is going to make me kick her ass."

"You and me both," Nora said, shaking her head.

As bad as Nora wanted to get some rest before the show, the loud sound of something falling to the ground prompted both of them to get up and check on it. Everything needed to be perfect today. There was a lot riding on it, and from the large crowd of people gathering outside waiting to get in, what they did today was going to determine the future of Thickums. The modeling field was nothing nice at all, and for the plus size woman, it was even more of a challenge. Nora had to make the best out of her first attempt to go public with Thickums.

Darleen had bagged up so much crack the previous night that her hands felt like they had arthritis in them. It was an all-night event, and if it wasn't for PooMan bringing Li'l Gunner over to help her, she didn't know how it would have gotten done. The good thing was, the product was already out on the street and was moving at an alarming rate. Crackheads were loving it, and it wouldn't be long until the entirety of North Philly heard about it.

"Damn, don't you gotta be somewhere?" Li'l Gunner asked as he stood at the kitchen sink washing his hands.

"Oh, shit!" Darleen shouted, realizing that it was the day of the show.

She grabbed her phone and immediately dialed Nora's number. "I done missed Andrea's calls too," she mumbled to herself, looking at the screen.

"Where the hell are you? We about to start in a few minutes," Nora snapped when she answered the phone.

"I know, I know, I'm sorry. I was taking care of something very important, but I'll be there in like twenty minutes," Darleen said, all the while gathering the packages of crack off the table. "I got a surprise for you too."

"Girl, just hurry up and get ya ass here," Nora shot back.

Darleen didn't say another word. After hanging up the phone, she shot straight to her bedroom. She took a shower, got dressed and was out the door in less than twenty minutes. Li'l Gunner was her driver for today, so she was able to do something with her hair while she was in the car. It was a good thing that she was only a hop, skip, and a jump away from the club because if Darleen was a minute later than what she told Nora, it was going to be a problem.

The lights in the club went dark, and Darleen was the first to walk out onto the stage. She was on her B-boy shit, rocking a pair of army fatigue capri cut pants, a black Polo hoody, and on her feet were a pair of three quarter inch Timberland boots. Her eyes were covered with a pair of black and gold Victoria Beckham shades.

She walked out to the edge of the stage, blew a kiss, then turned around and strutted back. The audience began to clap, loving how the show began.

I put on for my city, I put on for my city, I put on for my city, put on, East side, put on, South side, put on. West side . . . The Young Jeezy featuring Kanye West song blared from the speakers as Darleen did her thing.

Everyone in the building had their hands in the air, then out from the back strutted Nora. Her walk was the most fierce. She had on an all-white blazer that reached down to her thighs. On her feet were a pair of Saint Laurent pumps, and in her hand she carried a Gucci bag. She looked fabulous, coming out to the edge of the stage and striking her pose. Before she walked back, she gave her ass a little smack with a wink of the eye. The crowd clapped, and a couple of men even whistled.

Hat back, top back, ain't nothing but a young thug. HK, AK I need to join a gun club, big wheels big straps,

*you know I like it super-sized. Passengers a red bone,
her weave look like some curly fries. Inside fish sticks,
outside tartar sauce.*

Andrea took to the stage next, stepping out with a black
long sleeved dress, designed and made by herself. On her
feet were tan Jimmy Choos. and a pair of Gucci frames
covered her eyes. She stepped out, slinging her hips from
side to side, and when she got to the edge of the stage, she
posed, pulled out her phone, and snapped a selfie of her
and the crowd. Andrea spun back around, finger waved
with a smile, then backed up until she disappeared.

Darleen was right on cue, stepping back out onto the
stage with a different outfit on. Nora followed suit, also
switching her picture up. All three of the girls had done
a great job with their clothing selections, and they were
on point with changing into them. The other women they
had gotten to walk also did their thing, but the trio was
definitely the star of the show.

They managed to get off twelve outfits each, covering
just about every style. Retro, conservative, hood, formal,
casual, vintage and Darleen was bold enough to pull off
a cat suit for her last strut. For plus-sized women, they
made every outfit look good, and the crowd thought that
they rocked it too. They received a standing ovation. It
was surely a moment in time they would all remember.

"A'ight homie, just hit me back when you touch down,"
Wood told Teddy before hanging up the phone.

Today wasn't his day at all. First, someone stole five
bricks of cocaine from him, then he ended up having to
kill one of his boys. Now his connect wouldn't be back in
the city until sometime around the end of the month, and
Wood wasn't even 100% sure about that. Wood mainly
sold weight, so the single brick of coke he had wasn't
going to last but for a couple of days.

"Yo, I took care of that," Tech said, walking into Wood's office.

Tech was the type that didn't give two shits about anything, so it was nothing for him to drive Jesse into Fairmount Park and dump his body in a wooded area, and do it in broad daylight. That's how much love and loyalty he had for his boy, Wood.

"I gotta find a new connect. Not nothing permanent, just something to hold me over 'til my folks get back in town," Wood expressed, inhaling, then letting out a frustrated sigh. "Damn, I really wish I knew who came up in here and took my shit," he said, looking at Tech.

"Shit, nigga, it wasn't me. I was in Atlantic City wit' you all night," Tech responded with both of his hands raised.

Wood had to laugh at him. He already knew Tech wouldn't do no shit like that to him under any circumstances.

"Nah, homie, I was just thinking. That nigga had to have somebody here with him all night. If I know that creep muthafucka like I think, he had to have one of those two dollar bitches here wit' him," Wood said.

Tech sat there nodding his head in agreement. "So, what do you wanna do?" Tech asked, taking a seat. "People are starting to come in right now."

"Yeah, well, once everybody get here, I'ma call a meeting on the main set. If somebody was here wit' dat nigga last night, trust me, I'ma find out about it."

It took several hours after the show was over for people to start dispersing. Andrea's food and the open bar were to blame for that. All three of the girls sat down at one of the empty reserved tables, recapping how the day went. The event had turned out better than even they thought it would.

"I know one thing, my feet hurt like hell," Nora said, kicking off the flats.

"Oh shit, y'all, we blowing up the Internet right now," Darleen said as she tapped her phone.

It was true, so much so, that during the show, two hundred tweets a minute went out, and just about everyone there had posted pictures on their Instagram account. Facebook was poppin' too, and people couldn't help but to leave positive messages behind. The support kept flowing in, making Thickums an instant sensation.

"Excuse me, ladies," a male voice interrupted.

Everyone turned around to see a tall, dark, handsome man before them. Darleen bit down on her lower lip, looking at this perfect specimen of a man.

"My name is Reese," he said, extending his hand for a shake.

Nora snapped out of her trance just in time to avoid an awkward moment. "I hope you enjoyed the show, Resse," Nora said, accepting his hand.

"I did, and to be honest with you, I haven't been entertained like that in a long time," he replied, shaking Andrea and Darleen's hands as well. "Well, I'ma be real with you. I own my own modeling agency in Atlanta."

"Yeah, well we own our own modeling business right here in Philly," Nora shot back.

She didn't have any idea who she was talking to. If she did, she would have been a little more humble. Reese helped himself to the table, just to give the girls a little game that they could learn from.

"Tell me, Nora, what did you accomplish tonight besides just putting on a good show? Did you land another gig for the near future? Did you get a check cut for the clothes that you just advertised? Did you get any contracts, or hell, did you even make any money at all today? No, no, no. And you wanna know how I know? Because I was once sitting where you are right now, with dreams of starting a modeling agency. Let me tell you this, and then I have to leave to catch my flight. The modeling business is a multi-million dollar business, and more than likely, you probably lost money as opposed to making it. When you're really interested in getting into the game, give me a call," Reese said and passed Nora one of his cards.

It didn't take long after he left for the reality of the situation to kick in, all the way down to them not making any money from the show.

"I don't know about y'all, but I need a drink," Nora said as she walked over to the bar, which was still open.

Wood sat in his director's chair, looking around the room at all of his employees' faces. They had no idea what the meeting was about, but everyone in the room wished that it would get started. All the silence had started to become awkward.

"I'm only going to ask this question one time, and let me warn you that it's more than just ya job on the line," Wood began. "Who was here last night with Jesse?"

Joy didn't hesitate to answer that question, figuring that he already knew it.

"I was," she said, raising her hand.

Wood quickly dismissed everyone else, sending them back to work. Joy was led straight to his office by Tech.

Joy was a master at lying, so his fake-ass interrogation wasn't going to get Wood anywhere. In fact, before Wood could even ask a question, Joy explained how she and Jesse were fucking and smoking weed for half the night. She said that Jesse started inviting some people into the studio that she didn't know, so she took off. She made it look like Jesse was there having his own little personal party after hours.

"And you mean to tell me that you don't know none of those muthafuckas that was up in here?" Wood asked, trying to extract as much info as he could from her. "And don't lie."

"I swear. After a couple of them came in, I was out. I didn't feel like a threesome or getting gangbanged," Joy answered, looking him in his eyes.

He questioned her for about an hour, and after he figured he'd gotten all the information he was going to get from her, Wood dismissed her from his office. He was so mad, his blood pressure had shot through the ceiling, and he was only a few minutes from flipping out. A five-brick loss was a hard pill to swallow, even though Wood had plenty of money to blow. For right now, he was going to leave the situation alone, but he knew for sure that he was going to keep his eyes and ears open just in case the culprit behind the robbery dropped the ball somewhere. When that happened, Wood was going to be right there seeking retribution for his loss.

I been meaning to tell y'all something," Nora said as she and the girls were getting out of the car to go into Darleen's apartment. "I'm broke as hell, and I spent just about everything on this show today," she slurred as the drinks started to hit her. "But I got an idea. I'm going to get a loan from the bank, and we're going to do this thing right this time," she promised, feeling bad for not handling the finances right.

"I don't think you're going to have to do that. I think I have a way for us to make our own money to put in the business," Darleen said, reaching in and grabbing her keys out of her bag.

"Wait, what are you talking about? I'm not making any porno movies. You know I got cellulite," Nora joked and laughed at the same time.

Andrea seconded the notion.

"I'm not talking about no porn, y'all," Darleen said.

Once inside the apartment, she sat Nora and Andrea on the couch then ran back into her room. She could hear Nora and Andrea laughing and giggling about being porn stars as she grabbed the coke from her stash. When she walked back into her room, Darleen placed four kilos of cocaine on the table. All the laughing and giggling stopped, and it was as if the alcohol had instantly worn off. Nora looked from the cocaine back up to Darleen, wondering if she was serious.

"What in the hell is this?" Nora asked, picking up one of the bricks from the table.

"It's crack. Well, its powder right now, but it turns to crack after you cook it up," Darleen advised, digging in her back pocket and pulling out a package of the crack she had bagged up the night before.

Nora grabbed the bundle, examined it thoroughly then threw it onto the table with the rest of the coke.

"Girl, you must a lost ya damn mind," Andrea said, looking up at Darleen. "We're not drug dealers," she said and looked over to Nora for backup. "We're not, right?" she asked again after Nora didn't answer her the first time. "Oh my God, I can't believe that y'all are actually considering this shit. We can go to jail."

"Not if we're smart about it," Darleen cut in.

"How much is this stuff worth?" Nora asked before Andrea and Darleen could start debating.

"I got five of them, and you can make like anywhere from thirty-five to fifty thousand off each one of them, depending on how you get rid of them."

"Damn, that's over two hundred thousand. Do you know what we can do with two hundred thousand?" Nora asked, thinking about all the possibilities. "We can rent out office space, buy some materials for you to make our clothes, and put more money into the company."

"Yeah, but we can go to jail," Andrea yelled, trying to get the girls to understand that unfortunate aspect of the game.

Her rant about it did no justice because Nora had her mind made up the minute she heard the potential kick back on the product. In her mind, Thickums and its success were the most important things in her life right now. What was first an idea in Andrea's thoughts, a plus size modeling agency, had become a passion in Nora's heart. She had come too far, and it was way too early in the game for Thickums to go down in flames, and that's exactly what was going to happen if they didn't get some money rolling in asap. Nora definitely wasn't afraid to get her hands dirty for her new dream.

Chapter 10

Alice was the first person to notice Nora when she walked onto her old wing. Having been back to work since Saturday, she couldn't wait to see her good friend. Not only Alice, but the whole the unit had missed Nora, and it showed from all the hugs and smiles she got from everyone. Travis was probably the only person who wasn't feeling her presence, and that was because he was aware that Nora had been offered her position as head nurse back.

"Nora," Ms. Hill called out from the staff lounge. "Mr. Gant would like to speak to you in his office," she said, leading the way.

Mr. Gant was just about to have a meeting, but he was so eager to talk to Nora, he called his secretary and told her to give him five minutes. "I'm glad you came back," Gant said to Nora as he waved Ms. Hill out of his office. Look, in a nutshell, we were wrong for letting you go. Sometimes the administration gets it wrong."

"You don't have to explain. I understand," Nora responded.

"I don't think that you do. I let you go because as the director, I have a responsibility to maintain order in this hospital. I have to make all the tough decisions. Most of the time, I don't want to, but I have to in order to keep this hospital up and running," Gant explained.

Nora sat there listening, and the more that she did, the more she understood his position. Nora could relate to him in more ways than one. It was at that moment, she made one of the most difficult choices of her life.

"I'm sorry, Mr. Gant, but I'm not gonna be able to come back to work at this time," she said, shocking the hell out of him. "When you guys let me go, I obligated my time into something else, and I just can't see myself not following through. Don't get me wrong, I love my job, but—"

Mr. Gant waved her off with a laugh. "Nora, you don't have to go into all of that. Take as much time as you need, and when you're ready to come back to work, your job will be here waiting for you."

Gant could honestly say that he valued the work that Nora did at the hospital. If she needed some time to get her affairs in order, then so be it. That was the least she'd earned over the past years.

"Thank you, Mr. Gant," Nora said, getting up to leave.

Nora didn't expect the meeting to go as well as it did, and she appreciated Mr. Gant leaving the door open for her to come back. If she hadn't obligated herself to help get rid of the cocaine, she would have started back today. The fact was, learning the ins and outs about selling drugs was a lot, and Nora wanted to give it her undivided attention, especially with Andrea's scary ass talking about going to jail.

Darleen stood outside of her apartment building, waiting for her ride to show up. She had $3,500 worth of crack on her, and she planned to sell every single rock in one of the busiest projects in North Philly. Blumberg Projects was still one of the most popular crack spots that moved a lot of work. PooMan had the high rises on smash when he used to trap, and though he was out of the game, he still could do just about anything he wanted there. Letting his kid sister move some product wasn't going to be a problem at all.

A blue 2003 Park Avenue pulled up and stopped right in front of Darleen, getting her attention. Instead of it being Rodney, it was Joy from the studio. She rolled down the tinted window, and without a word, nodded for Darleen to get into the car. Feeling somewhat obligated to at least see what she wanted, Darleen walked around to the passenger's side and got in.

"Don't pull off, cause I'm waiting for my ride," Darleen said, looking in the rearview mirror for Rodney's car.

Joy put the car in park. "So look, I don't know how much you took from that man's safe, but I know it had to be a lot," Joy began. "They found Jesse's body in the park this morning."

"And what that gotta do with me?"

"I lied to Wood about what I saw that morning. . . ."

"Hold on. So what are you getting at?" Darleen asked.

Joy glanced over at Darleen then went back to looking forward. "I want my part of that money, or whatever you got out of there."

"Are you serious?"

"I figure that whatever it was, you can afford to pay the tab," Joy shot back.

"What tab?"

"Ten thousand," she answered.

Darleen wasn't feeling the shake down at all, or the way Joy was making her demands. She didn't even get a chance to start selling the stuff yet, and she was already in debt. Ten thousand wasn't no pennies either.

"What if I told you I'm not giving you shit? What, you gonna go and tell Wood what you know?"

"Yeah, and more than likely it will be your body found next. I don't care what you do, just have my money by the week's end, or you can start looking for a casket that will fit you."

Darleen wanted to reach over, grab a handful of her hair, and beat the shit out of her for talking like she was some type of a gangsta. She had Darleen hot under the collar, but Darleen took her time processing the whole situation and concluded that ten was a small price to pay for her silence. Just thinking about Wood and how vicious he was made her realize Wood wouldn't have a problem putting a bullet in her head, and if it came out that Joy was in on it too, he'd blow her head off as well. The best thing to do was lock Joy in with some money.

"I'll holla at you at the end of the week," Darleen said then got out of the car.

"Uh-oh, she got a serious face on now," Bugsy joked when he saw Nora bend the corner. "It's too early in the morning to be looking like that."

Even when she tried to be serious, Bugsy made her smile.

"Shut up boy, and come're," she demanded, grabbing Bugsy by the hand.

Nora pulled him around the corner and up the street to her house, all the while telling him that she needed to talk to him. Bugsy thought that it was her code words for wanting to fuck. It was something he had fantasized about on several occasions. He couldn't wait for the chance to slay her voluptuous ass.

Up the steps and into the house they went. She led him into the kitchen, where Bugsy wrapped his hands around her waist and squeezed. Nora jumped, not having been gripped up like that in a long time. She turned around and saw the sexiest grin on his face. That's when Nora realized that Bugsy thought they were about to have sex.

"Slow down, Bugsy, you ain't ready to ride the Nora train," she joked. "Nah, I brought you here because I needed you to help me with something."

"Yeah, I know you do." With a smile, he reached out for her waist again.

She playfully smacked his hands down, then pointed to the kitchen table. One of the two bricks of cocaine Darleen had given her sat out in plain view. One of Bugsy's eyebrows shot in the air.

"I know that's not what I think it is," he said, looking from the coke to Nora. "Is it?"

"It's cocaine. A brick, a slab, a bird or whatever else y'all niggas out here call it," she answered, taking a seat in the chair. "And please don't ask me where I got it from. I just need to know if you'll help me get rid of it."

Bugsy picked the brick up and sniffed it, making sure it was real coke inside.

"Damn, ya job got you selling coke now?"

Nora cut her eyes over at him.

"A'ight, a'ight, I'll help you get rid of it, but you're gonna owe me for this one," he said with a smile. Bugsy was in the streets hard body, so getting rid of a brick of coke wasn't going to be hard at all, especially since the city was dried up on the cocaine side of things right now. Nora could sell weight or bag the whole thing up, and she was sure to get rid of it asap. Bugsy liked Nora, and either way, he was going to make sure she got the most out of it.

Darleen hadn't been in the projects for an hour before the word got around that she had some bomb coke. Not only was the coke better then everyone else's, the rocks that she bagged up were twice the size of the norm. Even dudes who were in the neighborhood trappin' would come and buy bundles from her so they could break it down, re-bag it up, and double their money elsewhere.

"I hope you got some more of this shit," Rodney said, walking into the apartment Darleen was in. "It's chew-min' out here."

Darleen looked at him with a smile. "What da hell is chewmin'?" she asked as she began to count the money Rodney had just gave her.

Darleen had been around drug dealers all her life, but she had never been in the trenches this deep. She had to get caught up on the slang.

"Chewmin' means it's a lot of money out there," Rodney explained.

All of a sudden, right outside the door, a loud commotion began, raising alarm. Darleen reached into the cushion of the couch and wrapped her hand around a compact .45. She didn't know what was going on, but she wasn't about to play any games with whoever was out there. She cocked a bullet into the chamber then headed for the door. Rodney was right with her, pulling a .38 from his back pocket.

Darleen slung the door open, and to her surprise, two female crackheads were outside entangled in a vicious scuffle. Two other customers who had got off the elevator, walked right over top of them, not interested at all in what they were fighting about. They were coming to cop what everybody else wanted, which was the best coke in the projects. Breaking it up was out of the question. Darleen looked over at Rodney while stuffing the gun into her back pocket. She was down to her last four bundles, and by the looks of things, it was only going to pick up.

"Hold me down for a minute. I gotta grab some more shit," Darleen told Rodney then headed for the elevator.

At this rate, she was going to get rid of her product faster than she'd thought, and because she was protected by the name of her brother, there wasn't anybody in the projects who could do anything about it.

***

Nora sat in Bugsy's car, waiting as he grabbed a few items from the hardware store. Bugsy had a dope-boy car for real. It was a 2010 Chevy Impala with tinted windows and a clean grey leather interior. He kept it clean too, despite the fact that he sometimes dressed down.

"Who da fuck is this?" Nora mumbled to herself as she felt her phone vibrating in her bag. "Hey girl, where you at?" she answered, seeing that it was Darleen.

"I'm in traffic right now. On my way to pick something up. What's going on wit' you?

"I'm making it happen. We gotta meet up later so we can talk. Oh, and have you heard from Andrea? That girl ain't been answering that phone for nobody."

"I talked to her earlier, but she said she was taking care of some bank stuff."

Bugsy getting into the car caught Nora's attention. "A'ight, I got everything that you need. Now we gotta get you a throw away phone," Bugsy said.

"But I got a phone, and I like my phone."

"That's ya personal phone. You need a business phone, one that can't be tracked back to you. I'm probably one of the last niggas that stand on the corner. Everybody else trap off their phones. It's easier and safer," he explained.

Bugsy and Nora were so caught up in the conversation, Nora had forgotten that Darleen was still on the phone.

"Excuse me," Darleen yelled into the phone, bringing Nora back. "And who the hell are you talking to? He sounds cute."

"None of ya damn business," Nora said and chuckled. "And I have to go now, so make sure you call me later so we can all meet up. And if you hear from Andrea, tell that bitch to call my phone."

Nora quickly hung up the phone before Darleen could ask any more questions about Bugsy. It wasn't much to tell anyway. Bugsy was trying to put her in a position to win, and at that moment, that was all that really mattered.

Beyoncé's "Rocket" played softly in the background while Garnett lay on top of Andrea, caressing her from her neck, down to the center of her chest. He softly kissed her lips then the side of her face, until he reached her neck. Warm kisses to her breast and then to her stomach had Andrea's eyes rolling to the back of her head. As he continued to go further down south, Andrea jumped. She'd never been touched down there with a mouth before. Not even by Garnett when they were together. He was really pulling out all the stops.

"Wait," Andrea said, reaching down and grabbing his head before he got to her belly button.

Garnett looked up at her and removed her hands from his head. "Please," he begged, and then went back to work, kissing all the way down to her cave of wonder.

Andrea wanted to cry with happiness. He was showing love right now.

In fact, when Garnett's mouth landed on her sweetness, her eyes began to water. He pried her legs apart so that he could get better access. Stuffing his tongue inside of her, he twirled in a circle with the tip of his tongue then sucked the juices from her box. He spit it back out onto her clit, and then his mouth latched onto the soft pink ball of flesh, causing Andrea to reach down and grab the back of his head.

"Oh, Garnett. Yes, baby, right there," she cried, feeling her orgasm about to reach its peak.

Andrea tried to pull his head away as she began to cum, but he refused, pushing her hands away. It was the best orgasm she'd ever had in her life. Her body was in shock, and all she could do was stare at the ceiling and wait for the orgasm to pass.

By the time Andrea came to, Garnett was laying on top of her, rubbing his dick up and down the entrance of her pussy. She thought that he was about to pound away like he normally did, but Garnett had something else in mind. He wanted to take it slow this time around, and really explore her body. He wanted to show her how much he appreciated her body, and how sexy he thought she was.

Garnett wanted Andrea to know that she was beautiful and that he'd missed her. He was going to do something he'd never done before, which was make love to her.

Chapter 11

For the past week, things had been a little hectic, and the girls planned to meet up and discuss what was going on. Nora sat in Malcolm X Park eating a platter she'd bought from The Bottom Of The Sea. She was waiting for Andrea and Darleen, who had just pulled up in Andrea's car.

"I want some!" Darleen yelled out to Nora as she entered the park.

By the time she got up to Nora, there were only two Dungeness crab legs left.

"Greedy ass," Darleen said, taking the platter out of Nora's hand. "I don't have long either. I gotta get back to the jets. It's Friday, and it's chewmin'."

Nora didn't like Darleen being in the projects down in North Philly, but it was working because she was making good money. Nora wasn't doing bad herself, selling small amounts of weight from off her cell. She even gave Bugsy product to move on his corner, which he didn't mind, because he was getting it on the low.

"Here," Nora said, digging into her bag and pulling out a stack of money. "That's eight thousand. I should have more by the end of the weekend," she said, passing it to Andrea.

"What do you want me to do with it?"

"Put it in the company's account. We gotta start putting this money up, 'cause we got a gig in Atlanta next month."

"Atlanta?" both Andrea and Darleen asked at the same time.

"Yeah, I called that guy, Reese, and he said that he wanted us to do a show in his home town. He said some big names, and he assured me that if we impress, there will be some people who would want to sign us to a contract," Nora explained.

In the modeling world, contracts with different fashion companies were how models earned. This was a part of the game that Nora was starting to become familiar with. Next month in Atlanta was going to be the turning point, but the main goal now was having enough money to put on a good show.

"A'ight, y'all, I would love to stay and kick it wit' you, but I gotta take this boy back his car before he kills me," Nora said, getting up from the bench.

"Yeah, and why haven't you spilled the beans on ya new thing? I hope that nigga ain't got you dick whipped already."

"Girl, it ain't nothing like that. Me and Bugsy are just cool," Nora tried to down play. "I gotta get out of here," she said, looking down at her dope-boy phone.

Nora got away again without giving up the goods, but as soon as Darleen had the chance, she was going to find out about Bugsy. Unfortunately, she had other foolishness to deal with today, so that was going to have to wait.

"And why do I have to get a car?" Nora asked when Bugsy pulled up to Mike's Used Cars on Frankford Avenue.

Nora had her license, but she had never purchased a car. She'd grabbed a rental a few times, but that's when she had something important to take care of.

"You need a car because you're a hustler now, and you gotta be able to get up and go whenever your services are needed. Besides, I need my car. Plus, every time you bring it back to me it smells like a chick," Bugsy said, getting out of the car.

"So you don't like how I smell?"

Bugsy looked at her and smiled. "I love how you smell, just not in my car," he answered, walking Nora onto the lot.

Mike's wasn't a big time dealership, but he had every kind of dope-boy car a drug dealer could want. From a '96 Bonneville to an '08 Lacrosse.

"Damn, I think you'll look cute in this," Bugsy said, walking up to a 2008 Dodge Charger with the Hemi engine inside. The only thing that was wrong with it was the price tag. It was a little out of Nora's price range. She wasn't trying to spend no more than five thousand for a car.

"Oh, this is you right here," Bugsy said, stopping in front of an '06 Mustang.

Nora walked up on the car, leaned over and looked in. It was clean inside. Bugsy couldn't help but to look at Nora's fat ass bent over slightly. She raised up and stepped back to get a better look at the body of the car. She backed right up to Bugsy, who grabbed her by the waist.

"Better watch where you backing that thing up," he said, gripping her waist.

Nora turned around to face him, blushing from his comment.

"What you smiling for?" he asked.

"I'm smiling at you. You keep making these little com-ments, but as soon as I give you what you're looking for, you're not gonna be able to handle it," Nora said, smiling as she shook her head slowly.

Nora had to admit that over the past week, her outlook on Bugsy had changed. He was schooling her to different aspects of the game, which required them to spend a lot of time together. The way he talked and interacted with Nora, it was as if they were already a couple. Like they were on some Bonnie and Clyde shit. A few times, she'd even wanted to give him a shot of pussy, but the fear of the aftermath had prevented her from doing it.

"I'm not a hoe. I'm not ya average chick," she said, looking in his eyes.

"Yeah, I know, that's why I'm feeling you." Bugsy moved his hands to Nora's lower back and pulled her closer to him.

Nora didn't know how weak she was for him until this very moment. She leaned in and kissed him, wrapping her arms around his neck.

At that point, it seemed like nothing else existed. This was the first time Nora had been kissed this way. It was the type of kiss that made her eyes feel heavy. Bugsy was unaware of what he was doing to Nora in that moment, but in time, he was surely going to find out.

Darleen stood outside the gas station on Broad and Huntington, waiting for Joy to show up. She was starting to get frustrated because Joy was supposed to be there ten minutes ago. As soon as Darleen was about to pull out her phone and call her again, Joy's car pulled into the station and parked by one of the pumps.

"You took long enough," Darleen snapped when she got out of the car.

"Yeah, you can blame that on traffic. But anyway, do you have my money?" Joy asked, getting straight to the point.

Being smart and wanting to take her time, just like Joy did getting there, Darleen leaned against the back of her car and slowly took her time going into her bag to retrieve the money.

"It's crazy, Darleen, cause I never really liked you. Big girls don't have a place in the porn industry," Joy said.

"I actually thought you was cool, but I see you take advantage of any opportunity that presents itself," Darleen countered, pulling out the two stacks of money.

It looked like more than it was, and that's because crack money came in all types of bills. Darleen slammed it on the trunk then closed her bag. She was about to walk off, but Joy's next comment stopped her in mid stride.

"Same thing, same time next month," Joy said as she tossed the money into her car.

Darleen turned around and looked at Joy like she was crazy.

"Come again?"

"Come on, Darleen, you think I wouldn't find out that you took five bricks from that safe? If I would have known that in the beginning, I would have told you to give me fifty thousand instead of ten, but I guess as long as you make the payments for the next four months, I'ma get exactly what I want," Joy explained. "The first payment that you miss is when I go back and tell Wood what you did."

"Oh, you one of those bold bitches," Darleen said as Joy was getting back into her car. "Don't get in over ya head," she warned, walking up to the driver's side door.

Darleen was two seconds away from reaching in, grabbing Joy by her hair, and pulling her through the window. She couldn't believe this chick had the heart to shake her down for some extra money. Before Darleen could react, Joy pulled off, leaving her standing there, pissed. Joy had her stuck between a rock and a hard place with the information she was capable of providing to Wood. One or two things would have to happen. Either she would pay Joy the money, or end up killing her.

***

Andrea was on her job when it came down to handling all the business for the modeling company. After Nora gave her Reese's contact info, she immediately contacted him and discussed the event in Atlanta. This thing was going to be huge too, and as Reese explained it, this was going to be a one shot thing for Thickums, at least in that city. Several modeling agencies were going to be there, looking for somebody to stand out. The opportunity was big, not only for Thickums, but also for Andrea's potential clothing line. If done right, this could put the girls in a good position to do something crazy in the near future.

There was still a lot of work to be done. With that, a lot more money needed to be invested. Andrea wasn't trying to be a drug dealer, but she understood why Nora and Darleen were out there doing what they had to do. They were putting their lives on the line and faced going to jail. Andrea wasn't built for that type of life, but she respected her girls for going so hard for the cause.

Darleen walked into the projects to see her brother standing by his car with a few niggas standing around him. This didn't look like a casual get together, so instead of going into the building, she walked over to see what was going on.

"Ya sista really fuckin' the game up right now," Dirt complained to PooMan.

He wasn't just complaining for him, but for a couple of niggas in the Jets who wasn't eating like they used to. For them, fast money had slowed up once Darleen came out with dime rocks twice everybody else's size. Fiends came from all over after the word got around to the three high rises. The building Darleen was in did the most numbers.

"What, y'all niggas got a problem with what's going on?" Darleen asked, cutting into the conversation.

If it was anybody else coming through the Jets slinging coke like it was going out of style, the wolves would have been out, ski masks down and guns blazing. On the strength of PooMan, none of that was going to occur, at least not at this point.

"Look, if y'all niggas wanna eat too, I don't have a problem with that. It's enough money out here so we can all make some paper. How about this, whatever y'all niggas is buying right now, I'll give it to you for the best prices in the city."

Dirt spoke up since he was probably moving more coke than anyone else. "So what's the prices you talking about? I'm getting ounces for seven fifty right now."

"I'll sell it to you cooked up for six hundred an ounce. But that's just for the people who's standing right here. For everybody else, it's eight hundred."

Although the product was coming cooked up already, there wasn't a nigga in the city coming with better prices than that. Dirt wasn't stupid enough to turn that down. Plus, with those type of numbers, he could stretch out and make money outside of the projects. It was a win for everyone.

"You know ya brother had these projects on smash for a long time for showing love like this. You keep this up, and you're gonna make a hell of a name for yourself," Dirt said, giving Darleen the nod of approval.

Before he walked off, he gave PooMan some dap, and let Darleen know that he would be getting back at her later on. PooMan looked at his little sister, not proud of what she was becoming, but rather how she was handling herself amongst real men. He knew how vicious the streets were and how ugly things could get, but from the way things looked, his kid sister was a chip off the old block.

***

"Yo," Nora answered her dope-boy phone as she was driving down Fifty-second Street in West Philly.

Niggas in the hood couldn't get enough of it. They hadn't seen these kind of coke prices since the late '90s and early 2000s. In a week, she ran through just about a whole brick, and her clientele was only improving.

"I'll be there in like twenty minutes," she said then hung up the phone.

Selling drugs was like an adrenaline rush for Nora. She had to keep reminding herself that this wasn't going to be a permanent situation. Just like most drug dealers, she had a goal, and as soon as she met that goal, she was going to hang up her Pyrex pot. Unbeknownst to her, there was something lurking in the wings. Something that she least expected, but would probably be affected by for the rest of her life. Dope-boys all around suffered from this, and it ultimately ruined them. Heading down this path, Nora wasn't going to be any different, and neither was Darleen, for that matter. Once they got used to the life of a dope-boy, or girl, in their case, it was going to take something tragic or an act of God for them to get out the game.

Chapter 12

Darleen looked around the empty playground several times before jumping into Joy's car, which had just pulled up. Arrogant and cocky as always, Joy got right down to business.

"Where my money?" she asked, not even looking over at Darleen for eye contact. Darleen smiled, then reached in her bag and grabbed a wad of cash.

"Here," she said, throwing it onto Joy's lap.

By paying Joy, Darleen was hoping to get some very important information out of her. But just as she expected, Joy wasn't going to tell her what she wanted to know without some motivation.

"I don't know. Why you wanna know who Wood's connect is? You gone get yaself killed, and then you won't be able to pay me my money," Joy said as she counted the cash.

Joy clearly wasn't getting the picture. Darleen wasn't asking her a question, she was demanding to know. Darleen reached back into her bag and pulled out a chrome .45, and that's when Joy knew shit had just got real. Joy tried to stand her ground by acting like the gun wasn't that serious.

"I don't know him personally, but the guys call him Teddy," she informed. "Don't do nothing stupid."

"Where's Teddy from?" Darleen asked, not paying Joy's last comment any mind.

She was down to her last nine ounces of powder, and needed to re-up soon, or else she was going to lose the projects back to Dirt and his boys.

"I don't know where he's from, but he comes by the studio every Thursday."

Darleen began to tuck the gun back into her bag, but Joy's mouth made her stop.

"Next time you pull a gun out on me, you better be willing to use it," Joy said, setting the money in the center console.

Darleen chuckled then took the safety off. She'd had enough of Joy acting like shit was sweet. She was tired of Joy's mouth, and she was tired of having to give her money for a lick she pulled off.

"What, you gone shoot me?" Joy asked, looking at Darleen like she didn't have the guts to do it. "Pull the trigger then. You bad."

"Darleen had never shot anyone before, and really, until she took the gun out of Wood's safe, she'd never even held one in her hand. She was scared to death and wanted to pull the trigger bad, but she didn't.

"Yeah, like I thought," Joy continued to taunt. "Now the tab is up to seventy-five thousand for that nut ass stunt you just tried to pull."

Joy took it a step further and tried to reach out and take the gun from Darleen. She got her hand on the side, but that was about it. Darleen squeezed the trigger out of reflex. The bullet hit Joy in her side, knocking her back up against the door. The bullet crashed through her lung, making it hard for her to breathe. She looked at Darleen in shock as she tried to take in air. Darleen sat there staring at Joy, not saying a word, watching as she took her last few breaths.

Darleen was frozen, and she sat there for a minute, realizing what she'd just done. Oddly, she didn't feel the kind of guilt and remorse she thought she would.

After wiping the gun down thoroughly, she placed the pistol back into her bag. She grabbed her money from the center console, looked around to make sure the coast was clear, then got out of the car and walked off. It was crazy. After catching her first body, the only thing Darleen could think about was getting back to the Projects so she could make the rest of her money. She was on some real gangsta shit now, something that was already flowing through her veins.

Wood sat in his office in deep thought. It had been three and a half weeks since somebody stole the coke from his safe, but it was still fresh on his mind. He had even shut the studio down for a minute behind it. This was the type of loss he needed answers for. A knock at the door brought him back.

"Yo, what up?" Tech greeted, coming into the office. "Is we still going to the party tonight or what?" he asked, taking a seat in the chair in front of the desk.

"Yeah, we still goin'. But I'm not really in the mood to do too much of anything, so I'm not gonna stay that long."

Tonight was the party of the bosses, and anyone who was a pillar in the Philly drug game was going to be there. It was invite only, so the average nigga off the block wasn't going to be able to get in without rolling with someone of importance.

"Damn, you still mad about that situation?" Tech asked, seeing the stress in his boy's eyes.

"Yeah, homie, that's a tough pill to swallow. I lost money and some clientele behind that shit."

"I feel you, brah, but don't dwell on that shit too hard. It's still a lot of money out there to be made. Shit, it's going to be a lot of players at the party tonight, so you should be able to get back some of the clientele that you lost," Tech told him.

Tech was right, and dwelling on the situation would only have Wood on some other shit. He was down right now, and at this point, it was all about the get back. Despite being a stone cold killer, getting at a dollar was what he did, and if he wanted to climb out of this slump that he was in, that's exactly what he needed to do.

"Wassup, li'l sis," PooMan greeted when he saw that it was Darleen calling him.

"Let me ask you something, bro. Do you know a nigga named Teddy?" Darleen asked as she got on the project elevator.

As soon as he heard the name, PooMan was already hip to what she was on. Fortunately for Darleen, her brother didn't just know Teddy, he had done a bid with him, and was probably one of the only niggas in the hood who had his personal number. PooMan didn't want to get into his personal relationship with Teddy on the phone, but he was on point and had his little sister's back for what she was about to get into.

"I'ma come through there in an hour. I'll call you when I get outside," he said then hung up the phone.

"Oh my God, I can't believe I let you cum inside of me," Nora said, sitting up on the edge of Bugsy's bed.

"Shit, I can't believe you took this long to give me some pussy," he shot back.

Nora threw one of the pillows at him for his smart comment, which he caught then walked it back over to the bed and playfully hit her with it. He leaned over and rested his forehead against hers, then puckered his lips for a kiss.

"That's daddy pussy now, so I can do whatever I want to it," he said in a sexy tone.

Nora wanted to pull him back in the bed and get another shot of that good good, but Bugsy had to take care of something. "You can chill here as long as you want. Just make sure you lock the door on ya way out," he told her.

Bugsy had a nice house on Lime Kill Pike in Mount Airy, a nice distance from his hood. Resting his head where he did his dirt at was out of the question, and for the stick-up kids who wanted to follow him home on the late night, he had a specific route that he took that could shake anybody.

"I'll see you later," he said, leaning over and kissing her one more time before he walked out the door.

Nora flopped back in the bed, not really in a rush to get up and go anywhere. She was a little more than halfway through her second brick, coupled with the fact that it was the first of the month; Nora predicted that she was going to be done with everything by the end of the weekend. She looked over, hearing her phone vibrating on the nightstand.

"Damn, that's crazy. I was just thinking about you," Nora said.

"Shit, I was thinking about you too. We need to talk," Darleen said, looking out of the apartment window into the Jets. "I'm in the projects. Come get me in about an hour," Darleen told her, but then switched it up when she saw PooMan's car pulling into the parking lot. "As a matter of fact, you can come right now," she said as she headed toward the door.

"I'm on my way," Nora replied and jumped up from the bed.

When Nora finally pulled into the Blumberg Projects, Darleen and PooMan were leaning against his car talking.

"Hey, PooMan," Nora greeted, giving him a hug when she walked up.

"You know I'm shocked at you," PooMan told her.

She was the last person that he would expect to be selling drugs. She was one of the few friends he approved of Darleen having when they were younger.

"That's ya crazy-ass sister that got me out here," Nora laughed playfully and swung her bag at Darleen.

"Well, look, let me be the first person to tell y'all that I'm not okay with y'all being out here selling drugs. But since I know y'all gone do whatever y'all want, the only thing that I can do is point y'all in the right direction," PooMan said. "Now, with that being said, how far are y'all willing to go?"

Nora and Darleen looked at each other. Nora replied, "Until our modeling company get up and running and is able to sustain itself, I'm all in."

She had been thinking about this all night and had decided that she was in a great position to make a lot of money. Her clientele was growing day by day, and as they were sitting there talking right now, her dope-boy phone was going off in her bag.

Darleen felt the same way. She was showing the projects love, and in return, they were showing their love back. Everybody was eating and doing good. Darleen had even slowed down on her coke habit, mostly because she wasn't seeing much of Gordo these days. The new hustle had taken over, and for once in her life, Darleen was focused. Her only problem was that she'd run out of product.

"So look, it's up to y'all. If you really wanna be in a position to win, I can get you there. But once you're in, you're gonna be stuck in the game for a while," PooMan explained.

Darleen looked at Nora. "It's whatever wit' me. But I can't do anything if you're not gonna be wit' me on this."

"You know I'ma rock out wit' you. We came this far together, but as soon as Thickums is on its feet, we're done. I don't care how much money we got," Nora said.

Darleen smiled then raised her middle finger to the air. "Middle finger to the world," she said, interlocking her finger with Nora's.

Whatever choice Nora would have made, Darleen was going to follow her. It wasn't that she didn't have her own mind and couldn't think without her, Darleen just had a crazy level of love and respect for Nora, as if they came out of the same womb. One thing she knew for sure was that if it ever went down, Nora had her best interest, and it had been like that since the third grade.

Wood was on his way out of the office when breaking news came over his TV screen. Before Joy's picture even popped up on the screen, Pebbles fell into the office.

"It's Joy. It's Joy. Somebody killed Joy," she cried, falling to her knees.

Just as he turned his head, Joy's face popped up on the screen. The news anchor could only report what he knew, which was the fact that Joy had been shot and was pronounced dead at the scene. No witnesses had come forward, and no weapons were found at the scene.

"What the fuck is going on?" Wood mumbled to himself.

Naturally, the first thing that popped up in his head was that Joy's death probably had something to do with the drugs taken from his safe. He was suspicious as hell about any and everything, and the more he thought about it, the more the story Joy gave him about that night didn't add up. There was no way he could question her on it now, but the fact remained that something wasn't right. Wood vowed that he was going to find the person who took his coke, and he swore on it with his life.

***

The Boss party was on 1,000 tonight, and the magic started outside with a hood car show. Niggas was pulling up in all types of clean cars. BMW, Range Rover, Aston Martin, and when Teddy showed up, he was in a Rolls Royce Ghost. Nora and Darleen stood in front of the club in awe, looking at all the beautiful cars coming through.

"Come on, y'all, let's get inside," PooMan said, grabbing Darleen's arm. "Remember, y'all not here to party. It's business, and then you get out of here," he yelled over the music as he led them to the VIP section where Teddy was.

Teddy had his crew with him. He hopped up off the couch when PooMan came into the section.

"Aww, man, my fuckin' boy in the building," he said, smacking PooMan's hand then giving him a thug hug. He looked over at Darleen and shook his head. "I haven't seen you since you was yay high. Now look at you, all grown up."

Darleen was too young to remember Teddy. He used to stand on the street corners of North Philly with her brother, but she could see that he was one of the cool ones. After Nora introduced herself, they all went to sit on the couch.

"Drink?" Teddy asked, grabbing one of the bottles from out of the bucket of ice.

"Nah, we cool. We just wanna get right to the business," Nora declined as she shifted her Gucci bag to her lap.

Teddy respected that.

"So look, I'm not gonna lie to you, we're new to this drug game, so I'ma ask that you be thorough enough to not take advantage of us. In a nutshell, we want some good coke at amazing prices. It's not a one shot deal, we in it for the long haul, so you can expect for us to be doing a lot of business together."

"How much bread are y'all working wit'?" Teddy quizzed, so far liking what he was hearing from Nora.

Between the two of them, Darleen and Nora had about one hundred thirty thousand in cash, with some product still out on the street.

Teddy tilted the bottle to his lips, calculating in his head how he was going to bless them.

"On the strength of my man, PooMan—"

"Don't do it on the strength of PooMan. We stand on our own name and would ask that you respect that," Nora said, lightweight checking him.

It only made Teddy like her even more. He could see something in her, reminding him of the first time he had a sit down with his connect. He saw the hunger in her eyes, and for that, he wanted to look out.

"I can give them to you right now for twenty-one thousand apiece. That means you'll be the only one in the city getting it at that price. You let me know how soon you want it, and I'll get it to you," Teddy told her.

Nora took the Gucci bag and set it on the couch next to him. The one hundred thirty thousand was already on deck, and again, Teddy was impressed. He had just got to the party, but for that bread, he was about to leave. He too was about his money, and there were no days off for him.

"Yo, check it out," Tech said, tapping Wood's arm.

Wood had to look around the stripper dancing on his VIP table to see what was going on. He damn near pushed her off the table when he saw Darleen leaving the building with Teddy. He got up and walked all the way to the dance floor to see where they were going, and by the time he got there, Teddy, his crew, Darleen, and Nora were leaving out the front door.

"Wassup? What's going on?" Tech yelled, walking up next to Wood on the floor.

Wood stood there with a blank look on his face, trying to figure out why in the hell would Teddy have a chick like Darleen with him tonight. *The porn industry didn't give her that much exposure,* he thought to himself. Wood's spider senses went off, and in an instant, a conspiracy theory buzzed in his head. She wasn't before, but now Darleen was on his radar, and he was going to make sure he looked into it more.

A tired Andrea sat at the sewing machine running materials through it, as she had been doing for the past week. She had designed several outfits for them to model in Atlanta, and all of them were designed specifically for plus-sized girls.

"You still haven't thought of a good name for ya clothing line?" Garnett asked, walking up and placing his hands on her shoulders. "Thickums is a cool name for ya modeling agency, but I'm not sure about ya clothing line."

"Yeah, I know. I haven't had the time to run anything past the girls yet. I've just been so focused on putting on a good show for the people. This is our big chance."

"Calm down, baby. You're gonna do good," Garnett assured, massaging Andrea's shoulders.

His touch was relaxing and somewhat intoxicating as he rubbed. Financial help was the only thing that she'd been getting from Nora, but the rest of the business dealings had been left up to her. The time and effort that needed to go into building a modeling company was strenuous. It had only been a little more than a month since they started this venture, and Andrea was already thinking about taking a vacation. If it wasn't for the new and improved Garnett coming back into her life right now, Andrea didn't know how she would have made it through. His kindness and support went a long way, not to mention the incredible sex they'd been having on a regular basis. It was exactly what she needed at a time like this, and it felt good.

Chapter 13

Nora sat in her car in front of Pat's in South Philly, waiting for Bugsy to get their food. While she was sitting there, her personal phone began vibrating in the center console. She smiled when she saw that it was Reese.

"Hey, Reese, how are you?" she greeted.

"So, are you ready for Atlanta?" he asked, leaning back in his office chair.

This was really a temperature check on Reese's behalf. He wanted to be sure that Nora was still interested. "You mean, is Atlanta ready for us? We already got our plane tickets and our hotel reservations, so rest assured we are about to come and tear that runway up."

When Reese explained some of the new designers that would be showing up, it made her want to go even harder. Social media was buzzing too, in both Philly and in Atlanta, about Thickums showing up and potently showing out.

"A'ight then, Nora, just give me a call after the weekend," Reese said, ending the conversation.

Bugsy walked up and tapped on the window right after she got off the phone.

"I don't know why you like these cheese steaks. They too commercial," he said, passing her the food.

Nora didn't care anything about what he was talking about. She was hungry as hell.

"Oh, and I just got off the phone with Reese from Atlanta. Are you sure you don't wanna come with me? I can get you a ticket right now."

"Nah, I'm good. I gotta stay here and get this money. I'm not saying that it's you who has to sacrifice, but somebody gotta do it. That's the thing about being a drug dealer. We can party when our money is up."

Now wasn't the time for going out of town. They had the city on smash right now with these crazy prices. Word had got around quick about ounces going for six hundred a pop, not to mention Bugsy making it hard for niggas to eat around his way with nickel rocks that looked like twenty pieces. Crackhead traffic became some heavy, he had to move it to a back block close by so it wouldn't attract unwanted attention. Shit was turning up right now, and Bugsy knew that the only way they would be able to keep up is if they adapted to the changes. It was a must that he schooled Nora to every aspect of the game, and that's what he did all the time. Nora wanted to win, and he was going to teach her how.

It was nice outside, so just about the whole projects were standing out in front of the building laughing and joking around. Darleen had a small crowd of young cats around her, watching some of her footage from her porn page.

"Damn, D, you throwing that pussy back on a nigga," Rodney laughed, seeing that the nigga she was fucking couldn't handle it. "The nigga dick too small. That's the only reason why you gettin' out on him. Pick on somebody ya own size," he joked, grabbing a handful of his dick through his pants.

"Boy, please, I'll fuck ya li'l ass to sleep," Darleen replied, playfully smacking Rodney upside the head.

Everybody laughed and poked at Rodney until he started faking like he was getting serious. Darleen showed him some love though, giving him a hug and kissing him on the top of his head.

The niggas in the projects were feeling Darleen. They liked her because she wasn't the type to front on the less fortunate because she was up in the game. She looked out for the kids too, passing out dollars daily. She was thorough in every sense of the word, but she was also about her business and ran the jets with an iron fist when it came to selling coke.

"Oh, shit, y'all got Mama Love out here," Dirt said, walking up and giving Darleen a hug. While he was hugging her, he whispered in her ear that he needed four and a half ounces the hard way, then went back to play fighting with one of the young cats.

Darleen relayed the numbers to Rodney, who took off and headed to the building to retrieve the work.

"Aww, shit, what da fuck do this nigga want?" Dirt said, seeing his former connect pull up.

Darleen looked over and couldn't believe her eyes when she saw Wood. Before she came along, Wood used to serve a couple niggas in the projects, and Dirt was one of them. Darleen wasn't sure what he was there for, so she kept her bag unzipped for easy access to the brand new ten shot .40 cal she had bought a few days ago.

"Damn, what's good wit' you?" Dirt greeted when he walked up to the car.

"I ain't heard from you in a minute. I wanted to let you know that I was back on deck," Wood said.

Wood's prices were a little on the high side of things. For an ounce of crack, he wanted $800. Dirt told him that the only way he was going to cop off him was if he was going to sell it to him at the prices he was getting

it for now, which was $600 an ounce. Dirt fucked with
Wood, but not enough to be giving away his money to
him. Wood could have showed some love, but he was
greedy and wasn't going to change his prices for anything.

"I see y'all got Delicious out here wit' y'all," Wood said,
nodding over to her.

"Yeah, that's the big homie out here. She doin' her
thing."

"Oh, yeah? Hey Delicious, when you gone come back
and work for me?" Wood yelled out to her.

"Fuck you, Wood. You can't afford me, nigga," Darleen
shot back with a middle finger in the air.

Wood shot her the middle finger back then pulled off.
He wanted to probe a little deeper about her role out
there in the Jets, but now wasn't the time nor place. He
definitely was on her ass though, and his gut instinct was
telling him that she might've had something to do with
his coke coming up missing. More light would be shined
on the situation, and when it was, Wood was going to be
all over it like flies on shit.

Nora had a busy day ahead of her, so she had to cut
the lunch date with Bugsy short. She had so much to take
care of before she flew out to Atlanta, and wanted to get a
jump start on it.

"So call me if you need me," Bugsy said as he collected
his trash from Nora's car.

"Wait, hold on," she stopped him and grabbed her bag
from the back seat.

Nora reached in, pulled out a set of keys, and passed
them to him.

Bugsy looked at the keys then at her. "What's this?

"It's keys to my house," she answered.

Bugsy started smiling.

"Don't be smiling, nigga. It's only so you can house sit while I'm gone," she lied.

Their relationship was moving kind of fast, but as far as she was concerned, it was moving in the right direction. She didn't want to tell him, but Nora thought that she might be in love with him. Being with Bugsy, she never had to worry about her weight and size. The way he looked at her and complimented every part of her body, it showed that he appreciated what he had. Nora hadn't felt this wanted by a man since her junior year in college, when she was also sixty pounds lighter. The most important quality she loved about Bugsy was that she felt like she could trust him. That was huge for Nora, and for that reason alone, a key to her house was something small for her to give him.

Wood walked into his studio and stormed straight to his office, not speaking to anyone on the set. He had run into Teddy about twenty minutes ago and had an enlightening conversation with him about Darleen and Nora. Though Teddy refused to divulge their personal business about how much they were copping, he definitely let him know that they were in the game. That's when Wood got to thinking. He tried to place Darleen in the studio on the morning he was robbed. He remembered that she had given him the key back to the front door, but he had to make sure of it.

"Oh, I'm on ya ass now," Wood mumbled to himself as he sat in his chair.

He didn't have to look hard to find Darleen's key because he knew exactly where he put it when she threw it at him. He opened his second drawer, reached in and grabbed the key. A thorough examination was underway, and when he lined her key up to the key he had in his pocket to the front door, it wasn't a match. Just to be sure, he ran to the front door and tried it in the lock. It was to no avail.

"Bitch!" Wood yelled through clenched teeth. He stormed back into his office and caught the attention of Tech in the process.

"Damn, homie, what's good?" Tech asked, seeing the anger in Wood's eyes. "That bitch robbed me. That fat bitch got me," Wood snapped, popping open his safe and grabbing a seventeen shot Glock and cocking a bullet into the chamber.

Tech stood there, still a little confused as to who he was talking about. "What fat bitch?"

"Delicious. And I think that crazy bitch killed Joy."

Everything was hitting Wood at once, and the conspiracy theory that was manifesting in his head was becoming a little clearer. Everything started to make sense now.

"Whoa bro, hold on for a second," Tech said, stopping Wood at the door. "You working off ya feelings and emotions, and you're liable to do something crazy. Just hold on for a second and let me take care of it," Tech suggested. "You're no good to anybody if you get locked up."

Wood threw a temper tantrum, walking around his office waving his gun around. What Tech said held a lot of truth to it, and even if he was going to just flat out kill Darleen, it wasn't going to bring back none of the money he had lost. Teddy saying that she was in the game now, kept playing over and over in his head. If she was in the game, she had to be working with some nice weight, especially since she was dealing with Teddy. Wood wanted to capitalize off that as much as he could.

"I want my money, and I want those bitches dead," Wood ordered. "And I don't want you to play no games either," he said, walking over and passing Tech the gun.

Tech popped the clip out to make sure it was fully loaded, then he slammed it back in. "Fall back, brah, I got you," Tech said, tucking the gun away into his waist line.

"Girl, where are you taking me?" Nora asked Andrea, who had a smile on her face as they walked down Market Street.

They got to Seventeenth Street, where Andrea walked her into the Red Cross Building. Nora thought they were getting medical insurance, but this building had more to offer. They got onto the elevator and got off on the third floor. Andrea stopped right in front of a double door. Nora looked through the glass window and didn't see anyone, but then she turned and looked at Andrea, who had a key in her hand.

"Welcome to Thickums Modeling Agency," Andrea said, breaking out into her happy dance.

She opened the door and stepped to the side so Nora could enter first. It was a nice sized space. It had two offices, a conference room, a walk-in closet for filing space, a bathroom, and a small secretarial station by the door.

"What's the price tag on this place?" Nora asked as she walked around, peeking her head into all the rooms.

"It's thirty-five hundred a month with a security deposit for six months. We also get to use the waiting area down the hall," she explained.

There was no question as to whether the girls could afford it, because they could, with ease. Thickums was now an official business; it was time for it to start looking like one.

"I also got my eyes on a small studio that's about to become available within the next two months. I checked it out, and it would be a great place for our models to do photo shoots. Oh, and speaking of that, I think we should start holding interviews for Thickums models. That's the only way this place is going to make any money."

Nora listened while Andrea rambled on about company business. She was feeling the progress they were making, and she was also proud of Andrea for handling the business the way that she was. It seemed like that farfetched dream was finally becoming a reality, slowly but surely, and Nora was feeling and loving the vibe from it all.

Darleen wasn't big on smoking weed, but tonight she was blowing like crazy. What happened in the car with Joy had finally hit, and it hit her hard too. It wasn't the foul and disrespectful language that Joy used, nor was it the fatal shot that took her life. The thing that Darleen remembered the most was when Joy looked at her and took her last breath. The image was starting to haunt her. She couldn't get it out of her mind for nothing. It didn't matter how much coke she snorted, or how much weed she smoked, nothing could take her mind off of it.

The worst part was that she had no one to confide in. As much as she loved her girls, she couldn't bring herself to admit what she'd done. Hell, she could barely admit it to herself. Gordo was out of the question too. Darleen liked him a lot, but she didn't really feel that she could trust him with something this big. Since she'd started hustling and put their plans to branch out on their own in the porn industry on hold, things had changed between them. Gordo didn't seem as committed as he was before, but the sex was still on the bomb, so she didn't fuss.

Darleen never knew that she could be so heartless and not value the life of someone else. She didn't know what to think of herself, and in her heart, she felt like she was going to answer for what she did. It may be in this worldly life or in the hereafter. Either way, she knew that it wasn't going to be nice.

Chapter 14

Tech didn't go right at Darleen or Nora like Wood wanted him to do. Instead, he stepped back, evaluated the whole situation, and tried to strategize the best course of action to take. If Tech wanted them dead, it could have been done by now, but there wasn't going to be any financial gain in it. If they had cash and coke somewhere stashed away, he wanted it. In order to do that, he had to play his position and do all of his homework to see how they moved individually.

"You think that bitch crazy enough to have that shit in her house?" Gram asked Tech as they sat in a car about a block away from Nora's house.

"I don't know, but we sure as hell gone find out," Tech answered while he searched the Internet on his phone. "Look, these crazy bitches won't even be in the city this weekend," he said, showing Gram what was on Nora's Facebook and Instagram.

She was promoting Thickums and the show that they were about to put on in Atlanta. Social media could be dangerous for some people, especially drug dealers.

"Oh, shit, that's her," Gram pointed to Nora, who had pulled up in front of her door and got out the car.

Tech picked his head up to get a better look at her to see what she was up to. To his surprise, she ran into the house, but then came right back out and got back in her car. That's what Tech was waiting on.

"Follow her, and don't lose her," he told Gram, who gave her a nice distance before pulling out of his spot and tailing her.

Tech used to be a dope-boy, so depending on what move she made next, he would be able to get a better idea of if the coke was in her house. If she was stupid enough to keep it in there, Tech was going to be bold enough to run up in there while she was out of town. After that, he would lay and wait on her, then put a bullet in her head.

"I swear to God, I'm going to kill this girl if she ain't here in the next five minutes," Nora said to Andrea as they stood curbside at the Philadelphia International Airport. "This girl is gonna be late to her own fucking funeral."

Less than two minutes later, Gordo pulled up with Darleen in the passenger's side seat.

Nora let out a relieved sigh, but she was still a little upset about Darleen's tardiness. When Darleen stepped out of the car, she looked like she was red carpet ready. She had on an all-white, full length fitted dress, some black Christian Louboutin sandals, and an Eddie Parker clutch. Her hair was tossed up, and she had on a few accessories that set the dress off.

Nora and Andrea looked at each other and burst out laughing.

"Don't hate me cause I'm beautiful," Darleen said, strutting back and forth on the sidewalk to show off her outfit.

"Girl, ain't nobody hatin' on you. Yo' ass is about to be the only chick on this plane that looks like she's about to go on a prom or some shit," Nora joked.

Gordo even chuckled a little as he grabbed her bags from the trunk.

"I know one thing: if this plane go down, at least I'll be going down like the diva I am," Darleen sassed, snapping her fingers and striking a pose.

Nora and Andrea couldn't deny that at all. "I know that's right," Nora snapped back. "Now come on, and let's get our asses on the plane."

After a few hugs and kisses from Gordo, the girls headed inside. The show wasn't until tomorrow, but Nora had something special planned for tonight. She was going to make sure she got the most out of this experience in the ATL.

Tech had been on his job following Nora and Darleen around the city for the past couple of days, watching and mentally recording their every move. Wood didn't expect anything less from his boy, knowing that back in his time, Tech used to stalk, rob, and kill big time hustlers for a living. Hands down, he had more home invasions under his belt than anybody in the city.

"So do you think they keep the coke in their houses?" Wood asked.

From Tech's experiences, and seeing how Nora was moving, he was 95 percent sure that she had the dope in her home. How much, he couldn't tell, and as far as Darleen, he wasn't really sure, because she hardly ever stayed at her apartment. She was either in the projects all day, or she was at Gordo's place. If he had to guess, he would have thought that she kept her stash somewhere close to her, which more than likely would be in the projects. It was out of the question for Tech and his boys to run up in the Jets. Shit could get dark for him real quick, and death would come before he found out which apartment the stash was in.

"What about the other bitch? Ain't it three of them?" Wood asked, remembering Andrea from the day at the photo shoot.

"Yeah, but I don't think shorty in the game. I think she's taking care of all the modeling business."

Wood thought about it for a minute. "Don't exclude that bitch. Run up in her shit too. That's probably where they're keeping it."

Wood wasn't trying to leave any rock unturned. He wanted it all, and as soon as he got it, it was curtains for the girls.

The plane ride from Philly to Atlanta was only about an hour and a half, so they landed in the middle of the afternoon. The weather was beautiful, and from the looks of all the people outside, Atlanta was wide-awake.

"A'ight, by the time we check into the hotel and get dressed, the van should be here with our clothes," Nora said, looking down at the watch on her wrist.

Instead of bringing all the different outfits with them on the plane, Nora had paid someone to drive the clothes down to them. It was a little more convenient that way.

"I know one thing, I'm hungry as hell," Darleen said as they walked into the car rental place.

"I second that, and we definitely will be getting some Gladys' while we're down here," Andrea said as she scrolled through her phone.

They each had their own itinerary for the trip, but only one that was going into effect, which was Nora's. As soon as they got to the hotel, checked in, and got dressed, they were right back out on the town looking beautilicious. First stop on the agenda was The Underground. Men couldn't take their eyes off the three big, sexy women who looked like they were having a blast. Nora had never been hit on this much in her life, and Andrea couldn't stop smiling at all the attention she was getting. Darleen was only being Darleen, flirting as much as she could. Shockingly, one guy even noticed her from her XXX movies and got a couple of pictures with her.

The next stop was Gladys Knight's Chicken and Waffles, where the food was heaven. The girls didn't have to feel ashamed or uncomfortable about throwing down, because everyone was in there getting it in. They tore down, leaving behind nothing but chicken bones and syrup.

"Oh my God, I'm stuffed," Darleen said, now wishing that she hadn't worn the dress that was wrapped around her body so tight.

"I think I need to go back to the hotel and take a shit," Andrea said, making everybody at the table laugh.

Nora had to admit, it had been a long time since they had gone out and had a good time like this. This was only the daytime activity. What Nora had planned for the night was going to be so much more fun. The best thing any of them could do at this time was go back to the hotel and get some rest. They definitely were going to need it.

As the sun began to set, Bugsy planned to make one last trip to Nora's house to pick up some coke so he could serve some of the customers that had been blowing up Nora's work phone. He was starting to regret volunteering to hold her phone, because it seemed like he'd spent more time attending to her people than his own.

"Speak of the devil," he mumbled to himself, seeing her picture pop up on her phone. "You could have washed these dishes before you left," he said when he answered the phone.

Nora laughed at his fake attitude.

"I'm sorry, daddy. I'll make it up to you," she replied in a playful manner. "So what are you doing?"

"I'm at work, and it's busy," he answered, putting chunks of crack onto the scale. "And yo, don't worry about tomorrow, you gone knock it out of the park."

"Thank you. Why are you so nice to me?"

"'Cause I love you, that's why. And don't go getting on some lovey dovey shit, 'cause don't nobody got time for that," Bugsy said, making Nora smile even harder.

This was the first time Bugsy had professed his love to her, and though it wasn't in the most sentimental way, Nora felt the sincerity behind it. She wanted to say it back to him so bad, but she knew that once she did that, there would be no more barriers for him to break down. Nora was still a little bit afraid of that.

"So look, I wanted to give you a heads up that I'll be at the club tonight. I might not hear the phone ringing if you try to call. I'll call you in the morning, or if you still up tonight, call me around two o'clock. I should be back in my hotel room by then. And, I love you too," she said then quickly hung up the phone.

Bugsy looked at the phone and smiled. "Got you."

Bugsy got what he needed, put the coke back in the stash, then headed back downstairs. The moment he got to the bottom of the steps and saw that the front door was open, he knew something was wrong. At first he thought that it may have been the police, but when a hard object hit him in the back of the head, he knew it was the stick-up kids. The blow knocked him to the ground, and when he got his bearings back, he saw a masked man closing the front door.

The gunman walked over to Bugsy, who was holding the back of his head, and pointed a gun at his face. "I want everything, or you can die wit' it," the gunman spoke.

In the middle of being robbed, the one thing that came to Bugsy's thoughts after hearing the gunman speak was the French Montana lyrics, *We got a mask on, we coming for ya ice. Without the mask on, we coming for ya life.* These guys came with masks on, which meant that they didn't have to kill anyone. They could just take what they wanted and be on their way. But just in case they were faking, Bugsy had to try them.

"Y'all niggas got the right idea, but the wrong house," he told the gunman in front of him.

The gunman didn't say anything. He just reached up and acted like he was about to take off his mask. Bugsy stopped him before he could do it.

"Whoa, whoa. I haven't seen none of y'all niggas' faces. I'ma give you what you want, just don't rock me, dog."

"Where it's at?" the gunman said, pressing the gun against Bugsy's cheek.

It wasn't going to be that easy. "Nah, homie, I need you to give me ya word," Bugsy told him.

He knew this nigga was the real deal and prayed that he was the type to stand on his word. Fortunately for Bugsy, he was.

"My word," the gunman said, lowering his gun from Bugsy's face.

In return, Bugsy gave him the combination to the safe upstairs in Nora's bedroom closet. It was a little more than a brick of powder, a brick and a half of crack, and about eight thousand dollars. They took everything.

"Come on, dog, you gave me ya word," Bugsy pleaded when the gunman lifted the gun back up to his face.

The second gunman was already out the door with the goods, so it was nothing for him to put a bullet in Bugsy's head. He didn't, but just so Bugsy wouldn't be able to chase him down when he left, he shot him twice in the leg.

One to the shin and the second to the knee. Bugsy rolled off the steps and onto the floor in pain. By the time he looked up, the gunman was out the door.

Tech didn't even have to break into Darleen's because Gordo's slimy ass walked them right through the front door. "Tear this muthafucka up," Tech commanded his two men. He walked over and took a seat on the lawn chair Darleen had sitting in the living room. "So when are they supposed to be coming back?" he asked Gordo, who took a seat on the couch.

"Sometime on Sunday," he answered, kicking his feet up on the coffee table.

Tech's boys tore Darleen's room up but didn't find anything. Then they hit the second bedroom, the bathroom, the kitchen and the hallway closet. Still, they came up empty handed. They flipped the living room upside down, and still nothing. It wasn't a shock to Tech because he already felt like there wasn't going to be anything in the apartment anyway. Gordo was like a free pass to get into her place.

"I still get my money even though nothing was here, right?" Gordo asked as Tech and his boys were about to leave.

Unfortunately, Tech didn't give him his word like he had with Bugsy, and all he was right now was an eye witness who Tech knew would do just about anything for the right amount of money. He couldn't afford for Gordo to turn on him and alert Darleen to what was going on.

Tech pulled his gun from his back pocket in the blink of an eye and fired a single shot into his chest. The bullet hit him directly in his heart, and within seconds, he bled out and died. To make sure that he was dead, Tech walked over and put another bullet into the back of his head. He and his boys left the apartment and closed the door behind them.

"Yo, it's not here," Tech spoke into the phone as he walked down the hallway. "I'ma hit the other chick's house next."

"Nah, nah, nah. Leave shorty's crib for me. I'm going to take care of that one personally," Wood said. "I got a good feeling about that one. Shit just gotta get done right. Slide back to the studio. We on ice until these bitches come back."

Wood was a devious nigga, and Tech knew that whatever he had planned next wasn't going to be nice at all. His boy had plenty of tricks up his sleeve.

"Girl, if you don't get off the phone," Darleen said to Nora as they walked down the street toward the club.

When Nora got out of the shower, she saw that she'd missed several calls from Bugsy. When she got up from her nap, she kept trying to call him but didn't get an answer. He wasn't responding to her text messages either, which had her a little worried.

"Look, we gone go in here, have some fun, and you can call that boy in the morning," Darleen said.

"Yeah, call his ass in the morning," Andrea chimed in.

Nora agreed and finally put her phone back into her bag. Since she was going to have her bag on her all night, she put her phone on vibrate just in case Bugsy tried to call her again.

"Damn, Nora. You killing that dress," Darleen had to admit.

It was powder blue, short sleeved, and reached down to her thighs. It showed a lot of cleavage and the center of her back. She topped it off with some Saint Laurent pumps and a diamond ankle bracelet. Darleen rocked the same white dress she'd had on all day, feeling like it looked too good for her not to flaunt it at the club. Andrea, the fashionista that she was, made a pair of blue jeans and a white V-neck T-shirt look good off a pair of Jimmy Choos.

Like every Friday night, Magic City was off the chain, and pretty much everybody that was somebody was in the spot. Reese had hooked Nora up with some VIP passes, so she and the girls were set. It was a good thing, too, because the club was full to capacity.

"We doin' it big tonight," Darleen said, reaching into her bag and pulling out a wad of money.

She had a few thousand dollars in all sorts of bills. It was drug money, fresh off the block. Andrea was unprepared, not knowing they were going to a strip club that night, but Nora was on point. She pulled out a stack of twenty-dollar bills, totaling up to about five grand. Nora didn't even bother to count it out, but simply broke it in half and passed Andrea some of the bills.

"Shit, we ball together or we don't ball at all," Nora said, looking over and waving down one of the waitresses.

Darleen took it upon herself to go out to the floor and grab a couple of dancers for their entertainment. She made sure she grabbed three of the baddest pieces out there, too.

"Keep the bottles coming all night," Nora leaned over and told the waitress as she peeled off some money and handed it to her.

"Yo' shout out to Thickums Modeling Agency, holding it down in VIP," the DJ yelled over the music.

Nora and the girls couldn't believe it. What was even more shocking was how much love the people were showing them. It turned out that tomorrow's events were going to be bigger than what Reese had described it to be, and it was as if the whole city of Atlanta was waiting for the Thickums debut. Nora, Darleen, and Andrea took it all in, and tonight they were going to party like rock stars until the sun came up.

Bugsy kept trying to turn his phone on to at least get Nora's number out of it so he could call her. The phone was so dead it just kept shutting off. It got to the point where it didn't even come back on. He so desperately needed to let Nora know what was going on. Although Tech didn't take everything, he had put a nice dent in their product.

The Philadelphia police responded to a call of shots fired from Darleen's apartment complex. When they got there, a woman from the apartment above Darleen explained what she'd heard. The police waited for the landlord to come and give them access to the apartment, and when he did, Gordo's body was discovered. Within minutes, homicide detectives and the forensic unit were on the scene. They collected as much evidence as they could, and even tried to contact Darleen, whose phone went straight to her voice mail. She didn't know it, but she was automatically a suspect in the murder.

The neighbors tried to tell the detectives that Darleen was out of town, but all they did was make a mental note of it. In Philly, with this kind of crime, you were guilty until proven innocent, and Darleen wasn't no different than the rest of the criminals in the hood. Whenever she did wake up and check her messages, she was going to blow a fuse.

Chapter 15

Consistent knocks on Nora's door were the only things that woke her up from her deep sleep. Andrea was almost ready to call the front desk and see if somebody could come and open the door for her.

"I'm coming, I'm coming!" Nora yelled as she got out of the bed. She was still fully dressed from last night, and she almost broke her ankle, forgetting that she still had on her heels.

"Girl, we got an hour before we hit the runway," Andrea announced when she entered the room. "I been trying to get y'all up all morning," she said, pacing back and forth.

Nora came out of her heels and darted to the bathroom for a quick shower. She didn't even remember if she washed her whole body. Thankfully, Andrea had already gone down to Prince Hall to set up for the show, so the only thing that was left to do was get everybody down to the building.

"Oh my God, have you seen my phone?" Nora asked in a panic as she looked around the room. "Do you see it?"

It took a minute or two, but they eventually found it in the bathroom next to the toilet.

"Reese is going to kill me."

Nora had twenty-five missed calls, most of which came from Bugsy. She didn't have time for Bugsy right now, so she decided to call Reese back instead.

"You know you're getting ready to blow this," Reese answered. He was standing outside watching people flood into the Hall.

"I know, I know, I'll be there in twenty minutes."

"Make it fifteen, and make sure you're ready to hit the runway as soon as you get through the door," Reese said then hung up the phone.

Nora got dressed in record-breaking time, fixing and styling her own hair while she was on the move. When they got up to Darleen's room, it was as if everyone had stepped on the breaks. She answered the door with the same clothes she had on yesterday, and her hair was a complete mess. She turned around and walked back into the room where she was packing her things.

"Darleen, what's going on?" Nora asked, seeing what she was doing.

Darleen didn't say anything. She grabbed her phone off the nightstand and went straight to her voice mail.

"Hello, my name is Detective Turner with the Philadelphia Police Department homicide unit. Please give me a call or come down to Eighth and Race and ask to speak to me," the Detective said.

Nora had a curious look on her face, and so did Andrea. The next message gave more clarity.

"Hey, Darleen, this Tina. The cops found a body in ya apartment. I think it was ya friend. Girl, I wouldn't come back if I was you," Darleen's neighbor said in her message.

"Oh, shit, you think it's Gordo?" Andrea asked, taking a seat.

"I don't know, but more than likely it was. I don't know what the hell is going on, but I'ma go and find out," Darleen said as she closed her suitcase. "Y'all stay here and do the show."

"Fuck that show. We're coming wit' you," Nora shot back.

Darleen wasn't having it. She insisted on it, assuring Nora that she was all right.

"I hate to be the bearer of bad news, but if we don't do this show, we can kiss the potential contracts good-bye," Andrea spoke. She was only being realistic about the situation. Without any contracts and no connect like Reese backing them up, Thickums was going to hit rock bottom in a matter of seconds. Everything the girls had been working for was on the line right now.

"Seriously, y'all, I'll be good. Go out there and rock that shit," Darleen encouraged while grabbing the rest of her things.

Nora didn't want her to leave by herself, but the girls couldn't afford to lose out on this great opportunity.

"I swear, we'll be out of here on the next flight," Nora promised.

Darleen hugged both of her friends then headed for the door. Her flight was scheduled to leave in the next hour, and she couldn't miss it. Stressed the hell out, Nora and Andrea departed and headed straight for the Prince Hall to put on the show of their lives.

Nora didn't know how she gathered up the strength to go on with the show, but there she was in the dressing room, changing into her first outfit.

"Carly, do you have any experience with modeling?" Nora looked over and asked Darleen's replacement.

On their way to the hall, they searched the city for somebody who looked like Darleen to be able to model the outfits Andrea made. They couldn't find a single soul, but as soon as they pulled into the parking lot, they saw Carly, a cute Mexican girl who resembled Darleen to a tee. Carly was already there to support the plus size movement, and when Nora asked her if she wanted to be a model, she jumped at the opportunity.

"I never modeled professionally, but I know how to strut my big ass in some heels."

"Good, that's gonna have to do. Just follow my lead and pay attention to directions," Nora told her.

Right then, Reese walked into the dressing room and informed them that they were up. It was go time.

When Nora walked out onto the runway with Meek Mill coming through the speakers, the crowd stood to their feet. She strutted hard, swaying her hips side to side. She had on a cream linen two-piece suit and a white blouse designed and made by Andrea. On her feet were a pair of Salvatore Ferragamo pumps. She walked all the way down to the end of the runway, chucked the deuces, spun around, and headed back.

Carly stepped out and gave Nora a high five when they passed each other. She had on a baby blue linen skirt that reached down to the top her calf, a cream line button-up shirt, all designed by Andrea, and on her feet were a pair Monolo Blahniks. For it to have been her first time ripping the runway, she had the walk, the look, and the pose, along with a huge smile on her face the whole time.

Andrea hit the runway in a light pink linen short-sleeved dress that reached her upper ankle. On her feet were a pair of pink and white Air Max sneakers with no socks. She strutted to the end of the runway, hiked her dress up to show off the footwear, then headed back. The crowd went nuts, and even the judges nodded their heads in approval.

For the rest of the show, Andrea, Nora, and Carly let the people have it. All the outfits they designed were made by Andrea, and every plus size woman in the building had to have it. Nora gave the crowd everything they were looking for, burning the runway to the ground.

***

Darleen landed back in Philly a little bit after 4:00 in the afternoon. PooMan met her at the airport to make sure she got around safe. Instead of going to the police station or calling the detective, she went straight home to see what her place looked like. Cops were still sitting in front of the building when PooMan parked. She got out and walked right past them. Nosey neighbors were in the hallway when she got up to the floor, and on her door was a strip of yellow tape.

She walked into the apartment and saw that the place was trashed. A large bloodstain covered one of the couch pillows, and a bunch of trash from the paramedics was all over the living room. Darleen didn't even have a chance to make it to her bedroom because as soon as she was about to, a police officer walked into the apartment and stopped her in her tracks. He had been given precise instructions to call Detective Turner if Darleen came there, and that's exactly what he did.

"The detective would like to speak to you," the officer said, passing Darleen his cell phone.

She declined to talk but told the plain-clothes officer that she was on her way to Eighth and Race to speak with a Detective Turner. At first, the officer looked like he wanted to detain her, but Turner told the cop to let her go since she was coming to him.

Darleen left the crib in search of some answers as to what happened at her place.

Nora explained the whole situation to Reese and that she needed to get back to Philly asap. He understood the family emergency and let Nora know that he would be in touch with her.

While Nora and Andrea stood in the Airport, Nora's phone began to ring. She quickly answered it once she saw that it was Bugsy.

"I'm sorry, baby, I tried to call you back, but your phone was off."

"Don't worry about that right now. I'm in the hospital."

"What? In the hospital for what?" Nora asked.

Bugsy didn't want to go into details over the phone about what happened, but he did let her know that he'd been shot. That piece of information didn't do any justice because now Nora was freaked out.

"I'm on my way home, and I'm coming straight to you," Nora said before she hung up the phone.

The flight was boarding, and she didn't want to waste another minute. Her mind was racing, thinking about all the chains of events. Gordo being murdered in Darleen's apartment, and in the same night, Bugsy got shot. Nora was hoping that the two incidents weren't related in some way. If it was, who and why was all that she could think about.

The whole flight back to Philly, she tried to cipher through the madness. The hour-and-a-half-long flight seemed like forever, but eventually, the plane landed at Philadelphia International. She scrambled to the curbside for a cab.

"A'ight, I don't know what in the world is going on, but I want you to come with me," Nora said, waving down a cab.

"I gotta get home. I gotta check on Garnett," Andrea said.

Nora cut her eyes over at her. She hadn't heard that name in a minute. "I was going to tell y'all. He changed, and he's not the same as he used to be."

"A'ight, a'ight," Nora cut her off. "We'll talk about that later."

Nora didn't have time to go back and forth with Andrea, and from the serious look on her face, Nora knew that Andrea wasn't about to come with her.

"A'ight, you make sure you call me the minute you get in the house, Andrea, and if anything is out of wack, you get the hell out of there immediately," Nora instructed.

Needing to get to Bugsy, Nora jumped in a cab and headed straight for him. Andrea also got in a cab, en route to her house.

After Darleen was questioned at the police station and her whereabouts were confirmed, she contacted Gordo's sister to let her know what happened. It was one of the hardest things she had ever done. Explaining to someone that their brother had been shot and killed in her apartment while she was out of town was crazy.

"Ms. Grubbs, if you hear anything, please give me a call," Detective Turner said as he ended the interview.

Darleen was out of the state at the time of the murder, so the questioning was at a minimum. The house was flipped, and the detective did ask her if there was something in the house of value that somebody may have wanted. Darleen thought of the possibility of some stick-up boys trying to rob her, but she was not going to tell him about it. If that was the case, she was glad that it was Gordo laying on the cold metal table instead of her. It sounded harsh, but it was the truth.

On her way out of the police station, she got a call from Nora, who had just arrived at the hospital. She explained as much as she could about Gordo, but Darleen told Nora that she was on her way to the hospital so they could talk. Shit was getting crazy right now.

Andrea had tried to call Garnett several times, but she was unsuccessful in reaching him. When she got inside, the house appeared okay, but then she smelled the strong scent of a cigar as she walked into the dining room. She didn't recall Garnett picking up the habit. Nora's words came back to her, and she decided to take the safe route and get out. As soon as she turned around and was about to leave the house, Wood came out of nowhere and threw a right cross to the side of her face. She went down with ease, unable to even scream.

Andrea was knocked out cold, but she was awakened immediately by Wood throwing some cold water on her face.

"Wake ya fat ass up," he said, taking a seat on the arm of the couch.

Andrea sat up in the middle of the floor, wiping the water from her face. She looked up, saw the gun in Wood's hand, and instantly began to cry.

"Shut up? Shut up? If you scream, I'ma shoot you in ya fucking face," Wood threatened.

Andrea was scared to death.

"See, y'all bitches got the game fucked up. I want my fuckin' money," he said, stomping on the floor with every word. "I know you got something in this bitch."

Andrea's jaw was hurting, but she managed to answer him. "There's nothing here," she said, trying to flex the pain out of her jaw.

Wood didn't believe her at all, and he damn sure wasn't trying to wrestle around with her to find out. She only had one shot to come clean. His purpose for being there wasn't solely for the money anyway. He was there to make an example out of somebody. This part of the game was ugly, but fair, in most eyes. Wood got off the couch and walked over to Andrea. Outside, a car drove past with the bass thumping so hard, it slightly shook the windows. When he turned to look out the window, Andrea tried to run up the steps, but Wood spun around and shot her in the back before she got up two steps.

It slowed her down, but she kept trying to push. Wood shot her again, hitting her spinal cord and instantly taking her legs from under her. She tumbled down the steps backward, hitting her head on just about every step before she hit the bottom. Wood walked over and kicked Andrea onto her back. She looked dead, but just to be sure, he shot her in the face.

"That'll teach you fat bitches," Wood said before walking out the door.

"The niggas had on masks, and I didn't recognize his voice at all," Bugsy explained to Nora from his hospital bed.

Nora just sat there listening to the crazy story. She didn't care about the money or the drugs that were taken. She was just happy that the gunmen hadn't killed Bugsy. She would be devastated if that would have happened.

"I'm glad you're okay, baby," she said, leaning in and kissing his face.

Bugsy cracked a smile. "Man, this shit comes wit' the game. It's just time for us to relocate. It's never a good idea to eat where you sleep at."

Before Nora could say anything, Darleen knocked on the door and walked into the room. She looked stressed and exhausted.

"Girl, you need to get some rest. You look like you about to fall over," Nora said.

"I wish I could. Too much shit is going on for me to even think about closing my eyes right now. Oh, hey, Bugsy," Darleen greeted with a smile, almost forgetting to acknowledge him.

"Wassup, Darleen? Sorry to hear about ya folks."

"Yeah, about that, my brother thinks that we were targeted since our name is starting to ring bells in the city.

You know the wolves come out when they smell money."

Hearing her phone ring, Nora looked around the room for her bag. She remembered that she told Andrea to call her once she got home.

"Hey, I'm at the hospital. Where are you?" Nora asked, but didn't get a response right away. "Andrea!" she yelled into the phone when she didn't get a response.

Nora listened closely, plugging her opposite ear up so she could hear better. First, she heard heavy breathing, then she could hear Andrea's voice. "I've been shot. . . . He shot me," Andrea whispered.

Nora took off running out of the door without saying anything. Darleen took off right behind her without a second thought.

"Nora, what the hell is going on?" Darleen asked as they both raced through the hospital until they got outside and jumped into Nora's car.

She knew it was bad news because Nora's eyes were full of tears.

"Nora, you tell me what the fuck is going on now!" Darleen demanded, now realizing that the call was from Andrea. "Right fucking now, Nora!"

"Andrea's . . . Andrea's been shot!" Nora screamed.

"No, don't you tell me that. You take that shit back, don't you dare fucking tell me that. No!" Darleen yelled.

Nora sped out of the parking lot, recklessly dipping in and out of traffic, en route to Andrea's house in Southwest Philly. Her driving got the attention of a police car as she drove over the Grey Fairy Bridge, and within seconds, the red and blue lights were on.

"Don't you fucking stop," Darleen told her, pulling out her phone to dial 911.

Nora wasn't stopping anyway. She sped through the city at high rates of speed, attracting more cops. Darleen informed the operator that her friend was in danger and that the cops were chasing behind them. Nora was driving so fast, by the time she got to Andrea's street, she couldn't brake fast enough to bend the corner. She ended up running into a wall, causing minor damage. She and Darleen jumped out of the car and darted toward Andrea's house. Police officers ran behind them, chasing them up the street. They yelled for them to stop running, but Nora and Darleen kept chucking.

Up the steps and through the open front door they ran. Nora stopped and dropped to her knees when she came up on Andrea lying in the middle of the living room floor in a pool of blood. The cell phone was right by her face, and there wasn't a sign of life in her. Nora checked her pulse, but there was nothing. Darleen dropped to her knees as well.

Nora was about to administer CPR, but the cops ran into the house, guns pointed, yelling for everyone to get on the ground. It wasn't until they saw Andrea's body that they calmed down.

"No, no, get the fuck off of me," Nora yelled when they tried to pull her away from Andrea.

Darleen was dragged out of the house, kicking and screaming as well.

"They killed her! They killed her," Darleen yelled all the way out the door.

A few of the police officers felt sympathetic, but they had to do their jobs. They placed both girls under arrest for eluding police. They were placed in the cop car and taken to the police station. Both women were silent the whole way there, unable to get the image of Andrea lying dead out of their heads. Somebody was going to have to answer for this. Nora didn't know who right now, but her only mission in life at this point was to find them and deal with them.

Chapter 16

What it look like, my nigga?" Wood greeted, smacking Tech's hand when he got out of the car.

Since Andrea's death a few days ago, business had picked back up for Wood. Nora and Darleen were nowhere to be found and hadn't made a sale in the hood since. It wasn't the desired effect Wood had imagined, but it was profitable. He really just wanted to let the girls know how dangerous the streets could be when you out here in the game.

"So look, I'm having a party at the studio tonight. Make sure you come through, 'cause it's going to be crazy," Wood told Tech.

"I'm not making any promises. I'm still out here trying to find out where these bitches is at," Tech said, referring to Darleen and Nora. "Ain't no telling what these bitches gon' do if they find out we was behind that situation."

"You trippin', my nigga. No witnesses, no evidence, not anything that can tie that shit back to us," Wood reminded him. "And fuck, if they did know it was me, I wouldn't give a fuck. Dem bitches ain't scaring nobody over here," Wood flexed.

"Ain't nobody scared of those bitches, but at the same time, we gotta be smart. Homicide ain't got no statute of limitations on it, so if they did put two and two together, they could go straight to the police," Tech said. "That's why I'm out here looking for these bitches now."

Wood could see the point that Tech was making. The last thing he wanted to do was get smoked by some bitches, or get locked up for a body. Wood ain't have time for none of that in his life.

"A'ight, my nigga, whenever you run into those bitches, take care of that on sight," he instructed, sticking his hand out for a shake.

"You know I got you, my nigga. And as soon as I take care of this, we gone fall back and get this money," Tech shot back, showing Wood some love before jumping back in his car.

Darleen took a card and separated a line of coke on the coffee table, then sniffed the whole thing. She threw her head back and pinched her nose so the coke could run down the back of her throat. She was higher than a giraffe's ass and had been like this for the past few days.

"Aye, D, you can't do it like this, li'l sis," PooMan said when he walked into the living room.

She had been staying at his place until she found a new place, but PooMan really wanted to keep her close to him right now. His house was the safest place for her. Her getting high the way that she was made him a little concerned for her mental and physical well-being. Cocaine was a hard drug to kick once it had you, and he didn't want to see his li'l sister go back to being the cokehead she used to be.

"Leave me alone right now, PooMan. I'ma be all right."

"That's the thing, you're not gonna be all right. Look, I understand what you're going through," he said, sitting next to her. "And I know you're not gonna wanna hear this, but the fact of the matter is that she's gone. You're still alive, and that's how I want you to stay. You my baby sister, and I'm not gonna lose you, too."

Darleen listened to him but continued separating another line of coke. She didn't skip a beat, leaning back over and taking another line of the substance into her nose.

PooMan looked at her in sorrow. He reached over and grabbed the small sandwich bag of coke then blew the rest of the powder off the table. Darleen was hot. She began tussling with PooMan, trying to get the bag out of his hand. It was a struggle to avoid her as he got up and headed for the kitchen.

"No, Pooman, don't do that!" she yelled, trying to wrestle him down for the coke.

It had to be a little more than two ounces left in the bag, and Darleen would have to go through too much to get more.

PooMan loved his little sister and wasn't about to let her go out like this. He made it to the kitchen sink and poured it into the garbage disposal, then turned it and the water on.

"What da fuck are you doing?" Darleen snapped, punching and smacking PooMan's back while he made sure the machine ate the coke up.

Darleen kept swinging until she began to cry. PooMan turned around and gripped her up, wrapping her in his arms. As her big brother, he could feel her pain and knew from experience exactly what she was going through.

"I got you, D. We gone get through it together. Ya big bro here for you," he comforted.

The truth was, PooMan didn't know all that was stressing Darleen out right now. She had a lot on her mind. Guilt was eating at her because she felt responsible for Andrea and Gordo's deaths. He thought that the stick-up boys were responsible, but she knew better. It didn't hit her until she and Nora ran up in Andrea's house that

Wood was the man responsible for her death. The scent of his cigar was still in the air when they arrived. She knew the smell all too well, having been around it day after day in the studio. Andrea's death, along with Gordo's, was the result of something that she did. Bugsy was sitting up in the hospital as well because of it. It was killing her on the inside, and she could honestly say that she wished that it was her in the morgue instead of Andrea.

The chances of anybody knowing where Bugsy lived were slim to none, so he insisted on Nora moving in with him for the time being. She did, and for the past couple of days, she couldn't stay still to save her life. She cleaned the whole house from top to bottom, washed all of her and Bugsy's dirty clothes, cooked breakfast, lunch and dinner, complete with desserts, and she took time to redecorate Bugsy's whole bedroom. Bugsy had a pair of crutches to get around with, but he never had to use them, because Nora did everything for him. It was cool for the first couple of days when he came home from the hospital, but now it was starting to become annoying.

"Hold on, baby, what do you need? I'll get it for you," Nora said, seeing Bugsy trying to get out of the bed.

"I gotta take a piss," he replied as he grabbed his crutches.

"Well, wait, let me help you."

Bugsy had enough. "No," he yelled. "As a matter of fact, stay right there. Don't move!" he yelled again and crutched himself into the bathroom to take a piss.

When he got back to the room, Nora was sitting on the edge of the bed with her head lowered. She had a sad puppy dog look on her face. Bugsy wasn't mad at her by a long shot, he just hated seeing her like this. He took a seat next to her on the bed.

"I wanna tell you a story. Something that I never spoke about, except to God," he began. "A long time ago when I was a lot younger, I shot somebody for nothing more than to restore my pride. This guy kicked my ass in a one on one fist fight in front of everybody. He later died in a hospital as a result of a bullet that I put into his chest. After he died, it ate at me every day, mainly because I took someone else's life senselessly. Over the course of time, I came to realize that death is a horrible thing, and the feeling is even worse when you feel like you're the one who caused it. I bet I can tell the thoughts that are going through ya head. If I never started selling drugs, Andrea would still be alive. I should have went back to work instead of going getting involved in the streets," Bugsy said.

Nora looked over at him. Those words had plagued her all day, every day.

"But see, the thing is, no matter what you do, or how bad you try to busy yourself, the process can never be reversed, nor can the life be restored. The only thing you should be trying to do is let it strengthen you, then move on from it. Its sounds hard, but that's the only way you're going to be able to live ya life. If you let it eat at you, you'll be just as dead as Andrea," Bugsy told her.

Nora sat there and let what Bugsy said soak into her thoughts. He was right in so many aspects of what he said. Nora's phone ringing on the nightstand broke the silence in the room. She didn't even look at it. Nora hadn't been taking any calls in the past few days, but this was exactly what Bugsy was talking about.

He nudged her with his elbow. "Live," he said, nodding toward the phone.

Nora cracked a smile, reached over, and grabbed her phone.

"Wassup girl?" she answered, seeing that it was Darleen calling.

"I know who did it. Meet me at the Jets in two hours," Darleen said in a serious tone.

Nora automatically came alive when she heard that piece of news. It was like her prayers were answered. She wanted to know who could be so cruel to kill somebody so innocent. She wanted to look that person in his eyes and hopefully be the one to take his life. The anger, the hate, and the whispers of the Devil had Nora on one. Killing the person who did that to Andrea wasn't going to bring her back, but it was going to be a great start to the healing process.

"I'm on my way," Nora said, then hung up the phone.

Darleen had goons on deck in the projects, willing and ready to ride out for her. They were thirsty for the opportunity to put in some work, especially for somebody they had love for, which was Darleen.

"Answer the door, it's probably Nora," Darleen told Rodney.

Nora stormed into the apartment and walked right up to Darleen, who was standing by the window. All she wanted to know was one thing.

Darleen looked over at Rodney and his boy sitting on the couch. "Yo, let me holla at my sister for a minute," she told them. Rodney and his two homies got up and went to the back room, leaving them alone.

"I think you should sit down for this," Darleen said, knowing that what she was about to tell Nora was going to be mind-blowing. Nora refused. Darleen looked out the window and began to explain the whole situation about how Wood didn't pay her, which led to her stealing the cocaine. She told her about Joy catching her and shaking her down for cash. She even told her about what happened in the car when she shot Joy. She was convinced that Wood had put two and two together, then came after them to get his drugs back. Darleen wasn't sure if he was the one who killed Gordo personally, but she was more than certain that it was his call. She explained the whole theory and put it on her life that he was the one who shot Andrea dead.

After hearing everything, Nora had to take a seat. It was so much information to process at once. Her feelings were mixed about the whole thing. She was mad at Darleen for doing what she did and putting all their lives in jeopardy, but then Nora put herself in her shoes and concluded that she probably would have done the same thing if Wood didn't pay what he owed. The one thing Nora refused to do was blame Darleen for Andrea's death. If she did, she would have to blame herself equally. With all that being said, Nora wanted to unleash hell on Wood. That was where her thoughts resided, and everything else could be discussed later.

Darleen agreed 100 percent, and without further ado, it was on.

"Rodney," Darleen yelled out to the back room.

He strolled into the living room with a large Mack-11 in his hand. He looked at Darleen and already knew what was about to go down.

"Go get 'em," was the only words she had to say before Rodney walked back into the room, got his boys and walked out of the apartment without saying a word.

He had already been given his instructions earlier, so there was no need to go over them again. He knew exactly what he needed to do.

Chapter 17

Everyone in the studio stood around scared to death, watching as Wood got the shit beat out of him by Rodney and his boy, Blaze. Both of his eyes were swollen shut, his bottom lip had a nice size gash in it, and his right leg appeared to be broken. It was easy for Rodney to lift Wood over his shoulder and walk right out of the studio with him. None of the cast members, or even the solo security guard, attempted to do or say anything about it.

Wood was barely conscious, but he knew that he'd been thrown into the back seat of a car, and Blaze sat back there with him. He started thinking about how much money he had to offer for his life, or whether he should try to escape once he got his bearings back.

"How much do y'all want?" he asked in a groggy voice.

Neither of the men said a word, prompting Wood to ask again.

"I got one hundred K if y'all let me go right now," he offered after they didn't answer him.

Blaze was actually growing tired of his attempts to bargain with them, so he pointed his gun at Wood's forehead.

"Not another word," Blaze warned.

After that, Wood stayed quiet until the car came to a stop.

"Where the hell am I?" he asked, trying to get a good look out of the less swollen of his two eyes.

Neither man responded, but proceeded to drag him out of the car, around the corner, about twenty-five yards to the back of the project building, and finally up nineteen flights of stairs. Wood was out of it by the time he made it to the rooftop and was shoved to the dirt-filled tarp with force. When he finally came to, Wood looked up and saw Darleen and Nora both standing there with guns in their hands. He began to laugh through the pain his body was now in, not surprised at all by who was behind the beat down and the abduction. He knew this day might come to pass.

"Y'all fat bitches musta lost y'all fucking mind," Wood said, trying his best to get to his feet.

His legs wouldn't let him, so he ended up on his knees.

"All you had to do was pay me what you owe me, and we wouldn't be standing here right now," Darleen spoke calmly.

Wood spit a glob of blood out of his mouth before he spoke. "Well, you know, dis shit come wit' the game."

"Like you killing somebody I love," Nora shot back, clutching the gun in her hand a little tighter.

Wood looked up at her then smiled. "Like I said, shit come wit' the game."

Nora was done talking. She walked up on Wood, pointed the gun at his head, and took the safety off. She had never killed anybody before, but if she had to start, it was going to be now. The pain that she felt walking in and seeing her best friend's body laid out on the ground was overwhelming, and it was all because of the man who was now kneeling on his knees in front of her.

"Do you have any idea the kind of drama you about to bring to ya life if you kill me? Do you?" Wood yelled, looking Nora in her eyes. "You will never have this city. You will never live comfortably. I'm Wood, bitch."

Nora was done listening. She'd been waiting for this

moment all day, and her mind was made up. There was no going back at this point, and she honestly didn't want to. She pressed the gun against his head.

Wood looked up at his executioner and gave one last defiant smile. Next thing he saw was a quick flash. He thought that his life was over. He thought that he'd been shot, but it was only Rodney knocking him over the back of the head with the Mack 10. Wood was now face down with Rodney's knee in his back, and in no time, Blaze had zip tied his wrists together. He was then raised to his feet and dragged to the edge of the roof.

Nora walked over, tucking the gun into her back pocket. She could see the lack of fear in Wood's eyes as she stood in front of him. He still didn't care, gangsta 'til the end, just like Nora expected him to be.

"See you on the other side, Wood," she whispered in his ear before shoving him as hard as she could over the roof.

Nora didn't see it, but she could hear the fear pouring out of him as he screamed at the top of his lungs on his way down. His body hit the rim of the dumpster, cracking it in half before it rolled over onto the ground. Nora and Darleen walked over to the edge of the roof, glared down, and saw the end result. A huge relief came over both of them. It was a fucked up way to die, but like Wood had told Nora, it came with the game.

He definitely was right about one thing. His death was going to bring a lot of drama to their lives, but Nora knew that the moment she decided to kill him. The one thing he didn't count on was that she would be willing and ready to deal with anybody who tried to come at her and her girls. With Darleen and Andrea's spirit by her side, the city of Philly now had a serious problem on their hands.

The Minister

"Following him will lead straight
to the pleasures of hell."

By

Blake Karrington

Chapter I

"It's good, ain't it?" Kim asked as she bounced up and down on Kevin's hard dick.

For a woman in her mid-thirties with four kids, her pussy is still airtight, Kevin thought to himself. But he knew today he couldn't lose focus on the task at hand. This wasn't about the pleasure for him; this was about securing some cash. Capital One had been calling him for the past three weeks about his late car payments, and every attempt at getting the money from his Uncle Joe, or Bishop Joel Steele, as he was known to the Greater Charlotte area and his over three thousand-member congregation, wasn't working.

"Uncle Joe, why can't you lend me the money?" Kevin had asked.

"Kevin, I have nearly four thousand people who attend one of my three services every Sunday, 90 percent of whom are working women. Working women, whose husbands are either vintage workaholics or couch potatoes who spend their days eating themselves into early graves."

"What's your point, Unc?" Kevin asked. "I only asked you to borrow some money," he continued.

"What's my point?" Bishop repeated the question. "It's like this, nephew: I have given you an associate minister position, and I seat you up on the stage, which I call my pulpit, every week." He paused. "And you need me to let you borrow some money? Hell, no. I don't lend money to niggas who got women they can pimp."

With that, Kevin knew he wasn't ever going to get money from his uncle. He had to figure something out, and this was a good start. Kim was one of the first women he started dealing with at the church.

Because he had full access to all the church records, Kevin had begun his quest by looking through the church account books for the largest tithers. Also, his uncle had made it church policy for members to present their W2s so that the church could verify the 10 percent tithing rate.

When Kevin came across Kim and Keith Richardson, he knew he had struck gold. Both had jobs where they grossed over six figures of yearly income. To add to that, Keith was a marketing salesman who was on the road eight months out of every year, while Kim made money from home, meaning she also took care of the family's bills.

Kim started to notice something was keeping Kevin from his normal performance.

"What's wrong, baby? Why you getting soft?" she asked.

"I'm sorry, love; it's just that I'm going through a li'l something right now."

"Well, what is it, baby? Is there anything I can do?"

"Really, I don't even feel right talking about it," Kevin responded, trying not to make eye contact with Kim.

"Baby, you should know by now, you can talk to me about anything," Kim said while rubbing Kevin's freshly shaved head.

"Well, right now it's my car, and I just shake at the thought of having it repo-ed."

"Repo-ed?"

"Yes."

"Why, Kevin? How far are you behind?"

"Three months."

"Three months is not that bad, how much do you need to catch up the payments?" she asked with a concerned look.

"Fifteen hundred dollars, and I don't know how in the hell I'm going to get it."

"Baby, don't you worry about that. I will give you the money. You just give mama what she needs, and she will make sure you have everything you need."

Kevin smiled widely and then turned Kim over on her stomach. He immediately spread her legs as far apart as possible. While dropping to his knees, he used both hands to open her ass cheeks, fully exposing all her womanhood. He quickly began licking her vaginal lips from behind. Shifting his weight to his right elbow, Kevin moved his tongue up and down from her pussy to her ass.

Kim moaned loudly, trying to pull herself away from Kevin's active tongue, but he wasn't having any of it. He gripped her hips tightly and then buried his entire face in her ass. Kim had obviously put on some type of fruity lotion, because Kevin received a sweet taste every time his tongue entered her asshole. So much so, that he decided to toss her salad all the way. This only intensified Kim's moans and the constant twitching of her body.

"Kevin . . . wha . . . wha . . . What are you tryin' to do to me?" she panted.

Kevin's answer was a more intensified tongue assault. With a major orgasm building, Kim reached her finger down to her swollen clit and could feel her own wetness. She began furiously rubbing her clit in a circular motion as Kevin continued to give her a good reaming. Kim had one hand working her pussy, and the other one squeezing her right nipple. Kevin could feel that she was about to cum. Her moans had grown louder, her breaths shorter.

When her body suddenly tensed, Kevin started sucking harder on both her holes, trying to block out the fatigue of his tongue.

Finally, Kim reached her peak. Her body lost all direction as tidal waves of creamy cum escaped her sweet tasting pussy, only to become a prisoner of Kevin's waiting mouth.

With her vision blurred, and still somewhat fighting to find her breath, Kim's body finally went limp. Kevin moved his fingers around to her soaked pussy. He could hear her wetness producing its own music as he moved his fingers in and out of her. Pulling his hand from between Kim's legs, Kevin smirked at the long shiny threads of her cum between his fingers.

"How was it?" he asked, already knowing the answer.

"It was fantastic. I don't remember ever cumming so hard," Kim said, still trying to locate her breath.

Kevin slid both of the fingers he'd moments ago had inside of Kim, into his mouth.

"Got to have my protein," he teased, loving the taste of her juices on his tongue.

Kim looked over at the clock and realized she didn't have much time before her children would be coming home from school.

"Hey, baby, if you want me to get you off, we better hurry. My kids will be home soon." Kim uttered.

"Nah, don't worry about me, you already helping me out enough. I can get mine next time," Kevin answered in a sincere tone.

Kim got up, grabbed her purse off the dresser, and pulled out eight brand new one-hundred dollar bills.

"I only have eight hundred on me now, but I can meet you in the morning and give you the rest."

Kevin knew that Kim thought she was being slick. Being short on the cash was the perfect excuse for her to force him to come back over, so he responded quickly.

"I got a lot to do tomorrow, so could you drop by the church? I have to help Bishop out with some errands." Kevin knew she wouldn't press hard, knowing that he was doing something for his Uncle and her pastor.

"Okay, that's fine," she said, disappointment in her voice.

Kevin tucked the money in his pocket, then slightly bent his 6' 2" frame over and passionately kissed her.

"Humm . . . damn, that's good," he said after breaking their kiss.

Kim smiled.

"Call me," he said as he headed for the back door.

"I will," was the last thing he heard as he jogged to his car parked on the nearest side street.

Once inside his car, Kevin slumped his head on the headrest. *Damn*, he thought to himself, *I got to find someone to get this nut off on.*

It was too early in the day for most of the working women in his life. He began thinking of what other possibilities would be available at this early hour.

His phone interrupted Kevin's thoughts. He looked down at the screen and saw the name TONYA. Tonya was another one of the closet freaks he had picked up from the church. Although slightly overweight, she was very cute, and most of all had pretty teeth. Nice, beautiful white teeth. She also had the benefit of double Ds that sat up perky on her chest.

"Hey, what's good, lady? I was just thinking about you," Kevin spoke softly into the phone.

"Now, don't you know how to make a lady feel special?" she responded.

"Nah, for real, I really was."

"And what were you thinking, Kevin?" she asked, already knowing the answer.

"Well, I was just thinking of how good it would feel to have my dick in your warm mouth right now."

"Oh, really, and what would make you think I want your dick in my mouth in the middle of the day?"

"Because you a freak and you love the taste of my pipe," Kevin said with a laugh.

"Nigga, whatever. Where are you? You know I'm about to take my lunch break, are you close enough to come by?"

"Close by?" he asked.

"Are you close by my office?"

"Oh, yeah, I'm not far at all," he lied.

"Well, call me when you get downstairs, and I will come down and really show you how much I like the taste of that dick."

Kevin was already making a three-point turn in traffic, heading back down Interstate 77 to Tonya's office park, located off Tyvola Rd. Once he arrived, he tried to find a secluded parking area where he knew Tonya would finish off what Kim had started.

Grabbing his cell out of the center drink console, he redialed Tonya's number. "Hey lady, I'm downstairs."

"Damn, it took you long enough. I was hoping we could have at least gone and grabbed some lunch," Tonya spoke with a slight attitude.

"I have all the lunch you need right here, babe," Kevin responded.

Tonya could hear him slapping his dick up against his iPhone. "You so nasty, Kevin."

"Shit, you are too. Now get your ass down here."

"Okay, but it's not my fault you're late."

"I'm sorry, baby, but I had to stop by Uncle Joe's and grab some gas money just so I could make it out here to you."

"For real?"

"For real . . . you know a brother struggling right now."

"I know, baby, but it's going to get better for you, real soon."

"Yeah, they say it gets greater later. But damn . . . when, and how much later?"

"Right now, baby," she teased.

"Where you parked at?"

"When you get downstairs, look over to your left, I'm in the last spot on the second row."

When Tonya got into the car, she looked around to make sure no one was watching. Then she reached her hand into the crotch of Kevin's pants. She could feel his stiffness.

"You do miss me . . . don't you?"

"You damn right," Kevin said, already pulling out his massive dick. He brought his cotton boxers down enough to expose his lemon sized balls. She looked around once more, making sure the coast was clear, then ducked her head from view.

Kevin leaned his head back on the seat's headrest as Tonya's head bounced up and down in his lap. She was making loud slurping sounds, and he couldn't control his thrusting hips. Once in a while, Kevin's movements would cause his dick to push too deep in Tonya's throat, causing her to gag. Being 5'8" and 190 pounds, she was also a little uncomfortable in the small space, but Tonya was on a mission to see how fast she could make him cum.

Tonya used every trick she knew to get Kevin off. She nibbled on the underside of his dick and then ran her tongue along the main vein. Flicking her wet tongue really fast on the head brought Kevin's hips to life. Then, in one smooth motion, she took the entire length of his hardness into her mouth, applying just the right amount of pressure.

Kevin just looked at her in amazement. It wasn't often he'd met someone who could fully deep throat all eleven inches of him, but Tonya was one of the exceptions. He was also enjoying the sight of her sucking and licking the dick he'd just had nuts deep in Kim. Her juices were still all over him.

Tonya moved down to Kevin's balls, alternating them in her mouth. That was all Kevin could take.

"Damn, I'm about to cum!" he shouted.

"Cum in my mouth, baby!" Tonya screamed back before stuffing his dick back into her mouth.

"Aaaaaaaaaaahhhhhh . . ." Kevin groaned.

Tonya could feel the deep throb of his spasming manhood. Each one followed by jets and jets of hot cum. "Hummm . . ." Tonya moaned, fighting to keep his seed from spilling out both sides of her mouth. She continued sucking until Kevin's tense body collapsed and the twitching subsided in his love muscle. "You good, baby?" she asked around a mouth full of cum.

"Hell, yeah," he mumbled.

"Open the door for me," she said, wanting to spit the cum out of her mouth.

"Huh?" Kevin looked at her, puzzled. "I know you're not about to spit my seeds out on no parking lot pavement."

Tonya tilted her head back, making sure not to drop any of the liquid from her mouth.

"Stop playin' Kevin, before I get this on your seat," she said in an underwater voice.

"I'm not playin' with you, Tonya, and you better not get none of that shit on my seats. Just swallow it. It's not going to kill you."

"But I don't like the taste," Tonya said with her head leaned back and her mouth full.

"Do I say that when I'm eatin' your ass out, Tonya?"

"No."

"All right, then."

Kevin looked around and then grabbed a leftover Coke from his beverage holder that he'd been drinking with his McDonald's meal earlier.

"Here, chase it with this," he said while passing her the cup.

Tonya was upset, but she knew Kevin wasn't going to give in, so she swallowed the contents in her mouth and followed it with a gulp of soda. She had the look of a kid who'd just taken a dose of medicine.

"Damn . . . was it that bad?"

"Yes, it was. I have never swallowed anyone's cum before, not even Gerald's," she complained.

Gerald was her ex-husband and the choir director at the church. Kevin always thought he was gay, and was still convinced that he was.

"Well, I'm not your gay ass ex-husband, and I don't like my cum going to waste.

"What kinda shit is that to say, Kevin? I always go to the bathroom and spit it out, or spit it into the covers when we're in the bed."

"Yeah, I wish I would've known that. I would have set your ass straight! You know what the book says about planting and sowing seeds."

"Oh, so you just pick the things in the bible you choose to follow, huh? So tell me, bro minister, what does it say about me sucking your dick?"

"Thy rod and thy staff . . . they comfort me. That's what da hell it says. Now what?" he asked.

"It don't say nothing like that, Kevin."

"Look," Kevin said, tired of going back and forth with the debate. "Are you going to help a brother out with his car payment or not."

"I thought you said you needed gas money?"

"Well, what good is gas money going to be if I don't have a car?" Kevin responded, smiling.

"Kevin, you are crazy, and you lucky I like you."

"Negative . . . you like this," he said, squeezing his monster dick. As he did so, a tiny drop of cum oozed from its head.

"Tonya."

"What, Kevin?"

"You forgot some," he said, pointing to his dick.

"Boy, you a mess," Tonya said, then took one quick glance around the parking lot before dipping her head.

The sensations of her lips were too much for him, and Kevin had to force her mouth away from his sensitive head.

"Sssssssssssssshhhhhhhhiiiiittt," he moaned loudly. "That's enough. That's enough," he complained.

Tonya came up smiling.

"Here, I only have three hundred dollars on me now, but come by the house and pick up the rest Friday when I get paid. She dug into her purse and passed him the money. "Oh, yeah, and Kevin?"

"What is it?" Kevin asked while zipping up his pants.

"The company is hiring, and I could put in a good word for you."

"Thanks, but no thanks, ma. You know I'm focusing on the ministry right now. I can't be trying to work also," Kevin spoke as he grabbed the money out of her hand.

He leaned forward and started his car.

"Come on, let me drop you off at the front. You know I can't have my lady being late from her break!"

Tonya just looked at Kevin. She had to admit that he was a fine man. Everything about him was fine, all the way down to his manhood. Beautiful in her own way, but mentally abused by her ex-husband, she felt that there was no way a woman on her physical level could ever have a man like this without making some type of concessions. Helping him out financially was one concession she was willing to make.

Chapter II

On Tuesday morning, Kevin awoke at his normal time, 11:00 a.m. He sat up in his California king-sized bed, pulled his white satin sheets aside, stepped out in his black silk pajamas, and immediately planted his neatly manicured feet into matching slippers. There was no way he would allow his feet to touch the bare floor. Kevin was what most women would term a metrosexual, however, in his mind, he was nothing more than an honest playa. Honest in the fact that he didn't have to beat his woman to get his money.

Kevin walked into the bathroom and started the shower. After he'd completed his normal morning process, he looked into the full length mirror and marveled at himself. Indeed, God had put an anointing on his life, but it wasn't spiritual. No, the anointing he had received was the eleven inch, twenty-four karat gold dick that swung down just above his kneecaps. God had also not passed up his body when handing out his many blessings.

Kevin was six feet two inches tall, weighed two hundred twenty-five pounds, and was all muscle. His upper arms and chest were full of tattoos, which added to his bad-boy-gone-good persona.

"An apostle . . ." he began to think.

Maybe this would increase the membership at the satellite location his Uncle Joe had appointed him over. He certainly hoped so, because he was already struggling to pay the rent on the building, which was now his full responsibility. Luckily, he had converted a few elderly women who for some reason thought he was the second coming of Christ. Although Kevin had no desire to be a righteous minister, he knew it would be a viable tool in feeding his other addiction: the opposite sex.

Frequently, Kevin's morning would start off with him jumping on one of the many online social sites and leaving a powerful message. He enjoyed reading the many responses. Sometimes he would get an inbox from a female he already knew, and start a conversation that he hoped would lead to one inviting the other over to continue the discussion in person. Not today though. Today, he already had his victim in mind. She was a young, beautiful college student working at the nearby Waffle House. Kevin had gone into the Waffle House a couple days before and left a fifty-dollar bill on the table after ordering only coffee. He knew this would be the perfect bait for a young girl who had already expressed that she was working to pay for school, and had no other means of support.

"Excuse me, sir . . . I think you forgot your change," the young girl yelled as Kevin was about to step into his car.

"Nah, young lady, that's for you."

"But it's a fifty-dollar bill, and you only ordered coffee."

"Yeah, I know. Consider it a blessing. And you know what else, lady? I see something powerful in and around you."

"Really?" she asked with a quizzical look on her face, wondering who this nigga thought he was, talking about seeing something in her.

"Really! You got an aura about you, and I know some great things are going to happen for you. The Bible says, be careful how you entertain a stranger, because you could be entertaining an angel. You do believe in God, don't you?"

"Of course I do," Jessica blurted out, although she had not thought about God or her religion in quite some time.

"Well, take my hand," he instructed Jessica.

She immediately noticed how soft and well-manicured the man's hands were.

"Would you mind if I said a small prayer for you right now?"

"Ahh, yes, I would. I can pray on my own, thank you."

Kevin looked at the young woman with a perplexed expression. "Excuse me, I was just trying to speak something positive into your life. . . ."

"Thanks, but no thanks."

"Well, do you mind if I at least say, have a blessed day, with your beautiful self?"

"Naw, I definitely don't mind that," Jessica answered with a huge grin.

Kevin smiled, then opened the door to his car and climbed inside.

The young girl turned around and walked toward the front of the restaurant, thinking to herself, *Damn, he really thought I was gonna fall for all that?* She tucked the fresh fifty-dollar bill away in her pocket and headed back inside.

Kevin had been by the restaurant on three more occasions since their first meeting, and every time he left, he would try to leave her with more advice and another fifty-dollar bill as payment for his coffee.

Jessica was used to men leaving a large tip to impress her, but never this large. The other guys would always ask for her number immediately following the tip, but Kevin never asked for anything . . . just offered.

Not today though, Kevin thought as he climbed into his Caddy. It was time for him to collect on all the hard work he'd been putting in.

Kevin was in need of her help. He had already called up to the restaurant to find out her hours for the day and learned that she would be getting off in the next hour or so. He parked his black Cadillac Seville perfectly in the handicap parking space. For a minister, he enjoyed breaking all the rules and hated walking any further than he had to. Once inside the restaurant, he quickly located the young girl.

"Hey, how is my favorite lady doing today, Ms. Jessica?"

Jessica immediately lit up and showed Kevin to the available table in her section. "I'm doing wonderful, and how is my favorite customer doing today? Will you be having a cup of coffee, or will you be eating?" she asked.

"Just coffee."

"Okay, what about sugar or cream?" she asked in a semi-seductive manner. She and Kevin had been flirting in an undercover manner for some time now. Neither of them were bold enough to lay their cards on the table, so they had just been playing this game of playful poker.

"Both, please." he answered, matching her tone.

As Jessica walked away, Kevin couldn't help but admire her perfect body. She stood about five feet two, weighed around one twenty-five, of which at least twenty-five was all ass; Kevin was sure of that. Jessica didn't have an ounce of fat on her body. Indeed, the gene of youth was on her side, starting in the rear end! *That body was given, it definitely wasn't worked for!*

"Here's your coffee," Jessica said, interrupting Kevin's lustful thoughts. Her eyes seemed to understand him.

"Is there something wrong?" she asked, noticing the intense look on his face.

"No, not really . . . just having an issue with getting my sermon typed up."

"What type of issue?"

"Well, I can't type, and I have to do my sermon this Sunday. I have been having a hard time getting help."

"Oh, for real? I'll help you."

"But you work all the time, so when would you have time?"

"Well, actually, I get off in about forty-five minutes. I can help you then."

"Would you do that for me?" Kevin asked as if he were shocked.

"Sure I would. You have more then helped me over the past couple of weeks. It would be my pleasure."

"Well, thank you lady, and thank you, Jesus," he said. "I tell you, just like I tell all my members . . . God will answer prayers. . . ."

Jessica barely heard his final statement as she started to walk off. She enjoyed her and Kevin's conversations, but whenever he would try to run the religious game on her, she would become disinterested. Jessica had been around so-called men of God like Kevin all her life, so this was nothing new to her.

Forty-five minutes seemed like forty-five hours to Kevin as he anticipated what Jessica would look like outside of those clothes and straddled on top of him. He already knew that he was going to have that young firm body tied up all day and most of the night.

Jessica returned to Kevin's table to inform him that she had just clocked out and needed to get out of her work clothes because she smelled like fried food. She returned, wearing a pair of jeans and a collegiate sweatshirt.

"I'm sorry, I didn't really plan to go anywhere after work."

"Baby—I meant lady—you look fine," Kevin said with a smile, glad that he had caught himself before he revealed his true intentions.

He had to stop himself from staring because the jeans that Jessica was wearing looked like they had been air brushed on her ass. Once they arrived at the car, Kevin walked to the passenger's side and carefully helped her into the vehicle, then proceeded to the driver's side.

When he started the engine, the Bose system blared Power 98, which was a local hip-hop station. This definitely wasn't his everyday type of music. Kevin had intentionally placed it on this station, knowing the sounds would resonate with Jessica. Although he lived only twenty minutes from the Waffle House, it took more than thirty-five minutes because of the scenic route he took in order to ensure that the young girl couldn't find her way back without his help.

Once they arrived, the beautiful manicured lawn and house that looked like it belonged on *MTV Cribs* immediately impressed Jessica. It was just that big. But little did Jessica know, Kevin was eight months behind on the mortgage payments, had the lights rigged, and had bootlegged cable pumping into the place.

"Make yourself comfortable," he told her once they were inside his spacious home.

"Thank you," Jessica said before sitting down, as Kevin disappeared into one of the large arched doorways. As Jessica looked around the living room of the home, its beauty blew her away.

Ceilings, expensive human sized oak statues, plush imported sofas sitting atop gorgeous forest green carpet, and a baby grand piano decorated the lavish room. Jessica was surprised to see Kevin walk back into the room wearing a black silk robe with matching slippers.

Kevin noticed the timid look on Jessica's face and quickly tried to make his guest relax. Unbeknownst to him, this entire scene was an act, and she was not the innocent young girl he envisioned.

"I . . . I, ah, spilled something on my shirt," he told her, nodding toward the drinks in his hand.

Jessica simply smiled outwardly, but inwardly she knew it was all game. *If you spilled it on your shirt, why are you walking in here butt-ass naked? Minster, Pastor, or . . . what's the other word they liked to call themselves? Oh, yeah . . . Bishop . . . bull-shit.* She laughed silently.

Kevin didn't know that young Jessica had been raised in the church and had a strong Christian background. Her father was a minister, and she had witnessed first-hand the many extramarital affairs that most so called men of God carried on. Jessica could remember all the arguments her mother and father had about suspected love children he had fathered. With all the drama they had going on, her parents were still strict in their home. A home that she rebelled against at a very young age. With her virginity gone at the age of fifteen, young Jessica found herself pregnant just before her sixteenth birthday. What made matters worse, was that she was pregnant by her Sunday School teacher who was ten years her senior. After a hurried abortion and an even faster trial for the newly convicted sex-offender teacher, who happened to be married with three children, Jessica was placed in a school for girls until she was eighteen years old. Now, at nineteen, she'd been on her own and taking care of herself for over a year. Her parents didn't seem to care about her, so to Jessica, they were dead.

After enrolling at UNC-Charlotte, Jessica worked two jobs just to make ends meet.

The Waffle House was her second employer. Her first was a home office job she was able to pick up after she got her own computer. Neither job paid great, but she managed to get by. Jessica didn't label herself as a hoe or slut when it came to men. Actually, she'd been with only five men in her life, and so far, none of them had been able to replace the Sunday school teacher who had robbed her of her virginity. He'd taught her everything there was to know about sex, and the dick he had, she could've sworn it belonged on the horse, Big Red, in a movie she'd seen, or whatever his damn name was. He would eat her young pussy four days out the week, and most of the time, twice on Sundays.

For two months, he had sucked her pussy and asshole until she thought she was going to die from orgasmic stomach cramps. Then he would rub the head of that horse dick all over her pussy and asshole. The Sunday School teacher would work himself up to a point of explosion, and shoot so much cum on her inner thighs and stomach that it looked like he had spilled a milkshake all over her.

A few weeks later, he was so thirsty to feel his dick inside her, he'd completely forgotten about her virginity until it felt as if someone had hit him between the legs with a bush-ax. Then, the sudden waves of paralyzing pain were replaced with pure pleasure and ecstasy as he sunk inch after inch of his monster inside her tight vaginal walls. For close to a year after he'd been locked away, her young mind still remained so cloudy with memories of their fuck sessions that she would cum just thinking about him.

The very first time Kevin walked into the Waffle House, Jessica knew that he would eventually make a move on her. Hell, he would practically undress her with his eyes before taking one sip of his coffee. Sure, several guys would come inside the restaurant and leave a generous tip, but he had a different approach. Still weak, but different.

"My computer is in here," Kevin said, interrupting Jessica's thoughts.

"Excuse me?" she spoke back.

"I said my computer room is this way," he said, jerking a thumb over his left shoulder.

"Oh, okay, sure," Jessica responded, then stood and walked in his direction

"Would you like to get comfortable?" Kevin asked before producing another silk red robe from behind his back.

Jessica briefly gazed into Kevin's eyes before answering. "Sure . . . why not? Do you mind if I shower?" she asked as she took the robe from him.

"Huh?" Kevin answered, caught off guard by her request.

"Do you mind if I freshen up a little?" Jessica asked again.

"Oh . . . oh, no . . . The bathroom is down the hall on the right."

"Thank you."

Jessica turned and walked down the long hallway. She could barely hold her laughter as she felt Kevin's eyes burning a hole in an ass that she had been told on many occasions, was "fatter than a muthafucka."

As soon as she closed the bathroom door, Kevin began jumping up and down as if he'd hit the million dollar lottery.

"Yes . . . yes . . . yes!" he mumbled. "Damn, that was easy . . . Damn that was easy," he kept repeating.

Just then, Kevin's phone began to ring.

"Damn," Kevin cursed, looking at his phone. He saw that it was Tonya calling.

He thought about not answering but remembered that Tonya was supposed to be giving him the remaining money for his car payment.

"Yeah, what up, Tonya?" he answered in a low voice.

"Hi Kevin, why are you whispering?"

"I'm not whispering. What's good wit' chu, baby? I was just about to call you."

"Stop lying, Kevin."

"Aah, aah, aah, now, Tonya, you know it ain't right to call a man of the cloth a lie."

"Whateva, Kevin. I guess you're a strict man of the cloth when I be sucking your dick and licking them balls," she said sarcastically.

"Very funny, Tonya."

"Anyway, are you coming by tomorrow? You know that I'm off all day, right?"

"Do you have the rest of my money?"

"Damn, Kevin . . . is that all you think about when it comes to me? Money?"

"Noooo, baby, no."

"I can't tell," she responded.

No longer able to hear the shower running, Kevin sighed then quickly tried to end the call.

"Look, what time do you want me to come over?"

"Anytime. Gerald came by and picked up the kids today," she said, sounding a little better. "So I'm free all day."

"Okay, cool, I'll be there."

"The key will be in the same place, baby. I love y—"

Kevin hung up the phone before she could finish her last statement.

At that instant, Jessica stepped out of the bathroom and into the hallway. The soft silk robe seemed to be straining at every curve and contour of her sexy body. For a long moment, Kevin stood speechless, until the tingling sensation between his legs drew his thoughts to the little blue pill he'd taken almost an hour ago.

"Are you ready to get started?" she asked, interrupting his raging lustful thoughts.

"Oh, yeah, sure, right this way," Kevin said, leading her into his office.

The room was almost as big as her small apartment, Jessica noticed as she seated herself in front of Kevin's computer.

"My notes are . . . let me see," he said reaching over her shoulder.

Jessica couldn't help but to feel the heavy bump that slapped against her back. *Is that his dick?* She wondered. Her heart immediately began to pound at the thought.

"There they are," Kevin said, then grabbed a small stack of papers and passed it to her.

That was when she got her first glimpse of the monster that swayed back and forth between Kevin's legs. Jessica was literally helpless at the sight of his dick. Not only because of its size, but all the lustful memories of her Sunday School teacher flooded her brain. She found herself having to look up into Kevin's face, unsure if they could possibly be the same person.

Still intoxicated with the memory of her encounters with her past lover, Jessica's body transformed to an almost hypnotic state. Without hesitation, she reached out and grabbed Kevin's double digit manhood, just as she'd been trained by her Sunday School teacher.

Kevin had been so hungry and thirsty for young Jessica's body, it was impossible to keep his massive dick from poking her in the back as he leaned over her, fumbling for his paperwork.

"Damn," he mumbled when he brushed up against her the first time. *That enhancement pill was supposed to be only 40 mgs,* he thought. *It felt like it was one of them 100 mg joints.*

Jessica's soft hands interrupted Kevin's thoughts.

"What the fu . . . aaaaahhhhhhh."

Kevin's words were cut short by Jessica's warm mouth. He couldn't believe what was happening as he looked down at this young bombshell pulling and sucking on his dick. His head began to spin when he felt her take over half of his Alabama black deep down in her throat. Jessica worked on Kevin's dick for half an hour. Kevin could barely stand on his own legs, but Jessica still hadn't come up for air.

She looked up at the contorted face of the minister and inwardly smiled while thinking, *If this hypocrite mutha-fucka thinks that a simple man made pill can outlast these God given lips, he's soon gonna be sadly mistaken.*

Jessica relentlessly sucked Kevin's dick until she knew he was going to explode. Then she started working both hands at the same time. One jacking him, while tugging both cum-heavy balls with the other.

Seconds later, Kevin bellowed like a bull. Jessica tightened her grip and had to admit that his dick felt like a fire-hose pumping loads and loads of hot cum into her open mouth and nearly covering her face. Still, Jessica wouldn't let up. She took his semi-hard dick back into her mouth. Kevin didn't know whether to cry, scream, or moan, as his body was now under her control. For several more minutes, he whimpered, jerked and cried like a knocked kneed bitch.

Kevin looked back over at Jessica; his dick was beginning to get back to full erect status. He stood her up, got down on his knees, placing her right leg over his shoulder, and began to eat her. Jessica grabbed his head and pushed it further into her tight young pussy. As he ate her, he took his middle finger and slowly pushed it into her ass.

Jessica tensed up, but let out a moan that said she loved every minute of what he was doing to her. Kevin started to stroke Jessica's ass as he continued to flick his tongue across her clit. She came within seconds, covering his face with her cum.

Kevin looked up at Jessica. She had the look of "what's next?" in her eyes. With the size ass Jessica had, there was only one position that made sense—doggie style! She climbed up on the chair, got on her hands and knees, and lifted that juicy ass in the air. Kevin got behind her and slid his eleven inches into her wetness. He could feel the tightness of her walls and the cream of her earlier orgasm. Every time he grinded in and out of her pussy, he would smack her ass and watch it jiggle all over the place. Kevin grabbed both cheeks and opened her butt up, revealing her small anus. It was still a little dilated from when he had his finger in there. Then, Jessica said the unthinkable.

"Fuck my ass, Kevin. I love it up the ass." Those words were all he wanted to hear. He took his member from her wet pussy and placed the head up against her butt hole.

"Don't be gentle, ram it in there!" she yelled.

Kevin couldn't contain himself. Rarely did he ever have this invitation. Most women claimed to never do anal sex, and after they saw what Kevin was working with, he was surely never given the opportunity. But Jessica wanted it, and wanted it hard! Kevin did as he was told; he rammed his dick directly up her ass. He was surprised at how well she took it.

Jessica screamed with every thrust, as Kevin tried to touch her stomach from the back.

"Grab my neck and choke me, Kevin!"

Huh? he thought to himself. *Did she really just ask me to do that?*

Jessica reached back, grabbed Kevin's right hand, and placed it on one side of her neck. Kevin followed suit and placed his left hand on the other side.

"Now squeeze my neck! Harder, harder!" she yelled, gasping from the force of Kevin's strong hands. Kevin was so into the choking that he wasn't even paying attention to the cum that was about to explode at any moment. Before he knew it, it was at the tip of his shaft. He quickly pulled out and came all over Jessica's ass and back. She looked back at him with a somewhat disappointed expression.

"What's the matter?" he asked, almost out of breath.

"I don't like to waste cum. Get it off my back and feed it to me."

Damn, that is some shit I would say! he thought.

Kevin followed Jessica's instructions and began pulling up the milky white substance with his middle finger and feeding it to Jessica's waiting mouth. She played with it for a while in her mouth before swallowing everything. All Kevin could do was lay back on the sofa and shake his head in disbelief. This young girl had just turned him out. On the outside, he tried to maintain his playa image, so he acted like this shit was nothing new to him.

Chapter III

The sound of his ringing phone was the only thing that assured Kevin that he hadn't passed over into the afterlife. He tried to raise himself to a sitting position where he would be within reach of his phone on the nightstand, but his body was totally exhausted.

"Damn," he mumbled.

He then looked over at the still form of Jessica, who was sleeping peacefully. The shape of her young, tender body was still visible underneath the covers.

The phone started to ring again.

After a struggle, Kevin managed to answer.

"Yeah?"

"What the hell is going on, Kevin?"

"What . . . what . . . Who the hell is this?" he asked in an "I don't want to be bothered" tone.

"Oh, you don't recognize my voice, Kevin? Well, I guess you won't be needing my money for your car payment either."

"Oh, my bad, Rita."

"Rita? Oh naw you didn't! You didn't just call me some other bitch's name, Kevin! This is Tonya. Now, who the hell is Rita?"

Kevin cringed, knowing he'd fucked up by calling Tonya someone else's name.

"Damn," he mumbled.

"Well?"

"Well, what?"

"Say something, Kevin."

"What you want me to say, Tonya? I thought you were Sister Rita at the church."

"Rita from church? You talking about Rita Johnson's old antique ass, Kevin? Are you serious?" Tonya asked in a high-pitched voice.

"I said I was sorry. It was a mistake, Tonya."

"You damn right it was a mistake. How could you mistake my voice for a fifty-year-old dried up widow? Are you fuckin' her too, Kevin?"

Hell, no . . . she fucking the hell outta my black ass twice a week! Kevin wanted to say.

"No, I'm not fuckin' her." He finally answered.

"Well, what time will you be over since you're already an hour late?"

Kevin looked over at Jessica, who was just starting to stir.

"Give me about an hour and a half."

"An hour and a half? Kevin, I have an appointment at 10:00, and I've already canceled twice."

"All right . . . all right . . . all right! I'll be there in an hour."

"Just hurry up, daddy," Tonya purred.

Kevin didn't respond, he just disconnected the call. He rolled over and reached out his hand to Jessica's soft thigh.

"Jessica," he whispered.

Jessica had been wide awake the entire time Kevin was engaged in his phone conversation but pretended that she was asleep and Kevin had awakened her.

"Ye . . . yes?" she said in a groggy voice.

"We have to get up . . . I have to meet my Uncle Joe at the church," he lied.

"Okay, let me shower real quick."

Twenty minutes later, they were on the highway.

"Where do you live?" Kevin asked.

"I live off of Harris Boulevard, but you can just drop me off at work," she answered.

"Are you sure?" Kevin asked, hoping she wouldn't change her mind. He really didn't want to drive all the way across town and keep Tonya waiting with what he called his "weekly maintenance pay."

"The Waffle House is cool. I have to be at work in a couple hours anyway."

As soon as Kevin dropped Jessica off, he reached inside his glove box to retrieve his bottle of Super Man pills.

"Damn," he mumbled after dumping the remaining pills in the palm of his hand. He had only two left.

"Fuck it," he said, then tossed both pills into his mouth. "I'll hit Uncle Joe for some more later today." Before backing away, he watched young Jessica walk inside the Waffle house to work. Her body was flawless and seemed to be without blemish, but Kevin hadn't seen many porn stars with the type of sex game she possessed.

"And the pussy was—"

Kevin stopped and then thought about it. Hell, he didn't even remember getting the pussy. Just the thought gave him a raging hard-on . . . well, that and 200 mgs worth of his little blue pills.

Ten minutes later, Kevin was strolling up the walkway leading to Tonya's door. Without knocking, he walked straight into the house like he paid the bills there.

"What took you so long, daddy?" Tonya said before falling to her knees in front of him.

"Is this where you want me to start?" she asked while gazing up into his eyes.

"You know what I like."

"I sure do. Anything for you, baby," Tonya said, then pulled Kevin's dick out through his fly. "Hmm . . . nice and hard. Just the way mama likes it," she teased.

A clear drop of pre-cum escaped the large mushroom-shaped head of Kevin's dick. Tonya snaked out her tongue, catching it before it had a chance to hit the floor.

"Hmm . . . delicious," she mumbled before stuffing only the head in her mouth.

Tonya worked her tongue in and out of the slit, and all around the head of his dick. Kevin rolled his head from side to side, his body swaying back and forth.

"Aahhhhhh, shit!" he moaned loudly.

Kevin looked down at Tonya and envisioned that she was young Jessica sucking his dick. Just the thought of her young tender ass straddling him nearly carried Kevin over the edge. He could feel the cum leaving his balls, making its way up his shaft.

"Whoa . . . whoa . . . wwhhhhoooaaaa . . ." Kevin growled.

Tonya's lips made a loud sucking noise as his dick fell from her mouth.

"What's da matter, daddy?"

"Nothing. . . . Stand up," he said.

Tonya stood up.

"Now walk over to the couch and then turn around."

Tonya got on her knees, facing the back of the couch. Then in a rage of lust . . . and with Jessica's nude body imbedded in his brain, he pulled Tonya's ass cheeks apart and began feasting on her pussy. Tonya screamed to the top of her lungs at the unbelievable feeling of having her pussy eaten for the first time by Kevin. He continued feasting on her until her cries of passion were reduced to little more than whimpers.

Just as she thought his assault was over, Tonya felt the gigantic head of Kevin's dick slowly separate her pussy lips. She gasped for air when his enormous love-muscle began penetrating her tight hole. Tonya could feel every vein in his dick as he began thrusting in and out of her.

Long, slow, sanitizing strokes, allowing her to feel every inch of his hardness. Occasionally, he would speed up his pace, pounding her as if there was no tomorrow. Then he would slow back down, steadily rooting and pushing all eleven inches to the very max.

Position after position brought one shuddering orgasm after another, and it was close to midday when Kevin's Viagra-loaded dick decided it was time to let go. And let go, it did.

Ounce after ounce of Kevin's cum filled Tonya's swollen pussy, and for a long time, they both lay there in the middle of the battlefield of lust, their bodies covered with layers of sweat.

One month later . . .

Kevin sat alone at a table in the far corner of the Waffle house.

"Would you like a refill?" the waitress asked him, interrupting his thoughts.

"Please."

Kevin watched as the middle-aged white woman walked away from his table. He once again thought of Jessica.

"Four weeks," he said aloud. *Why hadn't she been to work in a month?*

Her boss had briefly explained to him that she'd asked for a leave, but today was the day she was supposed to have returned.

"Come on, Kevin . . . she's just another piece of pussy," he kept mumbling to himself, trying to get his mind off her, but it wasn't working. Kevin couldn't shake Jessica from his thoughts.

"But why?" he kept asking himself. "Why her?"

Maybe her sex game was above average, but he'd had plenty of above average sex partners. That wasn't it, at least not all of it. He kept thinking. Could it be the calm before the storm attitude? Whatever it was, he was determined to find her.

Kevin sighed and stood up to leave. Looking at his Rolex watch, he shook his head. "I'm late," he mumbled.

He had a meeting at his church with a couple of their newest members. Kevin hurried to his car and made his way to the church.

"You're late," his Uncle Joe said as soon as Kevin stepped out the car.

"Yeah, I know, Unc. I woke up late this morning. . . ."

"Long night?" he asked suspiciously.

"Yeah, you can say that," Kevin lied.

He knew that if he didn't give in to his Uncle's questions early, he'd be forced to answer a barrage of them for the rest of the day. After drilling him about responsibilities for another fifteen minutes, Bishop Joel changed the subject.

"Look, Kevin, the reason I called you over today was to discuss a few important issues."

"What's the problem, Uncle Joe?"

"There is no problem, nephew. Let's walk inside."

Inside Bishop Joe's office, he continued. "Look, Kevin . . . I want you to close the small church over on Sugar Creek Road."

"What? Uncle Joe, you know I can . . ."

"Hold it . . . hold it . . . let me finish," Bishop Joe said, stopping him.

"Kevin, you have been doing very well lately, and I've been thinking on this long and hard for quite some time now."

Bishop Steele paused a moment, then continued.

"I'm going to be opening a new church down in Atlanta, and I want you to take over here while I establish the new congregation."

Kevin's mouth dropped open. He was speechless.

"Did you hear what I said, Kevin?"

"Ye . . . yes, I heard you, Uncle Joe."

"Well . . . Do you think you can handle the position while I'm gone? You know you will be overseeing more than three thousand members."

"Three thousand," Kevin repeated.

"With new ones joining regularly, like today," he continued.

"Today?"

"Yes, today."

"We have four new members joining our . . . excuse me, *your* church while I'm away. That's if you're ready for the challenge."

"I'm ready," Kevin said, still somewhat surprised.

"Very well," Bishop Joe said, rising from his chair.

"Let's do it," Kevin responded, then he said, "Uncle Joe?"

"What is it now, nephew?"

"I just wanted to say thanks."

Kevin and his Uncle Joe smiled, then he said, "Don't thank me, Kevin . . . give all the glory to the Lord. Now, let's not keep our new members waiting."

After meeting three of his four new church families, Kevin was ready to leave. He couldn't believe his luck. His money problems were still in the forecast, but not for long. Now, the only thing he wanted to do was celebrate with a stiff glass of yak and some good pussy he could beat up on. His mind suddenly turned to Jessica. That's exactly what he needed

Kevin's thoughts were interrupted by the raspy voice of Kirk Franklin. Turning in the direction of the music, Kevin's attention was drawn to a midnight black Mercedes S63 creeping to a stop in front of him. He almost lost his lunch when the driver's door opened and out stepped one of the most beautiful women he'd ever seen. Although in her mid forties, this woman was fine, wearing a Stella McCartney form-fitting dress with a pair of Jimmy Choo heels. Her walk itself seemed to be one of Christian appeal: graceful and cultured.

"Aah . . . I see she did make it," Bishop Joe's voice broke in on his thoughts.

"Who is that, Uncle Joe?"

"Her name is Ms. Fuller, Ms. Beverly Fuller."

"Mrs. or Miss?" Kevin asked.

"She's a widower, Kevin. She lost her husband a year ago. He was one of the top bishops in the country. Let's go introduce ourselves."

After formal introductions were made, Kevin immediately found out that Mrs. Fuller was easy to talk to. Her conversation was smooth, not animated. Every so often, Kevin caught flirtatious glances from her eyes, which were barely visible behind Dolce and Gabbana sunglasses. Their short meeting quickly turned into an hour-long conversation that neither seemed too eager to end.

"Well, I must be on my way," Mrs. Fuller finally said, before standing to leave.

"Will I see you again?" Kevin asked, hating that his voice sounded so hopeful.

"Sure you will, Pastor Steele. I'll be here on Sunday," she said smoothly. With a smile, Mrs. Fuller extended her hand. "It was nice meeting you, Pastor, and I'm looking forward to hearing you speak."

"My pleasure, Mrs. Fuller, and I—"

"Please, Pastor, if you would, just call me Beverly. Sister Beverly will be fine."

"As you wish . . . Sister Beverly."

Kevin walked her back to her car, opened the door for her, and then closed it behind her. Once inside, she started the engine, then allowed the window to come down about halfway.

"I think that I'm going to enjoy the Charlotte area," she said

"It's a good city to live in. Oh . . . pardon me, here's my business card. Give me a call, and I'll be more than glad to show you the ins and outs of our beautiful city."

"Thank you, that is so kind of you, Pastor."

"Aah . . . just call me Kevin," he said, hitting her back with her own request.

"Okay, Kevin," she said, digging in her purse.

"Here's my info. Just call me when you have time to give me a tour of your little city."

"Little city?" he repeated.

"Yes, I'm from Chicago. The windy city," she said.

"Well, this is Charlotte, the Queen city," Kevin responded boldly.

"Call me," she repeated, then turned and walked away without looking back.

After leaving the church, Kevin decided to stop by the Waffle House for a cup of strong coffee. He'd already set up a meeting with Kim for later that night, so he was going home to drink a half gallon of yak and try this new Cialis pill on Kim's fine ass. Her husband was out of town for two days with the kids.

His thoughts turned to Mrs. Fuller. Damn, she was fine. A thing of beauty, and one could not forget the simple fact that she was single and filthy rich.

Kevin's thoughts were interrupted by a familiar voice.

"Would you like your usual table by the window?"

He looked up, and there she was. Just as beautiful as she was the first day he'd walked into the Waffle house and saw her.

"Jessica."

"Hello, Kevin."

"Jessica," he said again, then took her into his arms, not caring about the stares of everyone who knew him inside the restaurant. All he cared about at that moment was what he had wrapped in his arms.

Young Jessica. . . .

Chapter IV

Six months later

"I just don't understand where I went wrong," Kevin said as he looked down at the foreclosure notice he had received. The bank hadn't given him any warnings about falling behind on the building payments. At least not in his mind. Although he had a stack of mail that looked like it had not been opened in months, it seemed to him that they had waited until the tab got so high, it would be nearly impossible for him to pay it off.

Kevin had heard about banks that would use this method; it generally meant they had a potential buyer for the property. The First Baptist church was located in a prime area of Charlotte, commonly reserved for large businesses and Fortune 500 companies. But Kevin's Uncle Joe had purchased the property before the urban renewal had begun, and when there were only dilapidated houses in the area. So now, the property had tremendous equity already built into it, and the bank would have loved to foreclose on the church, knowing that they would have many potential cash buyers lined up to purchase the large property. Selling the property straight out was always better for banks, especially when the property was worth well over three million dollars.

"Bishop, you look stressed out," Catherine, the head usher said when she entered his office.

Kevin didn't want to tell the church business, but he knew Catherine was an exception. She'd been with the congregation since his Uncle Joe was preaching out of a shack down by the countryside. She was also one of Joe's first and finest hoes during his pimping days.

"I got to raise about one hundred and fifty thousand dollars, or I'ma end up losing the church," Kevin said, leaning back in his chair.

"How? I thought everything was going so well," Catherine said, looking shocked at what she had just heard "Have you called your uncle?" she asked.

"Hell no, and I'm not calling my uncle. He'll put my ass out faster than the bank!" Kevin responded.

Catherine walked across the room, grabbed the key from the top of the cherry wood cabinet, unlocked the bottom door chest, and grabbed a bottle off the shelf. She poured Kevin and herself a drink.

Although Catherine was a large woman, standing at about 5'7" and weighting close to three hundred pounds, she was a lot of woman to handle. Her breasts were 44Fs, and it seemed like most of her weight was in her thighs and ass. Surprisingly, she was prettier than a garden full of colorful flowers. Although she had seen the best days when she was working with Kevin's uncle, she still had a beautiful look about herself.

"One hundred and fifty thousand is a lot of money to raise," Catherine said, sitting on the edge of Kevin's desk.

"Yeah, I know," he responded, getting up and walking across the room. "And I need it within the next sixty days," he added.

Kevin began pacing back and forth across the office, trying to come up with an idea.

Catherine walked over, reached into her Alexander McQueen purse, and pulled out ten crisp one-hundred dollar bills. She reached out and stopped Kevin before he walked past her this time. Holding up the money, she said in a very seductive manner, "Well, let me be the first to donate. Now, you only need one hundred and forty-nine thousand."

Kevin smiled, but when he reached for the money, she stuffed the cash down into the front of her skirt and then shook her finger at him like a mother chastising a child. No, it's not that easy baby, I been hearing a lot about that big dick of yours for a long time now. How about you let me sample the goods?

Kevin smiled. He couldn't believe how hard his dick was getting from looking at the lust in Catherine's eyes, although he was not sure if it was her look or the money she had displayed. When he walked up to her, his dick got even harder.

"Since you heard about this dick, you should already know it can get expensively addictive," Kevin said while pinching Catherine's hard nipples that were now busting out of her blouse.

"Boy, your uncle didn't tell you? My pussy is made of money. Now let's see if you can hit the jackpot," Catherine said while slowly unbuttoning her shirt.

Kevin pushed her back onto the table, then violently undid her skirt and yanked it off. *She is a big sexy red bone*, he thought to himself, and all of her thickness was proportioned well. Catherine was also confident, wearing a light pink thong and bra that matched. Kevin pulled both of them off of her, catching the money before it hit the floor.

"Jackpot," he said, taking the wad of cash, placing it in his pocket and then dropping his pants.

He wrapped his arms around both of Catherine's legs and pulled her to the edge of the desk. She had already started rubbing and licking her nipples, making her box nice and wet for him. Her pussy was fat and pretty, and when he spread her legs and pushed them back, her canal opened up about as wide as her mouth now was.

"Don't be scared," Catherine teased, seeing the look on Kevin's face.

Kevin didn't even have to guide his dick inside of her. It was as if her pussy sucked it in. It was so soft and wet, Kevin had to pull out after he got about a little more than half of his rod inside. He looked down at his glossy dick then back up at Catherine, who was smiling while she sucked her nipples.

Feeling like Catherine was trying to make a mockery of his fucking abilities, Kevin took in a deep breath, tightened up his stomach, and pushed his dick back deep inside of her. This time he slammed all eleven inches in her, plus an additional half-inch from stretching it at the base. Catherine let out a grunt then looked at Kevin with the mad, but pleased face. She had underestimated the size and girth of the young minister.

"Don't be scared now." He smiled, pulling out and pushing his long thick rod back inside of her, ever so slowly.

Kevin held on to Catherine's fat thighs and began to pound and dig his dick deep inside of her. Her wet pussy was so gushy, it made a sucking sound every time his massive dick went in and out of her.

Catherine moaned and tried to keep from screaming out his name, but she just couldn't. "Kevin!" she yelled, sitting up on the desk, but keeping her legs hiked as far up in the air as possible. "Yeah, Bishop, fuck me good," she moaned, breasts bouncing everywhere.

Kevin put his index finger over her mouth and shushed her. "Don't use that kind of language in the Lord's house," he said in a joking manner, as he continued stroking. "Now, cum all over this dick," he requested, feeling himself about to cum as well.

"Oh, yes, Bishop," she moaned, lifting her right tit into his mouth.

Kevin bit down around her areola and sucked on her nipple. It brought Catherine to the peak of her orgasm. She came all over Kevin's dick and onto the desk, causing Kevin to bust off himself. He pulled his dick out and jerked it, squirting streams of cum on to Catherine's stomach and thighs.

She looked down, saw Kevin's dick for the very first time, and almost had another orgasm just by looking at it.

"Boy, the lord has surely blessed you." She smiled, shaking her head in awe as Kevin reached for his trousers.

Bishop Joe sat at his desk, looking into the sky, mumbling some words and dabbing the sweat off his forehead. His cell phone vibrating on the desk caught his attention immediately. In the nick of time, he reached out and grabbed his phone before it fell to the floor. He looked at the screen and noticed it was the bank calling him. He answered the call immediately.

"Bishop Joel Steele," he said, trying to get control of his heart rate that seemed to be going up and down.

"Hello, Bishop Steele, this is Angela Prillaman calling from Bank of America. You have fallen behind on your payments for the property here in Charlotte, and I was wondering if it was anything we could do to resolve this issue and bring the account current," the bank manager spoke.

"Behind on my payments?" he responded in shock.

Angela pulled up his file on the computer screen and began telling Bishop Joel about what was going on over the last four months pertaining to the church and its financial breakdown. She gave him a rundown on the church's account, and the many withdrawals and lack of deposits that plagued it. It wasn't anything too serious at the moment, but the lenders wanted to make sure that everything was running smoothly, especially when millions of dollars were at stake.

"Don't worry, every dime I owe you will be there before the month is out," Bishop Joel assured the young bank manager and then hung up the phone.

"Is everything all right, Bishop?" a young woman's voice asked.

The bishop looked down at Sister Rebecca, who had his dick in her hand, stroking it and kissing it softly. She stopped briefly to hear his answer to her question.

"Yeah, everything is fine. Now you get back to work," he said, grabbing the top of her head and pushing it back down on his dick.

Rebecca took the whole length of the Bishop's dick into her mouth and shoved it deep within her throat. She was an animal at sucking dick, taking it in and making all ten inches disappear into thin air. That wasn't the impressive part. Not only did Bishop Joe have length, he also had girth. It was damn near as fat as a sixteen-ounce soda bottle, and Rebecca never grazed her teeth against it.

"Let me call this damn fool," Bishop Joel mumbled to himself, scrolling through his phone.

Rebecca simply continued to suck and swallow pre-cum and spit during the call.

"You better have a good damn reason why the bank is calling me saying you're behind a little more than a hundred and fifty thousand," Bishop Joe spoke into the phone when Kevin answered.

"Uncle Joe?" Kevin responded, shocked to hear his voice.

"Uncle Joe, my ass. Nigga, what's going on up there?" he snapped.

"Everything's good, Uncle Joe. Sister Beverly will be making the deposit at the end of next week. You know we just had the largest retreat in history, plus we did a lot of stuff for the community over the past few months," Kevin explained. "Every now and again, we gotta give back something to the people who believe in the word of God."

"Yeah, well giving back ain't gon' do no good if we don't have a building, son," Bishop Joe said, looking down at Rebecca, who was focused on her task. "Look, nephew, I don't like when the bank calls me telling me that I owe them anything. Get that money to them by the end of next week, and make this the last time I get a call from the bank," Bishop Joe yelled, then hung up.

The Bishop ended the call fast because Rebecca was going crazy on his dick. Her head was bouncing up and down, and he could hear the sound of spit splashing around in her mouth. She looked up at the Bishop and could see the pleasure all over his face. It only made her suck faster, knowing he was about to cum.

Cum is what he did, shooting his load into her mouth. She swallowed the first batch then he shot the rest of it on her cheek and over her lips.

The Bishop was stuck. "Damn girl, you nasty."

Kevin wasn't lying when he said that he gave back to the community, but he did leave out the details of overspending at times. The holy retreat for a week cost the church every bit of eighty thousand dollars with ease. Kevin took over a small island in the Bahamas and all five of its hotels and resorts. He had over three thousand members in his congregation, but only a little more than a thousand made the trip.

Kevin had paid for top-level entertainment including TGT and Mary Mary, which took almost half of his budget. His hotel accommodations and first class airfare absorbed another portion, then the rest was in food and fun for the whole week. The retreat was so big it made the local news.

Kevin didn't stop there. After the retreat, he came home and purchased himself a new toy in the form of a white Bentley GT coupe. Within six months, Kevin had managed to spend almost every dime in the church's bank account, and since everyone was getting used to being spoiled by the church, people slacked on Sundays when the collection plate went around, or when it was time to give that 10 percent tithes. Kevin needed to get the congregation back in the spirit of giving, and soon.

"So, what are you gonna do, Bishop?" Catherine asked, looking at Kevin and thinking about how he made her pussy tingle every time she thought about his dick. "I don't think you can find and fuck a thousand sisters like me for a thousand dollars a pop, within the next thirty to sixty days." Catherine smiled.

Kevin had a twenty-four karat dick, but even he knew that a goal like that was impossible, plus he had to have the money at the bank by the end of the month, despite the bank giving him sixty days to catch up. If he didn't pay the tab by then, Uncle Joe was going to pay it, but Kevin was going to be out on his ass.

"I see I'ma have to take this pimpin' shit to a whole other level," Kevin said getting up and walking out of the room.

He knew exactly who to call. Kevin scrolled through his contacts until he came upon his buddy and child-hood friend, Cedric, or Ced as everyone referred to him. Cedric's upbringing was similar to Kevin's, in that it was his father who had gotten Kevin's Uncle Joe into the ministry. But unlike Kevin, Ced's father took care of everything for him, so he never had to worry about money. Instead, he was able to use all of his time chasing women and working on his music career. He had a couple of near big deals that always seemed to keep falling through, mainly because although he had some talent, he was not talented enough for true stardom. Luckily for Cedric, his father was the bankroll of all of his endeavors, so he was able to continue, even at his age.

"Ced, my man, what's going on with you, brah?" Kevin asked.

"Nothing much, my friend. You know, just doing what I do," Ced responded. "But on the real, Kev, what's popping with you? Pops told me that your uncle was telling him that you was going through some financial shit over there and that you had been wilding out and got the church all tied up in debt," Ced spoke with a laugh.

Kevin was kind of pissed that his uncle had shared his money issues with someone else. Joe knew how competitive the ministry game was, and Kevin didn't want any of the other pastors knowing about his financial situation.

"Man, you know my uncle. He always got something to say, and it's always worse than what it really is. Although keeping it real, I do have a situation that I'm gonna need your help on, but it's nothing that I or we can't handle."

"Bro, you know I'm always here for you. Just let me know what you need, and I got you."

Kevin ran down his plan of how he needed to get a hold of some young men and women who could help him in stepping up his game. He needed them to be down for whatever, and able to keep his shit under wraps.

Ced knew exactly where to find some recruits that would fit perfectly into what Kevin was about to embark on. Ced had already assembled a small crew that he would call on whenever his father called ministry retreats. Because his father was the head bishop in the area, Ced had grown up around all the top ministers. They trusted him and were always calling on him to set them up with a nice piece of ass or point them in the direction of the church hoes when they visited the city. Some preferred men over the women, so Ced had both on speed dial.

Ced had to admit that Kevin really might have something with this idea. He knew the type of money that flowed through the mega churches and their members. If this were to come off like they planned, it would mean plenty of money and women for both men.

Before they hung up, Ced assured Kevin that he could trust him. He had his utmost loyalty. "Look, Kevin, give me about three days to get everything situated. I got a friend over at the Hilton hotel; he will give us the private suite so we can make sure that we get the right people for the job. You just make sure that you look out for your brother once you get everything popping."

"No question," Kevin responded. He sat back and smiled, knowing that although things were not perfect, they at least were looking up.

If all worked out the way that him and Ced planned, it wouldn't be long before not only would he have the biggest church, but also one of the biggest financial hustles going on in the city of Charlotte—shit, maybe even the state of North Carolina. Hell, probably the East Coast.

Chapter V

Thursday was possibly the least active day of the week in the church, so Kevin took this opportunity to do what he and Ced called, "First Class Interviews." They had spent the last couple of days, along with Catherine, scanning through the Craigslist and Backpage ads, looking for men and women who were advertising for adult services. Their plan was to bring them in under the guise of his new outreach and security staff. The Men would be called "The Men of Steel" and the ladies, "The Women of Steel." He had made sure that the potential applicants were individuals he could trust with the sensitive nature of their new jobs.

When Kevin walked into the large hotel suite that he had rented, seven of the males stood in a line against the wall. Sister Catherine sat in chair off to the side, scrolling through all of the applicants' pictures on her iPad. When she saw Kevin and Ced enter the room, she turned the device off, got up, and walked over to them.

"All right, listen up, gentlemen. I handpicked each and every one of you because I see potential in you," Kevin said, walking down the line of fine, healthy, young men.

"This here is a very sophisticated and delicate operation, and it's going to require you to have special abilities that you may already have, or you can obtain through our guidance," Kevin continued, looking each young male in the face as he passed by them. "Now, without further ado, let's get this show on the road," he said, snapping his fingers.

Having prior knowledge about what was about to occur, each man stripped down and got completely naked. The ages of these men ranged from twenty-one to twenty-five, and for the most part, their bodies were physically fit. This alone wasn't enough. In fact, they had to be blessed down below in order to make the cut. This was the part of the interview that Catherine enjoyed the most. Her mouth watered at the sight of all that meat in front of her.

Kevin and Ced walked down the line looking each man up and down from head to toe. Far from gay, they either gave them a nod of approval for the required length or simply instructed them to put their clothes back on.

Catherine walked behind them, giving a second opinion from a woman's perspective. When Kevin walked up to a kid named Javon, he almost lost his cool. Javon was hung like a horse, and if he wasn't bigger than Kevin, he was about the same size.

"Shit, you might not even be allowed in the church." Kevin laughed as he spoke to Javon, a little intimidated by his size.

Catherine was loving it; she already knew Javon was packing a heavy bat. That's why she picked him. As Kevin moved on with the interview, Catherine walked over to the door of the suite's adjoining room and opened it. In walked seven of the cutest, thickest, country-fed women. Catherine and Ced had handpicked them, knowing how freaky and money hungry these girls were.

The women came in, lined up in front of the Men of Steel, and began peeling off their clothes. Breasts flopped out of bras, while asses dropped out of their jeans. Each of the women had a body to remember. With the signal from Catherine, they all dropped down to their knees right in front of the men. A female named Lacy was the first to engage, grabbing Javon's massive dick and taking it into her mouth. Kevin, Ced, and Catherine just sat back and watched.

"You got five minutes to make your partner cum," Kevin announced, looking down at his watch.

Lacy lifted Javon's long, hard dick and licked up and down his shaft before kissing the tip with her full-sized, glossy lips. Already thirty seconds into her five minutes, she didn't panic. Her mouth was wet, and when she took Javon's dick back into her jaws, she went until her bottom lip was touching his balls.

Javon felt nothing but soft, warm, wet tissue covering his pole. She knew how to deep throat for real, pulling back only a couple of inches before shoving his dick back down her throat. It felt so good, Javon started to get weak in the knees, and about two and a half minutes in, he was spraying his cum down her throat.

Lacy continued sucking Javon's dick, draining him of all his fluids. She had broke Javon's big ass dick down to the point where he had to hold onto her head with both his hands in order to keep from buckling to his knees.

All the other girls did well too. Some used the bobbing and weaving technique, while the others jerked and sucked at the same time. Dexter didn't allow Kelly to make him cum within the five minutes. The way she sucked and jiggled his balls felt so good, he didn't want her to stop. They were the only group who continued after everybody else was done. Kelly was determined to make him cum. She grabbed his hand and placed it on the back of her head, forcing him to guide her.

"You gon' work for dis nut," Dexter said, speeding up her head strokes.

Dexter started fucking Kelly's mouth like it was some pussy. Her mouth stayed wet, and her jaw remained loose, sucking and slurping away. She looked up at Dexter, begging him to go deeper into her throat. Everyone turned and watched the show, silently rooting for their sex to be the most dominant in this cat-and-mouse game of chasing a nut.

"Arggggggggh!" Dexter grunted, feeling himself about to explode.

Kelly looked up and saw that she had him. She knocked his hand off the back of her head and started slow sucking, taking the whole length of his nine-inch member down her throat. She was making love to his dick, and Dexter couldn't take it anymore. Right before he let loose, Kelly rolled over in the doggy style position and told him to cum inside her ass. She lifted her ass up to give him a clear shot.

Dexter squirted some of his cum onto Kelly's back, unable to hold it, but dropped to his knees and rammed his cum filled dick clean inside her back door. The cum around the head of his dick was like a lubricant, so it slid in with ease.

"Damn, she's a freak," Kevin leaned over and told Ced.

"A'ight, y'all got five minutes to recuperate before we move on to the next exercise," Kevin said, pulling out his cell phone and walking to the other side of the room.

Seeing Kelly take it in the ass had made him think about his appointment with Mrs. Fuller. She was Kevin's cash cow, and he had her wrapped around his finger, despite the fact that she was into some real kinky, freaky shit that he wasn't used to doing. With the kind of money she had to throw around, right now, Kevin didn't have a problem accommodating her.

"How long is it going to take you to get to my house?" Beverly asked, walking toward her car.

Kevin looked at his watch then over at his eager students who were awaiting his next sexual command. "I guess I could be there in about two hours," he said, rubbing his dick through his pants.

"Well, think about this on your way. By the time you pull up in front of my house, I'll be lying in my bed with some fishnet thigh highs on, heels, no panties, no bra and my two middle fingers digging in and out of this sweet wet pussy you love so much," Beverly whispered, rubbing her pussy through her jeans.

Kevin's dick got hard just thinking about it. Beverly was definitely in the top three for the best pussy he ever had.

"Oh, and just so you know, all of my doors are locked, and I'm not getting out of the bed. So if you wanna taste my sweetness, you gotta find ya own way in," she said then hung up the phone.

Kevin shook his head and smiled. That was just some of the kinky shit she was into. He walked back across the room and directed everyone on to the next phase. All the females were instructed to lay on the beds in any position they chose.

Kelly went right back into her doggy style position, while Renee and Tia chose to lay on their backs. Olivia and Kelsey laid on their sides, only waiting for further instructions. Tiffany sat on her knees, hoping she would be able to ride somebody. Lacy was on her back too, but she had her legs so far back, her toes were touching the pillow right by her head. She made her pussy wink at Javon, then bit down on her lower lip. His dick rocked back up immediately.

"You niggas got ten minutes to make ya partner cum . . . twice," Kevin said looking down at his watch.

Javon wasted no time dropping to his knees, holding Lacey's thighs back and planting his face in her pussy. His tongue was long, damn near curling up to her G-spot, and he lunged it back and forth inside of her nectar jar viciously. Within the first minute of licking and sucking her wetness, Lacy was at the peak of her first orgasm.

Dexter rubbed his swollen bat up and down Kelly's pussy before pushing it inside her. She arched her back and spread her knees apart so he could go in up to his balls. Kelly had a fat ass, and it jiggled every time it clapped against his stomach. He grabbed the top of her shoulder with one hand, gripped her inner thigh with the other, and pounded away like she was a human battering ram.

"I'm cumming," Kelly yelled out, looking back at Dexter.

Dexter could feel Kelly's walls tightening up around his dick. She began throwing her ass back at him, then reached down and grabbed a handful of her breasts. Dexter grabbed a hold of her hair and pulled her head back, fucking her and beating down on her walls. Kelly couldn't hold it anymore. Her pussy busted, releasing her fruit juices onto Dexter's long black dick.

"Beat dis pussy up," she said through clinched teeth, looking back at her ass slamming against Dexter's stomach.

Dexter came for the second time, pulling out of Kelly's pussy and squirting his thick cum all over her ass. He wiped his cum up and down her pussy lips then pushed his dick right back inside of her. He wasn't going another round though, he just wanted to play inside of her until his dick went soft.

When Tiffany straddled Tim, Kevin had to adjust his semi-hard dick in his pants. Her smooth, dark chocolate skin complimented her juicy red lips and her light pink pussy. She reached back and spread her ass cheeks apart before sitting all the way down on Tim's nine-inch sword. Tiffany leaned over, rested her elbows on Tim's chest, and began bouncing her ass up and down on his member. She bounced her pussy all the way up to the tip of his dick, then let it crash down to his nuts.

Her pussy was so wet, Tim's dick looked like it had a fresh layer of wax on it. Tiffany had a treat for Kevin, who was directly behind her looking on. Looking down at Tim and feeling herself about to cum, Tiffany licked her lips.

"Dis how ya make it rain," she said, speeding up the bounce. "Ohhhhhh shhhhhhiiitttt," she screamed, taking one of her breasts and putting it in her mouth.

Cum shot out of Tiffany's pussy and drowned Tim's dick and balls. It looked like she was pissing on him, but it was pure 100 percent orgasmic fluids. Shit got so slippery, Tim squeezed off his load inside of her without Tiffany even knowing. She was in her zone. She sat up on Tim's dick and continued riding him, hips rocking until he couldn't take it anymore. He had to literally lift Tiffany up off his dick to get from up under her.

Having a rearview front seat of the action, Kevin nodded his head in respect of Tiffany's squirt game. *I got to get me some of dat,* Kevin thought to himself.

Ced and Catherine sat back in their chairs and watched the crazy sex session going down.

For the most part, everyone was finishing up, except for Lacy, who was having trouble taking all of Javon's dick. He kept her legs pinned all the way back as he banged all eleven and a half inches of his hammer deep into her canal. He wasn't showing her any mercy either, fucking her like he was an official porn star.

"Call me Jack Hammer," Javon requested as he pounded away. "Say it," he demanded.

Everyone seemed to tune into Javon and Lacy's battle for dominance. Lacy wasn't trying to submit and scream out the name he wanted her to, but the more she resisted, the deeper Javon drove his dick into her. He had her legs locked, so Lacy couldn't go anywhere. She was at his mercy and wasn't even able to reach the peak of an orgasm. This was a pure slaughter for the stunt she pulled when she made Javon buckle from her dick suck. She couldn't take the beating anymore.

"Jack Hammer! Damn boy, Jack Hammer," she screamed trying her best to crawl from under Javon.

Javon finally let her legs down, and when he pulled out of Lacy's swollen pussy, he shot his cum all over her body. It seemed that the more he jerked his dick, the more cum he released. It was everywhere.

Kevin was impressed. One by one, he looked at the pleasure written all over the faces of every female in the room, including Catherine. He was more than satisfied at what he saw from both the males and the females. It was official. From here on out, this was his crew. "First Class" was the name he gave them, and with over two thousand adult members in his congregation, most of whom were sexually deprived, Kevin and his young sex stars were about to take the church by storm.

Chapter VI

On his way over to Beverly's house, Kevin decided to stop by the bank and have a little word with Angela, the account manager for the church at Bank of America. Having a good relationship with her from being a member of the church, Kevin wanted to direct her to call him from now on when there was a problem with the finances pertaining to the church.

"Bishop Steele, so glad to see you. What brings you this way?" she said, getting up and pointing to the seat in front of her desk for him to sit.

Kevin didn't normally indulge in the white meat, but he had a thing for Angela. She was sexy as hell for a white woman, and she would always flirt with Kevin after the service.

"Hey, Angela. I just wanted to stop by and let you know that I'll be making those payments by the end of next week, hopefully," Kevin said, taking a seat and putting his bible on the desk.

"That's no problem. I wasn't rushing Bishop Joe. You know all eyes are on me these days, so I gotta do my job," she said glancing over at the tellers' booth where jealous eyes wandered in her direction.

Kevin couldn't stop himself from staring at this gorgeous snow bunny sitting across from him. Every time he saw Angela, she reminded him of the super model Kate Upton. Angela was just a little thicker in the hips, and her eyes were blue. She sat there with her breasts busting out of her shirt, and her lips were shiny from the lip-gloss she applied regularly.

"When you gon' let me take you to dinner?" Kevin asked playfully.

Angela blushed and shook her head at the gesture. "You are a mess, Pastor. I heard about you, and I can't afford to be tempted by the devil," she chuckled.

Kevin smiled and grabbed his Bible before getting up. He wanted to stay and play, but he had to get over to Sister Fuller's before she started without him.

"Will I see you in church on Sunday?" Kevin asked, tucking his bible under his arm.

"Don't you see me there every Sunday?" Angela asked in a flirtatious way, applying some lip balm to her already glossy lips.

In a split second, Kevin thought about all the things he would have done with her lips and the places he would have put his own if ever given the chance. She didn't know it right now, but Kevin had her locked in as a target, and nine times out of ten, he never missed his mark. "I'll see you in church," he said, then left.

"What was all that about?" Lacy asked, sitting down at the table with Javon in the hotel restaurant.

"What are you talking about?" he responded, taking a bite out of his sandwich.

"You fuckin' me the way you did in front of everybody."

Her sucking his dick until he damn near buckled was a little fun and games, and when Javon ate her pussy and made her cum in a minute, Lacy thought that they were even. The way Javon fucked her face to face and stuffed his tongue down her throat in the process, Lacey felt like it was personal. He looked into her eyes as if they were the only people in the room.

"Yo, I'm not gonna lie to you, Lacy. You got some good pussy and some crazy head. If we weren't in the situation that we we're in, I probably would have made you my girl. I've had a thing for you for a while, but . . ."

"But what?" Lacy asked since she had been feeling Javon in the same way.

Javon looked at Lacy and took another bite of his sandwich. It was impossible for them to actually be together, now that they were a part of something so sinister

"We're First Class, now. Just leave it alone," he said, getting up from the table and leaving the restaurant.

Kevin pulled into Beverly's driveway and parked his Bentley GT right next to her Mercedes Benz CLS63. Whenever Kevin went out to her house, he was amazed by something new every time. This time it was the change in her landscaping—she had added a fountain to the front yard. It was a statue of a naked woman covering her breasts and vagina with her hands. The water came out of her mouth and landed in a basin at her feet.

Kevin walked up to the front door and rang the bell a couple of times. When Beverly didn't answer, he remembered what she had told him about finding his own way inside. Going around back, Kevin walked up to a door on the side of the house that led to the backyard. It had multiple small windows. After looking in and seeing nothing, he looked around before knocking out one of the windows with the backside of his elbow.

Kevin took another look around at the neighboring houses before reaching in and unlocking the door. Sister Fuller always had him on some bullshit, and triggering the silent alarm was a part of her plan. Kevin didn't even know what he had done.

When he got upstairs to her bedroom, he walked through the door and was stunned. Mrs. Fuller was lying in the center of her bed with her legs spread apart, playing in her pussy. She was finger fucking herself with one hand and rubbing on her nipple with the other, moaning and biting down on her lower lip in pleasure. Seeing Kevin walk through the door, she slowed down, pulled her two fingers out of her pussy, and began sucking on them.

"I see you started without me," he said, placing his keys on her dresser and walking over to the bed.

Kevin wanted to dive into the bed and slay her on the spot, but he had to establish some very important business first. He kept his cool and put his serious face on. He was kind of dampening the mood in the room, but it was very much necessary in order to establish what he needed.

"What's da matter, baby?" Sister Fuller asked, sliding down to the edge of the bed, where he stood.

"Church business," he said in a sad tone. "If it ain't one thing, it's another."

"Tell mama all about it," Beverly said as she unbuckled Kevin's belt. She unzipped his pants and pulled out his semi hard dick, taking it into her hand and kissing his large mushroom head.

Kevin could barely stay focused, looking down at this beautiful woman about to put his dick in her mouth.

"The church may be in need of a loan in order to stay open," Kevin began. "I think I might have overdone it with that retreat, and now I'm a little behind on the building payment.

"Well, how much money do you need to borrow?" she asked, kissing and stroking his massive dick.

"We need one hundred and fifty thousand dollars," Kevin said, looking down and waiting for her reaction.

Beverly wasn't shocked at all by the number he threw out. She continued kissing up and down the shaft of his dick until she opened her wet, warm mouth and began sucking it.

Kevin looked up to the ceiling, and as bad as he tried to control himself, he couldn't. The deeper into her mouth she took him, the harder his dick got. Mrs. Fuller looked up, and Kevin and could see the pleasure written all over his face. She took his dick out of her mouth and rubbed her lips up and down the side of it. Then she licked his large golf ball-sized nuts.

"As your loan officer, you need to convince me why I should loan you that much money," she said in a seductive manner, crawling backwards onto the bed.

Kevin's dick stood at attention. He removed the rest of his clothes and climbed into the bed with her. He was going to give Beverly something totally different than what she was used to getting. Something that was sure to have her head twisted.

"Let's pretend that I'm your husband," he said, gently kissing her lips. "And today, neither of us have to go to work," he continued, kissing her again. "Until the morning comes, I just wanna make love to you," Kevin told her, looking into her eyes as he kissed her again.

Beverly tried to roll from under Kevin, thinking about her late husband who used to start off making love to her in the same manner. Kevin stopped her, grabbed her wrists, and pinned them to the pillows beside her head. He leaned in and kissed her again, then moved to her neck. He bit down on it then sucked it softly, causing her to go into a trance. This was Beverly's spot, and at this point, it was impossible for her to stop him.

"Ohh, Kevin," she moaned, feeling his warm kisses travel down the center of her chest and onto her stomach.

Kevin licked inside Beverly's belly button, then went down further until he reached her throbbing kitty. He took his tongue and licked from the bottom of her pussy, straight up the middle until reaching the tip, unveiling her clitoris, hiding inside the top of her pussy lips. She moaned in pleasure looking down at Kevin's head between her legs. It felt so good, she attempted to crawl up onto the bed even more, but Kevin wouldn't let her.

Beverly arched her back, feeling a tingling sensation in the pit of her stomach. In the blink of an eye, the orgasm hit her like a freight train.

"Ohhhhh, Kevin!" she yelled out, grabbing the back of his head and pushing his face deeper into her pussy.

Kevin could feel her body shaking. Moments later, Beverly's cum oozed out of her kitty, into his mouth, and onto his chin. She ripped the sheets off the bed from the bone cracking orgasm she was still having as he licked his way back up her stomach and to the center of her chest.

Kevin stopped and cupped one of her breasts, biting down on it like it was a juicy peach. She moaned, still feeling the ending of her orgasm.

"Dis daddy pussy now," Kevin said, grabbing his dick and rubbing it up and down her tunnel.

Beverly hissed as the oversized mushroom head pierced her entry point. Inch by inch, Kevin pushed his dick inside her wetness, all the while looking in her eyes. It was slow and passionate, and with every long, deep stroke, Kevin kissed her and wrapped her body tighter in his arms.

Beverly was submerged in his clutches, and couldn't understand why it felt so good.

"I love you," Kevin whispered in her ear, then pushed his dick inside her as deep as he could go.

Those words, along with feeling his dick damn near in her stomach, made her cum yet another time. She screamed out in ecstasy, biting and sucking on his shoulder.

In the heat of the moment, she said some words she had not said in years. "I love you too," she whispered back in his ear while sucking on his lobe.

Kevin was shocked that she said it, but since she did, it was time for him to put the icing on the cake. He sped up his strokes slightly, only so he could cum too. She screamed out his name and clawed into his back.

Her orgasm lasted even longer once she felt Kevin's warm cum enter her sensitive canal. He let out a loud sigh, and right when he was in the middle of letting his load go, the bedroom door came crashing in with a man's voice screaming at him words he couldn't believe.

"Charlotte Police Department!" the uniformed officer yelled, pointing his gun at Kevin.

He looked back at the cop then turned back around to face Beverly. She sat there with a huge smile on her face, and if Kevin's dick wouldn't have shriveled up out of her pussy, she would have had another orgasm.

Being caught in the midst of having sex was a part of her original fantasy for today's sex venture. She knew that if Kevin broke in, the alarm would go off and the cops would respond immediately, only to find her with her legs in the air. Beverly had some shit with her, but for a $150,000 dollar loan, Kevin would play along with whatever came to her mind.

"I'm sorry, officer. It was just my husband," she said and smiled.

Chapter VII

Kevin had just given one of his best sermons, having his whole congregation stand out of their seats, clapping and praising. It was a packed house too, and as the choir sang gospel music on stage, he walked out and shook hands with his moneyed members. It was something about the word today that had people in the mood of giving . . . that and a few other things that were going on behind the scenes.

"Bishop Steele!" an older woman called out as she walked through the crowd.

The closer she got, the more Kevin recognized her face. He didn't know her name, but he was sure he had seen her many times in the dining hall after service.

"Bishop, is it too late to request a meeting for this week?" she asked, walking up and extending her hand to him.

"No, ma'am. It's never too late for me to spend some quality time with my members," Kevin said, reaching out and accepting her hand.

It was innocent at first, but then the woman swiped the back of his hand with her thumb and gave him a sinister, but lustful look. Kevin gave her body a quick scan then glanced around the room. He laid eyes on Catherine, who was standing off to the side, giving him the nod of approval. It was a nod to say that she was wealthy and didn't have a problem paying for some good dick. All Kevin had to do was seal the deal.

"Here's my number. Call me when you're ready to extend me some true counsel." The woman leaned in and whispered in his ear.

She disappeared back into the crowd of people who were all gathered around to speak with the Bishop. He tucked the number away in his pocket and proceeded to hug, kiss, and shake hands with the rest of the congregation.

Kelly stood in the rear of the church bus, bent over on the back seat while Brother Johnson fucked her from behind. His pants were down to his ankles, and he was pumping away, chasing down the nut he felt coming on. Kelly's ass bounced with every stroke, and knowing that he was about to cum at any minute, she took one of his hands off her waist and brought it up to her bare breast hanging out of her bra.

"Harder, harder!" she moaned, pushing her ass back onto his dick. "Give it to mama," she said, looking back at him. "You gon' make me cum all over this dick."

Brother Johnson sped up. With a hand full of titty and her fat ass clapping against his stomach, he shot his load into the lubricated condom. He fell face forward onto her back to avoid buckling to his knees.

Kelly let him stay there for a few seconds until he got his footing right. She turned around and grabbed his dick, jerking the rest of the cum he had left into the condom. Brother Johnson looked beat.

"Are you satisfied, Brother Johnson?" Kelly asked, ready and willing to go another round. "Dis pussy's yours right now."

"Girl, you sure are a blessing for an old man like myself," he said, rolling the condom off his dick and pulling his pants back up. "I gotta get back inside with my wife," he said before courteously getting off the bus.

Brother Johnson couldn't go another round with the young, energetic Kelly if he wanted to. At the age of fifty, he felt every bit of father time. He was a one hitter quitter, and it didn't even take him that long to get to his point. Kelly had him on that bus for about eight minutes and it was over. She didn't mind fast money like that, but at the same time, she wanted to nut too.

Unfortunately, he wasn't big enough or could last long enough to give her what she wanted. She would later get her orgasm from the cash he gave to Cedric, who was now the official pastor's assistant. As far as everyone in the church knew, Kevin wasn't involved in the sexual deviance that was going on. He saved his secret for only the most elite and wealthy members. Ced's job was to be the setup and collector for all transactions.

The service was great, and afterward, those who normally stayed behind, gathered in the dining hall to enjoy a nice, hot meal, courtesy of Sister Jackson, the church's head cook. Kevin walked through the door and got another round of applause for his sermon. Although he had his own private table in the dining hall, he decided to sit amongst the people today, and his reason for doing so was because a pretty young face had caught his attention.

"You came to church today," Kevin said, taking a seat in the empty chair next to Jessica.

For the past couple of months, they hadn't really been in touch, and that was mainly due to Jessica going to visit a cousin who lived up in Durham. Kevin had went up to see her a few times, and each visit was a sexual explosion. Jessica was everything in the bedroom, but that wasn't what he needed right now. He needed someone who had money, so for the last month, the communication between the two had dwindled to the point that there wasn't any at all.

"Yeah, I was in the neighborhood, and I figured I'd stop through before I head back to my cousin's," Jessica responded. "You gave a great sermon today. Hell, you moved me to put some money in the collection plate."

Kevin smiled. "You're still as beautiful as they come," he complimented. "You know I miss you. I think about you every day, hoping and praying that you come back into my life," he said, spitting some of his finer game.

Jessica was eating it up. She had to turn away from him because she didn't want him to see her blushing the way she was. Kevin had to turn his head as well, because he didn't want the people to see him staring at Jessica.

"So, are you going to stay for a while, or am I going to have to relocate my church out to Durham in order to spend some time with you?" he asked. "I need to be with you. I miss you."

"You wanna spend time with me?" Jessica asked, knowing exactly what that meant. "I'd love to, but . . ."

She knew Kevin wanted some pussy, and he did, but not just any pussy right now. Kevin wanted some of that soft, tender young pussy that tasted and smelled like a citrus, almost as if it produced its own fruit juice. The only female who ever gave him that was Jessica.

"I gotta be at work in the morning, but maybe on my next few days off we can spend some time together," Jessica said, putting her hand on top of his, with a sad look on her face.

Kevin moved his hand from under Jessica's, but not because of the unnecessary attention it would bring. Kevin moved his hand because he was disappointed she had shot him down. Jessica could see it in his face.

Before she got a chance to say anything or give him a time and date, Kevin blessed the food on the table, got up and walked off.

Jessica just sat there, a little embarrassed. With her appetite completely shot for the rest of the afternoon, she too got up and left.

Catherine was in Kevin's chamber counting all the money from the collection plate and the monthly 10 percent checks given by most of the members. There was even money in the anonymous charity box at the front door. Hardly anybody ever put money in that box. The sermon Kevin gave on charity and giving for the sake of God really did the trick. Not to mention some sexual favors to some wealthy people, which brought in some nice money as well. The church did good today.

"Oh, I'm sorry," Javon said, opening the door. "Where's the Bishop?"

"He's in the kitchen. But wait a minute, Javon. Come in here for a minute." Catherine waved with a fist full of money. "You know we got a new member to the church. Her name is Georgia-May Atkins, and she just moved up here from Columbia, South Carolina."

"Oh, yeah. She had a little entourage with her today," Jovan said, remembering her getting out the back of a Rolls Royce Ghost. "So, what's her story?" he asked, walking over and taking a seat in the chair in front of the Bishop's desk.

Catherine put the money down, got up, and walked around to where Javon sat. Her big wide ass wobbled with every step she took. Once directly behind him, Catherine leaned over and slid her hands down the center of his chest. Her extra-large breasts contorted to the back of his neck, lightly draping over both his shoulders.

"She wants what every woman wants," Catherine said, kissing Javon softly on the side of his neck with her thick, full lips.

Javon's dick got hard within seconds, and Catherine could see it bulging through his slacks. She leaned in a little further, reached down and grabbed him through his pants. Javon jumped up out of his seat and tried to laugh it off.

"You ain't ready for this, big momma," Javon smiled, grabbing his large package that was riding down his leg.

"You think I hand-picked you without having a reason," she asked, walking toward him. "I knew you had potential the first day you walked through these church doors."

Catherine stood in front of Javon, reached down, and grabbed his package. She was horny as hell and wanted to sample Javon's goods, and she really didn't care about the cost.

"Don't bite off more than you can chew," Javon warned.

"Yeah? Well, I got a big appetite." Catherine smiled and pushed Javon backwards to the couch.

Dexter left the dining area and began taking his stroll through the church, hoping to see the choirgirls taking a swim in the church's pool like they did every Sunday after the service. The Bishop's chambers were en route to the pool, and since he saw Kevin leave the dining hall, he figured he'd stop by to see if he had any work for him.

Dexter knocked on the door twice before opening it. He walked in, looked to the left, and saw Catherine's bare body straddling somebody on the Bishop's couch. He couldn't see who it was because her back was facing him.

"Damn, my bad," Dexter said, turning around and heading for the door.

Catherine looked back, saw who it was, and stopped him.

"Come here, Dexter, and lock the door behind you," she said, slowly grinding her hips back and forth on Javon's dick.

For a big girl, Catherine could ride a dick. She sat all the way down on it with her knees spread far apart so she could take all of it inside of her. Dexter walked over to the couch, rubbing his dick at the sight of her fat, round, wide ass moving back and forth. Looking down, he almost didn't recognize Javon. The breast he had in his mouth covered the whole front of his face, and her other one covered the side. He had his arms wrapped around her ass as far as they could go, pushing her down onto his dick.

When Catherine turned around to tell Dexter that she wanted him too, he already had his dick in his hand between her chest and mouth.

Javon couldn't lie, he needed some help with her big ass. She was a monster.

"You fucked up good this time," Dexter said, pushing his long, thick dick in Catherine's mouth.

She grabbed it and began jerking and sucking on it, while at the same time, bouncing up and down on Javon's dick. Javon reached up and grabbed both of her tits, squeezing them and pinching her nipples. Catherine was going crazy fucking and sucking two dicks at the same damn time.

To get better leverage on Dexter's dick, Catherine turned around repositioned herself, riding Javon cowgirl style. She bounced her big ass up and down on Javon's dick, grabbing both of her breasts and squeezing and pinching her own nipples while she continued to suck Dexter's dick.

"Mmmmmmmmm!" she moaned, looking up at Dexter.

Catherine pulled Dexter's dick out of her mouth, got up off Javon's dick then sat back down on it. This time she slid Javon's massive dick into her asshole. She moaned and endured the pain of sitting all the way down on it, but eventually she got all of him into her back door. She leaned back on Javon, who held her up with his forearm, then put her feet up on the couch, giving Dexter a clear path to her big, fat, pink pussy.

"Jovan, you good back there?" Dexter asked, giving him a warning that he was about to go in.

"Yeah, I'm good, nigga. Just watch ya balls," Javon told Dexter as he pushed his dick deeper into Catherine's ass.

Dexter kneeled down and rubbed his dick up and down Catherine's wet pussy before pushing it into her. She frowned and hissed as he inched his member inside. Once the length of his dick was in, Dexter leaned forward, held on to the back of the couch, and started stroking Catherine. Javon was underneath her, guiding his dick in and out of her ass. After about a minute into it, all three of them found their rhythm.

Catherine lifted her breast up into Dexter's mouth, and once he started sucking on it, Catherine reached her peak. She threw her head back and began cumming all over Dexter's dick. Javon pushed his dick further inside of her only to let his load off after feeling the inside of her ass get moist.

"Oh my fuckin' God," she cried out as her body trembled at the peak of her orgasm.

Feeling her cum dripping down his balls, Dexter pulled out and squeezed his dick, stopping his cum from shooting out. He grabbed Catherine by the top of her head, pulled her face up to his dick, and shoved it into her mouth.

She gladly took it, rubbing on her clit as his cum oozed into down her throat. She sucked and swallowed every drop he had in him, and as she continued rubbing her clit and squeezing down on her nipples, Catherine brought herself to her final orgasm.

Chapter VIII

"A'ight everybody, listen up," Kevin said, silencing the room.

Everyone was there. Cedric, Catherine, Lacy, Javon, Dexter, Tim, Kelly, Tiffany, Olivia, Stacy, Christian, Dante, Jasper, Eric, Monique, and Riley, all stood around the office, waiting to hear what he had to say.

"We did good last week, and everybody pitched in one way or another," Kevin began. "The collection plate did well, and members felt comfortable giving their monthly ten percent. Our wealthier members also seemed to be in a generous mood, thanks to First Class, and for that, I got a little som' for y'all," Kevin said, reaching down by the side of his chair and pulling up a Louis Vuitton carry bag. "Like I told y'all before, we gone take this church over by storm. The only way that's going to happen is if we look the part," Kevin said, dumping the contents of the bag onto his desk.

One by one, he separated the small manila envelopes, tossing one to everyone in the room. When they opened it, nobody was surprised that it was money inside, but when they pulled it out, that's when the shock kicked in. There was nothing but Franklins, and a nice stack at that. It was way more than what they thought they'd earned.

"How much is this?" Tiffany asked as she started to count.

"It's ten grand, and every last one of you earned it," Kevin said, reaching into his drawer and pulling out a folder.

"Treat yourselves. Buy some new clothes or get a new car. I don't care. You guys do whatever you want with the money, because that's nothing compared to the kind of money you'll be making in the near future."

They all paused to look at the money but were snapped back to earth by Kevin knocking on his desk. He had bigger plans for First Class, and if he wanted to execute his master plan to the tee, he was going to need them to be focused. There were some key people in the congregation that he wanted to target. After doing some homework, he found out that there were some very influential people sitting in the pews, and he wasn't just talking about the wealthy.

"Seduction is going to be key," Kevin said, taking some photos out of the folder and spreading them across the table. "These are your targets." He pointed to the pictures of ten men, ages ranging from thirty to sixty.

All the girls gathered around the desk and took a good look at the photos. Some of the men were cute, while others were ugly, and in two instances, very fat.

"There's one thing that sells no matter where on this earth you travel, and that's sex. Men will always pay for pussy, no matter how you look at it. The thing is, I need these men to want and desire your pussy more than anything," Kevin said, locking his fingers across his stomach.

"Aye, Javon," Kevin said, nodding for him to come over. "Take that," he said, referring to the folder.

Javon picked up the folder and looked at how thick it was. It had to be at least an inch thick, and when Javon opened it up, there were nothing but pictures inside. It was young women, old women, tall women, short women, white women, black women, Puerto Rican women, Asian women, fat women, skinny women, short hair, long hair, fat ass, no ass, big chests, small chests, and any other kind of woman God created.

"Who da hell are all these women?" Javon asked.

"These are all the women I had sex with in our congregation. Some are married, some are single, but all of them got money. You can call that my little black church book." Kevin smiled. "If you make these women happy, they are going to bless you. You might have to deal with some freaky fantasies here and there, but in the long run, it will be well worth it."

First Class sat around observing the pictures and taking in everything Kevin was telling them. He was putting the food out there, and all they had to do was go get it. Eager and hungry for more Franklins, First Class was on one. Kevin didn't tell them just yet, but if everybody played their part and did everything they were supposed to do, the church, along with Charlotte, was going to be eating out the palm of their hands.

"You need a ride?" Lacy asked when Javon exited the church. "Javon!" she yelled, seeing he didn't hear her because he had his headphones on.

"Yo, what up, Lace?" he said, looking over at her standing next to her red Nissan Altima.

"You need a ride?" she asked again as she put her gym bag into the trunk.

Javon was trying to avoid having a conversation with Lacy because he knew exactly what she wanted to talk about. Being in a relationship with her was out of the question, especially since she was on team First Class. He wanted his significant other to be a little more innocent and sophisticated, and definitely not a type that was fuckin' everything moving in the church for a check.

"Thanks, but no thanks," Javon responded, putting his headphones back over his head.

Lacy watched as he walked away, shaking her head before getting into the car. She couldn't figure out for the life of her why she liked him so much. Could it be his good looks, his humble attitude, and his quiet dominance among the Men of Steele? Or maybe it was the way that he walked or the way that he talked, or maybe it was the way that he fucked her brains out the day of the First Class interviews. Whatever it was, Lacy was hooked, and she wasn't about to give up on him yet. The attraction she had for him had become too strange for her to give up.

When Kevin got home, he kicked his shoes off the second he stepped foot inside his bedroom. All he had time to do was take a quick shower before he had to leave right back out. He had an appointment with Beverly, and tonight, she wanted Kevin to escort her to a fundraiser dinner in downtown Charlotte. Kevin agreed to it, mainly because she was going to introduce him to some very important political people who ran the city.

Right before Kevin was about to get in the shower, his doorbell bell rang. He looked at the clock on his wall and saw that it was only 4:36 p.m. He didn't have to be at Beverly's house until 7:00, and he definitely wasn't expecting any company.

"Who da hell?" Kevin mumbled, wrapping the towel around his waist and heading down the stairs.

When he got to the door and opened it, Jessica was standing there with a tan trench coat on with her hair pulled back in a ponytail. It was cloudy outside, so he thought that she was only dressing for the weather, but when she undid the belt around her waist and let the coat fall open, his jaw damn near hit the ground. Jessica stood there with her birthday suit on and a pair of pink Saint Laurent metallic peep toe pumps.

"You gon' make me stand on the porch?" Jessica smiled, waiting for him to invite her in.

"Damn, my bad," Kevin said, standing to the side, watching her strut by him like a runway model.

As soon as Kevin closed and locked the front door, he was all over her. She didn't make it to the stairs before he grabbed her by the arm, turning her around to face him. His towel dropped to the floor, and in one swoop, Kevin wrapped his arms around Jessica's waist and lifted her into the air. Her legs wrapped around his waist and her arms around his neck.

"Damn, I missed you," Kevin said looking up at her.

Jessica leaned in and kissed Kevin, throwing her tongue into his mouth. They were locked in, and instead of carrying her upstairs, Kevin walked her over to the kitchen, sitting her on top of the island. Jessica's body was crazy. He opened her coat and grabbed both of her soft 34B breasts then continued tonguing her down. She started to take the coat off, but Kevin stopped her.

"Nah, leave it on. Leave everything on," he said, leaning her back on the countertop. "I want you just like this."

Still standing in front of her, he lifted her legs up and sat them on his shoulder. Kevin started licking and sucking on Jessica's pussy lips, getting her juices flowing real good. She had one hand on the back of his head, while her other hand spread her pussy lips apart for Kevin to lick the hole of it.

"You miss dis pussy, don't you?" Jessica asked, looking down at his head swaying side to side.

Kevin didn't answer her. He just kept nibbling away. Jessica bit down on her lower lip, feeling the sensation of an orgasm forming in her gut. She couldn't hold it any longer once Kevin started flicking his tongue at high speeds on her clit. When she came, Kevin could see the clear fluids leaking out of her pussy and onto the counter top. His dick turned into the Arm & Hammer baking soda arm.

"Gimme dat dick, daddy," Jessica said, pulling him up onto the island. "Make it hurt, baby."

She didn't have to tell Kevin that, because he had planned on doing it from the moment he opened his front door. He guided his long, banana-curved dick right into her honey pot and lifted her left leg between his forearm. Turned on by the trench coat and her heels in the air, Kevin pushed himself deep inside. Jessica let out a loud moan, leaning up and sticking her tongue back into his mouth. Kevin towered over her, speeding up his strokes. No matter how many times they'd fucked, Jessica could never get used to the size of his dick. It always hurt in the beginning, but after a while, it became easier for her to manage. She raised both of her legs up and rested them on his shoulders, her heels dangling right beside his head.

"Beat dis pussy up, nigga," she pleaded, grabbing and squeezing both of her breasts.

Kevin honored her request and wasted no time slaying her. The top of his thighs clapped against the back of hers as his short, but deep strokes knocked down her walls. Jessica got everything she was looking for and then some, and as her eyes rolled to the back of her head and the whole of her body locked up, her honey pot cracked wide open, lubricating the giant chocolate muscle that dug deep within her.

Javon sat on his front steps, smoking on a blunt full of Grand Daddy Kush, something he enjoyed doing every now and again when things were going well in his life. The extra ten grand from the Bishop had come at a good time. He really needed it to catch up on his bills, plus rent was due in a couple of days. If it wasn't for Kevin, he would've had to call up his boy, Mark, and trap for a few days to get right.

"You can't be serious," Javon mumbled to himself, seeing Lacy's car pull up in front of his house.

He almost choked on the weed watching her get out of the car and walk up to his steps.

"Come on, Lacy. What are you doing?" Javon asked, a little irritated about her coming there busting his relaxation high.

Lacy stood there with her hands in her pockets and her head down, like she was ashamed of her stalker tendencies. She looked up at Javon with the puppy dog face and spoke.

"I'll stop," she said in a low tone.

"Stop what?" What are you talking about?"

"I'll quit First Class if I have to. I didn't even have sex with anybody yet."

Javon gave her a doubtful look.

"No, I swear. You're the only person who I had sex with in that whole church," Lacy responded, walking up and taking a seat next to Javon on the steps.

Lacy was telling the truth. Out of all the fucking that was going on in and outside of the church, the only time she had got her hands dirty was with Javon. At Sunday dinner, she did reach under the table and grab Brother Samuel's dick, but it was only to get him worked up for a later date. It wasn't that deep, so she didn't feel the need to share that with him.

"Why me? Out of everybody in that church, why me?" Javon asked, taking a toke of the weed.

"Javon, I been liked you. You was just too stupid to see it. I practically threw myself at you on several different occasions, but you was nothing less than a gentleman," she said, nudging him.

Javon didn't know if it was the weed smoke, but concept of him and Lacy ran through his mind, and he actually liked the thought of it. She was young and beautiful with a crazy body. Not only that, but Lacy was well educated, having graduated out of the same high school as Javon with honors, and was finishing up her last year in college. She was definitely a catch, but there were a few obstacles still in the way.

"Even if you do stop, I'm still gonna do me in First Class," Javon told her. "Shit, I need da bread, and the last time I checked, regular jobs wasn't giving out ten grand bonuses."

"I understand that, and if you give us a chance to be together . . . under one condition of course," Lacy said, holding up one finger.

"Yeah, what's that?" Javon asked, curious as to what she was about to say.

"All I ask is that you put a condom on when you fuckin dese bitches. Dis pussy should be the only pussy you go in bareback," she said, giving him a stern look.

Javon chuckled at her demand. It was asking a lot, but it was respected. He took another puff of the weed, looked over at Lacy, and passed it to her. Lacy didn't smoke, but she took it anyway, only hoping that it would relax her nerves. She took one puff then tried to inhale, but began choking uncontrollably. She coughed so hard she couldn't even gather herself to pass the weed back.

Laughing at Lacy, Javon had to grab her wrist and take the weed out of her hand. After she finally finished choking, Lacy and Javon sat there on the step laughing at what had just happened. Although Lacy was high as hell off that one puff, she was still conscious and waiting for Javon to give her an answer to her proposal.

***

Kevin and Beverly stepped into the ballroom looking like a power couple. Kevin had on a grey Hermès suit, a white Tom Ford shirt, and a pair of golden brown Salvatore Ferragamo shoes. On his wrist was a black Hublot, and on his face were a pair of basic ready frames. Beverly had on a white Diane von Furstenberg knee length cocktail dress and a pair of red Rupert Sanderson satin pumps. In her hand was a red and gold Alexander McQueen clutch. Her hair was curled and draped over her shoulders. She looked elegant and had all eyes on her.

It took every bit of thirty minutes for Beverly and Kevin to get to their reserved tables. That was due to the pre-meet-and-greets both Beverly and Kevin entertained.

The Bishop was already familiar with a few faces, and those who did know him showed him love. Beverly was impressed.

There was no need for a menu because it was only a couple of dishes to choose from, all of which cost $2,500 a plate. Kevin had been to a few fundraisers, but this one was on some big boy shit. He looked around the room and realized that out of the few hundred people there, every one of them was rich. The first thing that came to his mind was that he wished that First Class was in the building.

"Mrs. Fuller!" a tall, light skinned gentleman walked up to the table and greeted.

Beverly immediately introduced the man to Kevin. "Bishop, this is David Young from L and I," she said.

"A friend of Beverly's is a friend of mine. If you ever need anything, just give me a call," David said, passing Kevin his card. "You two have a good night," he finished, then walked off.

Throughout the entire night, people walked up to the table greeting Beverly. Kevin didn't know that she knew so many people; and these weren't just the regular rich people. These individuals had power throughout Charlotte. Doctors, high powered lawyers, judges, District Attorneys, Assistant United States Attorneys, the Governor, the Mayor, Fire Chiefs, and all sorts of business men and women who kept the wheels of Charlotte running. Beverly made sure to introduce Kevin to every one of them.

"Are you okay?" Beverly asked, seeing the blank look on Kevin's face. "Are you ready to leave?" she said as she kicked her heel off under the table.

Kevin was in the zone, thinking about all that he could do if he had individuals of this caliber in his pocket. The sky would be the limit. He snapped out of his deep thought, feeling Beverly's small foot sliding up and down his leg under the table. He looked at her and could see so much lust in her eyes that they appeared glossy. Kevin reached down, grabbed her foot, and began massaging it.

Beverly's pussy got wet at the touch of his big, manly hands rubbing her feet and calf muscle. "Before I forget," she said, reaching for her clutch on the table. "You don't have to rush to get this back to me, but I do expect that you'll be responsible in returning this," she said, digging out the check and passing it to him.

Kevin looked down at the check and saw that it was for $153,941.89

"Wow," he said, thinking about how good he was going to fuck her tonight.

This was how much Kevin owed the bank to the number. Being honest with himself, he didn't think Beverly would do the full amount. It made his dick hard just looking at the check.

"Thank you sooo much, baby," Kevin whispered in her ear. "Tonight, I'm going to have to do something very special for you," he added with a wink.

"Yeah, that's just what I was thinking," Beverly responded with a seductive scowl.

"How so?" Kevin asked, trying to think of a new way to give her his massive dick. In his mind, he had fucked her in every way imaginable, but he knew with Beverly, shit wasn't just about the fucking, it was more about the thrill of the hunt. So, he was hoping she would be direct, but not too crazy with her request.

"Well, as much as I would like to have you tonight, my little friend has decided to inconvenience our plans. I think the fucking we did last night brought my little friend down for an early visit. But you know I still need my fix," she continued while smiling.

It wasn't like Kevin had never fucked a girl while she was experiencing 'mother nature'; however, he figured Beverly had too much class for this teenage type shit. But for the type of money she was kicking out, shit, he might even give her some head before he hit it.

"That's no problem, my lovely lady. It's just going to make it extra gushy." Kevin responded.

"Oh, Lord ,no, I didn't mean like that!" Beverly voiced. I was hoping you could fulfill one of my other fantasies. . . ."

"And what would that be?"

"I want to see you perform. I want you to fuck some young, hot girl in front of me while I direct you two. I want you to show mama everything you want to do to me. Can you do that for me?"

Hell yeah, Kevin thought to himself. But he didn't want to seem too interested just in case Beverly was setting him up. He had never received a request like this one before. Although he had had a couple of ménage's before, never had someone sat on the sideline and just watched.

"Well, do you have someone in mind?" he asked, hoping that she had some beautiful new pussy for him to stroke.

"No, I was hoping you had somebody. I want her to be a real freak because you know I can be, and who knows, I might want to taste her myself," she added.

Kevin's dick was now starting to pulsate at the thought. He knew exactly who he was going to call. He excused himself from Beverly to go and give Jessica a ring, hoping she had not left to go back to Durham yet. Pulling out his cell phone and searching for her number, he took a deep breath before pressing her name.

"Hey, what's up, sexy?" Jessica answered in a seductive tone.

"Nothing much, beautiful. I'm just in need of your help."

"And what can I help you with? I thought after our last session, I had given you everything you needed and more." Jessica responded with a giggle.

"That you did, baby, that you did. But now, daddy needs you even more than ever."

"Anything for you, love, just let me know what you need me to do."

Kevin took his time breaking down the situation to Jessica. Although she did have a freaky side to her, she wasn't sure if this was something she wanted to do. Before she made her decision, she had to ask a couple of questions. First and most important being, what was she getting paid? No way was she was going through with all these theatrics and not receive some type of compensation, and she knew that if Kevin was doing it, there had to be money involved.

"Okay, so you know I have no problem with helping you with this, and you know I have no problem with my performance. So all we have to do is agree on the amount and just tell me the time and the place."

"The amount is five thousand, the time is tonight, and I will text you the place as soon as we get off the phone. Oh, and baby, come like you did before, nothing but the trench coat and stilettos," Kevin added before hanging up the phone and going back to tell Beverly the good news.

After a few more dances and brief introductions to some more key people, they quickly whisked themselves out the door, heading to the valet to retrieve his keys. They drove back toward Beverly's place. On the car ride over, Kevin couldn't help but to imagine himself stroking and filling young Jessica up while Beverly stood by and watched. He was hoping that she could maybe come up with something he and Jessica had not already done, but he was coming up short with ideas. Beverly definitely had age and experience over both of them, so who knows?

Pulling up into the large circular driveway of the home, both Beverly and Kevin got out, eagerly wanting to go and prepare for their guests to arrive. Just in case it was a long night, Kevin went into his pocket and discreetly pulled out two of his Cialis pills and tossed them down his throat. He was going make sure that if the performance wasn't top-notch, it wasn't on his part. Although he knew that the sexual chemistry he and Jessica shared was on such a high level that something like that could never happen, he wasn't leaving anything to chance with a six-figure check still stuffed in his pocket. Kevin was trying to make sure that behind this one, another would soon be on its way.

"So, baby, you never told me who the young lady is that we are expecting. Is she someone that you have fucked before, or something new?" Beverly asked

Kevin again tried to play it cool, unsure of how Beverly knowing that he had relationships going on with other women would affect their current situation. He gave her a quick and short end answer.

"Oh, I've known her for a little while, nothing too serious though."

"Okay, I just want to make sure there won't be any awkward moments. I'm looking to have a very memorable and special night, as I hope you two planned on doing as well." Beverly uttered while getting a bottle of wine from the neatly stocked bar. She took out two glasses and partially filled both before extending one to Kevin. He quickly swallowed the sweet white wine.

"Baby, do you mind if I go to the restroom and freshen up a little bit? You know daddy has to be on point for you and our guest."

"Not at all," Beverly responded as Kevin walked away, heading towards the bathroom.

Kevin reached under the sink and grabbed one of the hand towels. He placed it under the lukewarm water and grabbed the soap to gently lather it up. He pulled down his pants, figuring he would give his balls a quick cleaning since he had been sweating while dancing at the event. Satisfied that he was now ready for whatever the night had in store, he wrung the towel out and placed it on the towel rack as he was exiting the bathroom.

Hearing the doorbell ring caused a smile to stretch across Kevin's face as it brought back all the excitement that he felt on the ride over. He couldn't wait to see what the night's festivities had in store. As he was walking toward the door to answer it, he noticed that Beverly had beat him to it. Looking over her shoulder as she slowly opened the door all the way, he noticed Jessica standing with her trench coat wide open and her beautiful body fully revealed.

"Jessica?" Beverly asked in total shock.

"Mom?" Jessica responded, equally surprised, while quickly closing the trench coat.

Kevin stood there like a deer stuck in headlights, searching his mind for the right words, but there were none. Even with his 24-karat dick and his solid gold tongue, he knew that it was going take more than one slick sentence to get him out of this one.